SECRET CACHE

BOOK FOUR OF THE THOMAS YORK SERIES

BOOKS BY SHIRLEY BURTON

HISTORICAL FICTION
Homage: Chronicles of a Habitant

THRILLERS
Red Jackal
THOMAS YORK SERIES:
Under the Ashes - Book One
The Frizon - Book Two
Rogue Courier - Book Three
Secret Cache - Book Four
The Paris Network - Book Five

MYSTERY
Sentinel in the Moors
INSPECTOR FURNACE MYSTERIES:
Mystery at Grey Stokes
Swindle: Mystery at Sea

CHRISTMAS
Clockmaker's Christmas
Christmas Treasure Box

FANTASY
Boy from Saint-Malo

shirleyburtonbooks.com

SECRET CACHE

BOOK FOUR OF THE THOMAS YORK SERIES

SHIRLEY BURTON

HIGH STREET PRESS

HIGH STREET PRESS
Calgary, AB
www.highstreetpress.com
First printing 2014

This book is a work of fiction. Names, characters, places and incidents are the product of the author's imagination or are used fictitiously. Any resemblance to actual events, locales or persons, living or dead, is entirely coincidental.

Printed in the United States of America
Available in eBook formats.
Cover photo licensed Shutterstock.com.
Design and edit Bruce Burton

Library and Archives Canada Cataloguing in Publication.

Burton, Shirley, 1950-, author
        Under The Ashes / Shirley Burton

(Book Four of The Thomas York Series)
ISBN 978-1-927839-00-3 (pbk.). —ISBN 978-1-927839-01-0 (bound)
ISBN 978-1-927839-02-7 (ebook)

    1.   Title. II.Series: Burton, Shirley, 1950-, Thomas York Series; bk. 4.

PS8603.U778S43 2014   C813'.6   C2014-907079-9
                                            C2014-907080-2

Dedicated in remembrance of my Grandmother
Agnes May Smith (1887-1969).
She encouraged me to find excitement in reading
Starting with Old Yeller. For every Christmas and birthday, she gave me
books like L'il Rascal, Trixie Belden, and my favorite, Nancy Drew.
She was on the trading list for Nancy Drew books with my grade three class.
It was such fun.

Thanks, Grandma!

SECRET
CACHE

ONE

Normandy, France

Flashing red lights caught Daniel's vision as he eased on the brakes. A flagmen in orange made eye contact and waved him down. No other vehicles were in sight.

Daniel looked at Pascal and continued into the cell phone. "I'll call you back, Emily!' Looks like an accident ahead." Before the call went silent, Emily heard the echo of sirens, then raised voices at the car. She dialed Daniel back but it didn't ring.

"He must have gone out of cell range." Emily mused.

Standing at the kitchen island, Joseph didn't hear Emily approach. She wrapped her arms around his shoulders.

"In the middle of my call with Daniel, the scene went haywire. Should we be concerned?"

Joseph stopped and laughed. "No need to worry. Daniel can take care of himself."

Locked in the darkness, Daniel's eye's adjusted and he knew he was in the trunk.

How long have I been here? And what happened to Pascal?

His bonds were tight, and the numbness spread up his ankles and wrists. A black hood was pulled over his head, and he shook it to be able to breathe.

The tow truck and a second vehicle pulled away from the fake blockade, leaving the kidnapping site as mere tire marks on the shoulder of the road.

As the Mercedes hummed into the night, Daniel listened for anything else and heard only a distant train.

It must be a secondary road. How could I let them take us? The man had a Dutch accent. And why? The Frizons are gone and no one is on my tail. That I know of . . .

At the hairpin turn, they swerved to avoid a transport truck coming in the center lane. The tractor-trailer skidded and jack-knifed across the pavement, pinning the truck driver inside.

With only seconds warning, the Mercedes tires screeched as it swayed, and from inside the trunk Daniel felt the sensation as it became airborne. As it thrust back to the pavement, his head was slammed to the floor into unconsciousness.

The country roads of Normandy were veiled in darkness, pierced by the hiss of the dying engines. From the highway, the flicker of the tail lights in the ditch were barely visible through the grass.

Hugo turned to his partner and extinguished his cigarette.

"The beacon is still on and it hasn't moved in half an hour. Their GPS indicator shows the vehicle must be at a full stop about two kilometers ahead. But slow down . . . the road is dangerous with these sharp turns."

Yannick nodded. "Something's wrong. They should've been at the rendezvous by now!"

"Hold on," Hugo said. "I see a flicker of light ahead."

Yannick squinted on the object.

"I see it too, Hugo. Pull up on the shoulder. There's a truck jack-knifed on the road. The GPS signal is close; they must be there too."

With barely room on the shoulder to park the van, Yannick jumped to the loose gravel.

"Whoa, we are right on top of an embankment! There are dim flashing taillights down below. Get the flashlights and I'll go down to the car. Can you check the truck?"

Sliding down the steep ravine, Yannick arrived at the beacon attached to the undercarriage of the Mercedes.

"Mon Dieu! The driver is dead and pinned behind the wheel. The other must have been thrown from the car."

Hugo jumped down the hill beside him. "The truck driver is also dead."

With a long stick, Hugo paced through the brush and found the passenger. "Too late for him. The heat light from the tracking helicopter indicated three people, there must be one more."

They got the Mercedes doors open and walked around to the trunk.

"Hugo, blood's dripping from the trunk!"

He pried the catch open.

"It's a faint pulse, but he's hanging on."

Yannick worked over Daniel's limp body, performing heart massage, and Hugo scrambled to get a tarp for a stretcher.

Time was important to keep Daniel alive, and they lifted the stretcher sideways up to the van. His twisted leg appeared to be broken. He was unconscious and bleeding from head injuries. Yannick stayed in the back to monitor his pulse.

"Call for a medical team to meet us at the boat ramp," Yannick said. "His pulse is at thirty-five and he's in a coma."

Hugo sped up for the two hour drive to Normandy, beyond the beaches of Dieppe. Shreds of sunlight touched the horizon over the small fishing village, and the sandy beaches had pock marks from breathing the low tide. A cluster of French cottages rose up onto cliffs, looking over the fishing docks and warehouses.

Hugo peered through the binoculars. "It's the yellow and red boat on the marina side."

Napa Valley, California

As Zach turned the ignition, a ball of flame split the sky. The explosion of the truck engine echoed through the vineyard, followed in seconds by a second explosion. A plume of soot blanketed the ground, falling on workers running to help.

Addie heard it from the house and ran outside to see the fireballs.

She took off on foot from the back porch, shrugging off the hot ash landing on her back. At the shed she climbed up on a tractor. Like a vision of Florence Nightingale, Addie's hidden thoughts were wild and frantic.

Addie called for her husband as adrenaline surged through her body.

"Zach! Where's Zach?"

She started the tractor and accelerated down the lane toward the service house. Her mind was like a trance as she saw the truck, torn and mangled. A fire truck careened past, and its blaring horn sharpened her senses.

Eclipsed in time, the world around her moved in slow motion. People rushed toward Zach, yet she couldn't make sense of the chaos. Shouting his name again, she couldn't see him anywhere.

A second fire truck arrived and the hoses simplified the scene to smoldering metal. The adjacent concrete house was charred and beginning to buckle. Zach had been taken by EMS workers away from the embers.

Addie's face was white.

That can't be my Zach!

His body lay motionless on the ground with an oxygen mask on his blackened face. She stood beside the paramedics, with her hand over her mouth.

He opened his eyes. They seemed so white, with the rest of him black in soot; then they closed, wincing in pain. There was a lot of blood, but she couldn't see where it was coming from.

"Zach!" Addie dropped to her knees, yelling his name over the noise, assuming he was deaf from the explosion.

Squeezing his hand, she leaned close to his ear. "I love you. Everything will be alright."

The firemen continued with apparatus and sedation.

Zach whispered for Addie. "It is murder." He closed his eyes again and his voice drifted to an incoherent mumble.

"No, it can't be, Zach. It's going to be okay. I know it." The grip on his hand released and his eyes closed.

"Zach!' She yelled again, "Zach!"

Addie turned slowly to the field foreman. "Jonas, what happened here?" She grabbed his arm for support. "I don't understand."

The world was spinning around her, with voices echoing from all directions. People she didn't know rushed to her, and with all the attention, she had never felt this alone before.

Addie glanced at Jonas's hands.

"Gracious, Jonas, your palms are burnt. You need medical attention."

The medic interjected. "Do you want to ride with us, Madam?"

"Yes, yes." She stepped into the back of the ambulance and stood to scan the crowd for Maria, her housemaid. She waved, to come over.

"Maria, you'll be in charge of dinner."

Jonas assured her that he'd check the service huts and vehicles, but he concealed his own pain.

With gardening gloves and barbeque tongs, he examined the truck's remains as they hissed and cooled. He reached through the rubble to a six inch metal mechanism, like one he remembered when his uncle booby-trapped a shed infested with skunks. The memory flashed and he grimaced.

He was alone but spoke out loud. "This is a home-made contraption, but it was powerful enough to cause this!"

Sliding onto Addie's tractor, Jonas called to two workers to hang on to the sides. They maneuvered down the main lane, deep into the vineyard toward the back service station where another truck was parked. Cement block houses were positioned mid-point in each of the eight fields, serving as a cool relief on hot days, and storing gasoline, water and tools.

Police roped off the crime scene prodding the workers for any tidbit of evidence. Under a bush at the back of the garage, they found an oil rag and a cigarette butt; they bagged them into brown manila envelopes. It was too late to check for footprints that were destroyed by the influx of contamination by the well-intended.

The ambulance whisked them away, with Addie still numb as she watched Zach's quiet body. She held his hand and prayed that he was only asleep.

"Who would do such a thing? Zach doesn't have an enemy in the world."

They were taken directly to ICU. Before surgery, the doctor explained Zach's injuries to Addie, but the words filtered through her head without cognition.

Addie Ducharme was a strong, beautiful woman of fifty-five, tall and slender with emerald green eyes, and thick blonde hair with wisps of grey tied at the back. Only Zach saw the golden cascade of waves she took down at bedtime.

The years of hard work had weathered her porcelain aura and added worry lines to her youthful complexion.

A strong burly man of sixty years, Zachary Ducharme had an indecisive reddish-brown beard, a weathered tan on his muscular six foot frame. Addie declared he had the Ducharme jaw indicating his strength, and called him the guiding light in her life.

As a lad, Zach was taught the secrets of the Bordeaux grapes. The crop year ran religiously on a tight schedule to produce award-winning quality Bordeaux and Chardonnay wines, always aspiring to be the envy of other vineyards.

Ducharme ancestors from France had nurtured the eager stock into the current bumper. Zach had an intimate relationship to his vines and the soil. It was his life.

On many evenings, Zach slipped into the fields with his flashlight to measure the nitrogen in the soil, like a Papa Bear. Often he would clip a small cutting, and lovingly massage its leaves and inspect every pore of the stalk. The slip was then planted in a tin can leaving it to adolescence on the window sill.

In the past year, Zach had seen increased nighttime activity in the back west fields. He thought it might be teenagers, but noticed it more in the past month.

The sound of a truck woke him one night, and with binoculars he watched the movement of flashlights in the field. The next morning, at the site of the commotion, he discovered several rows of his grapes had been tampered with, taking fresh cuttings from his vines. A sack of cuttings had fallen to the side by the culprits, with the name emblazed into the burlap, 'Delacriox'.

He decided not to tell Addie of his suspicions, it would worry her too much. However he had confided in Jonas, his head foreman.

I guarantee I'll get to the bottom of this.

TWO

Paris, France

Thomas and Rachel returned to their Montmartre loft in Paris from rainy London, perplexed by their last meeting with Daniel. They now had insight into the surreptitious 'Angels of Providence', although it seemed too unbelievable.

The unraveling of the diamond theft in London left them feeling deceived by Daniel's sting, but also amazed at his talents in master-minding such an intricate ploy.

"When Daniel revealed the truth to us, Thomas, it was a total shock. I'm understanding the depth of his connections working for Interpol and supporting his pledge to assist poverty. I wonder if he really did go to Bangladesh to help with reconstruction."

Rachel shook her head. "He didn't call me back. He said he would. I know something is wrong."

Thomas smirked at the thought. "Daniel likes to ride around on a white horse, but I'm not convinced about all his charitable deeds."

"Thomas, in New York, Daniel was your guardian angel. He saved you from Sanderson, and rescued the Frizon from unscrupulous dealers. And out of nowhere he came to your aid when I was kidnapped by Simon Charbonneau. But what kind of organization is his 'Angels of Providence'? Is it even real?"

"It's like a Robin Hood premise, to take from the rich criminals and give to the poor. What I don't like is he thinks you're his Maid Marion."

Thomas thought his gentle sarcasm would be amusing, but his tension and gaze revealed his jealousy.

"What does he want from you, Thomas?"

"The Frizons have run their course bringing out the collectors of forgeries. The Sauliere and Baker scheme is on track, and now Daniel has turned to piracy. The head of the 'Angels of Providence' organization in New York is orchestrating an international surge of retribution."

Thomas was hesitant to tell her yet, but it seemed like the time.

"Daniel asked me to become his partner," he said.

"I don't want a clone of Daniel, I want you." Rachel held his arm tightly, and leaned her head onto his shoulder.

Thomas's thoughts vanished as he felt her body press next to him. With her face in his hands he kissed her and stared into her blue eyes. Words were not needed.

Napa Valley, California

Addie struggled to get away from the hospital waiting room's hive of activity, as a bus crash had turned the floor into a triage hub.

She wished a friend would join her as a comfort right now, and was relieved when Maria stepped off the elevator.

"Hello, Mrs. Ducharme, I wanted to come and be with you through the wait."

Maria put her arm around Addie's shoulder, and at the touch of tenderness, Addie burst into tears.

"Thank you, Maria. Yours is a welcome face with all the commotion."

"How is Mr. Ducharme?"

"I haven't seen him yet; he's been in surgery since we got here. What time is it?"

"Almost ten. Can we get a cup of coffee and sit at the end of the hall, away from this noise. The nurse will find us."

"You know, Maria . . . Zach has always been the leader; we work as a team. It never came up that someday all those decisions could fall on me. Funny after being together for thirty-eight years!

"When I was young, I looked forward to Saturday night events with zeal. I met Zach and his brother Pierre at a barn dance in the valley, and we were married six months later on Valentine's Day. If only I could turn the clock back.

"We lost our first son in his first few weeks of life, a grief that no mother should bear. Our treasure, Melissa, was born two years later, then our second son, Jacob Jr., two years after Melissa. He was valiant and determined to serve his country. I thought the hardest thing was watching him go to Afghanistan to fight the President's War. But I was wrong. It was when they presented me with the flag of my country in gratitude for his service. He was a child of eighteen when his patriotism took him. That was the worst."

Addie's tears flowed from a past world as she grasped her memories. Maria held her hand patiently.

"I mustn't be so sorrowful, we are so blessed with Melissa and her family, and we love each of our staff."

"We all feel loved by you, Addie," Marie said.

"The new generations are different. The vineyard business isn't in Melissa's blood. Not many kids get to feel the soil of their land run through their fingers. Instead, wee ones are attached to phones and computers, even while they eat."

"Do you have other family who could come and stay for a while?" Maria asked. "Is there anybody I can call?"

"I was about to say no . . . but perhaps my sister, Marion, and her . . ." Addie drifted away in thought.

"No, Maria, we don't need to send for anyone yet. I'll call Melissa, but she doesn't need to come right now. Zach will be back to the vineyards in no time.

"Zach taught Jacob, Jr. to whittle, and to catch fish in the creek. They'd skip rocks on the pond, and do the other things fathers and sons do. One day I found the two of them on their stomachs watching a string of ants marching in a line, each with tiny bits of grass. They lost sight of the ants under a branch, but would stay watching the row coming back empty. Zach loved to tell that story. Can you imagine, Maria, they stayed there until I insisted they come for supper.

"But, Melissa was Zach's little girl; she loved following him down each lane on his evening walks. I watched them from the veranda, holding hands and singing about a lemonade song they made up. On other evenings, Zach and the children sang the 'Rubber Tree Plant' song." She laughed. "Of course, I joined in."

Addie paused. "I'm wondering about my niece."

Her words ended abruptly as Zach's surgeon walked briskly in her direction. A claw of fear clenched her stomach and a lump formed in her throat.

The somber face stopped at her chair.

"Mrs. Ducharme?"

"Yes, call me Addie."

There was still no smile as the doctor took the empty chair beside her and reached to lay his hand on hers.

"Addie, we did the best we could, however there was more damage than expected. The surgery took too long and I'm afraid Zach went into cardiac arrest. We tried to bring him back . . . I'm sorry, Addie, but he's gone. Do you have relatives you need to call?"

For an instant, Addie froze. Her vision left her body to look down from a distance, her mind was detached. She needed Zach to help her through this; it was too much to bear alone. She had no opportunity for goodbyes.

This is not happening! That is not how life ends.

"Ma'am, please say something," Maria said, rubbing her back. "If you have Melissa's number, I could call her from the end of the hall." Addie wrote it on a napkin.

The surgeon rose to return to his surgical vacuum. "Mrs. Ducharme, do you have pre-planned arrangements? When you are ready, please let the head nurse know of your wishes. I'm sorry for your loss."

Addie nodded and remained seated.

She said, "Maria, can you call Jonas to come for us. I'll wait here."

Addie took a deep breath. She felt ready to take charge, like her internal control switch was back on. She had many thoughts, but only one wish.

Dear God, please give me my Zach back.

Maria was back in ten minutes. "Jonas is on his way. And I reached Melissa. She was in shock with the news and she'll be here in the morning with the little ones."

"The hospital wants to know about the arrangements, so I need to go home to think. Zach always told me the important papers were in his desk drawer." She rambled to stall the tears. "I was never tempted to look, but I expect there are instructions there."

She recognized Jonas's tall silhouette in the hall. He was quiet-mannered and likeable, in his early fifties, with solid morals. Zach and Addie had been a source of strength for him, when he lost his wife, Isabel, several years before. Isabel had been close to Addie, having tea together most afternoons swinging on the porch while snapping peas or peeling carrots.

"Addie, I am so sorry. Zach was like a brother to me, teaching and encouraging me every day." Jonas knew he had said enough and gently took Addie by the arm.

"Jonas, your hands! Did you soak them in Greek yogurt with warm water like I suggested? It works like magic!"

He looked up like a young boy. "I haven't had a chance."

"I'll fix him up, as soon as we get home, Addie. No need to worry," Maria chimed.

The drive back to the vineyards was solemn with Addie gazing into the darkness.

"What time is it, Jonas?" She closed her eyes.

"It's one o'clock in the morning."

The crunch of the gravel in the lane sounded comforting and she knew they were home. The porch lights were on and a glow of consolation exuded from the kitchen.

"Jonas and Maria, would you mind coming into the house for a bit?"

Jonas took Addie's coat. Maria put on a pot of tea to soothe their nerves and returned with the potion for Jonas's burnt hands.

"Jonas, you'll need to call a meeting of the workers in the morning to announce Zach's passing. The vineyard will continue as usual under your guidance and mine. We'll leave business matters until after the funeral. Close for business the day of the funeral out of respect for Zach. Our staff will be welcome to attend if they wish, but otherwise it will be a family affair."

Addie opened the desk drawer and shuffled through Zach's papers. She removed bank statements, letters, and a legal envelope labeled 'My Will'.

In the sitting room, she quietly read a letter Zach had written to her of his undying love and gratitude for the life they shared. She didn't recall a time when Zach had ever written her a letter.

On the second page, Addie found the unexpected, and for a moment, she froze, glad that she had witnesses.

Looking away from the letter, she recalled Zach's past words of caution to her, "If it ever comes to that, remember the script."

She wondered to herself if she had the strength to stick to the defense plan. Too exhausted to object, she skimmed over the letter, by a hand unfamiliar to her.

> . . . *It breaks my heart that I have held a secret from you all these years. I was married once, two years before I found you. My wife died in childbirth. We had a son that was raised by my brother's family. Matthew is my son. Once he was grown, I talked to him on a few occasions over the years. He never held a grudge but said he wished he had been part of the family.*
>
> *Matthew promised me if anything ever happened, he would take care of you. When the lawyer reads the Will, you will find I have bequeathed half of the vineyard to him. It will be good for both of you, my dearest. Forgive me!*
> *All my love,*
> *Zach*

Addie muttered under her breath, "Rubbish to you, Zachary Ducharme, you never had a wife, but me."

She handed it to Jonas to read. "Jonas, would you mind calling Matthew Ducharme. His name is in my address book by the telephone, under 'Charles'. I'm not sure if he's at that same address, perhaps the operator can find him. I must speak with him in the morning."

"Maria, would you please stay in the upstairs guest room tonight. I'd be grateful of the company. I'm afraid the house will seem empty tonight."

"Of course, Ma'am. You need your rest."

"Jonas, thank you for being so kind and helpful. I know you have pain too. Zach relied on you, and now I will rely on you. Please come to the house in the morning and we'll talk more. Did the potion help your hands?"

"It's much better, thanks."

Addie turned and left them. She carried herself painstaking up the stairs to her bedroom, the bed she shared with Zach nightly. There was an old fireplace against the east wall that hadn't been used for over fifty years. Bricks and mortar filled the hearth. All that it was used for now was a row of family pictures in antique frames, resting on a hand carved mantle.

With her finger, she traced their faces on their wedding portrait, then picked up a family photo from when Zach's parents lived in the house. Such an aching enveloped her heart that she thought she might break. Jacob Sr. and Jacob Jr. were together and little Melissa sat on her own lap. She felt like the tears of a hundred angels fell upon her.

Lying awake, her thoughts collided. Then the tears came, racking her body and her broken heart. She held Zach's pillow close, remembering how he smelled and craving the slightest memory.

She allowed herself to drift to sleep. When the morning rooster beckoned, Zach's pillow was still cradled in her arms.

Reality smacked her awake and she stared at the ceiling. The confusion around the explosion would have to be solved before any sense of normalcy could return, and so much responsibility awaited her beyond the bedroom door.

She opened the door an inch to hear the clatter of dishes in the kitchen below. It was reassuring over the silence of her heart.

THREE

Addie felt the weight on her to take control of the vineyard, but even the funeral arrangements were as much as she could grasp. She sipped her tea and ignored her toast. The stress challenged her calm demeanor.

It's too much for one person. Today I have to transport Zach to the funeral parlor.

Taking down a simple black dress, Addie looked in the dressing mirror and saw a face she didn't know, overwhelmed by sadness. Wisps of blonde and grey hair framed her face, and her bright emerald green eyes were now faded, mottled by grief.

Preparing to go to the funeral home on her own, she left instructions with Maria to send the lemonade and sandwich wagon to the service huts at noon.

Business in town would take a chunk of her day. It was now just seven in the morning, too early for the sleepy town of Charron. Passing the time, Addie wrote lists of those to be notified. At 8:30 she called Paterson's Funeral Home in Vallejo, then the head nurse at the hospital.

Zach's letter said that arrangements were made for both of them at the Vallejo Cemetery, in a plot beside his parents. He bought the plots at the time of his mother's passing, and Addie recalled the jolt of hurt that he hadn't discussed these sensitive matters with her.

She decided to make a point of personally approving both the plot and stone regardless of his predetermined choices.

In the night, Addie had thought at length about her sister Marion in upstate New York. Her mind wandered over each family member, finally focusing on Marion's daughter Rachel. Marion had boasted that Rachel, the eldest, had become a real detective, somewhere in Europe.

Rachel always kept in contact with her younger sister, Amy.

When Rachel and Amy were small, they were frequent visitors to the Napa Valley vineyard for summer vacations and during harvest. Addie envisioned them romping in the fields and learning to pick grapes the proper way.

Away from the city, they became tomboys, walking on their hands, with their bare feet in the air. She smiled at thoughts of the summers of laughter and cartwheels, a time when Zach told old stories that held them spellbound that even Addie had never heard.

In later years, they grew more distant, with college and their own paths. Some years passed with barely a Christmas card and an occasional telephone call that would always brighten Addie's spirits.

Her mind was made up.

I need Rachel to come.

A knock on the kitchen door broke her train of thought.

"Can I come in?"

Before she could get up, the screen door opened and Matthew Ducharme stepped in. He was freshly shaven, five foot ten, burly like the Ducharmes, but his cough showed his nerves.

"Of course, Matthew. My goodness, you do look like your father, much more than I ever gave thought over the years while you were growing up. You've got the Ducharme's thick brows, and I certainly recognize the family smile."

"What would you like me to call you, Mrs. Ducharme? Addie?" He hesitated. "Mom sounds a bit weird."

They both managed a relief laugh.

"Dear boy, I'll call you Matt and you call me Addie. Is that alright with you?"

"Good." His face was red and his tone awkward.

Addie broke the silence. She was curt. "It seems we have some business matters to discuss. Finding the estate envelope in Zach's desk took me by surprise. I was only aware of the documented Wills that he and I prepared years ago. What could make him change his mind recently, I don't know."

Addie looked into Matthew's eyes for a reply but he was silent. She continued, "However, there was a letter explaining who you really are."

The tension dissipated and Addie sighed without taking her eyes off Matthew. She was overcome by his resemblances to the Ducharme men.

Matthew gathered his courage, eager to embrace his newly found providence. "It's too bad that Zach didn't explain this before. I promised him I would always help the family in any way." He followed Addie to the coffee maker where Maria had brewed a fresh pot.

Addie deliberating avoided responding to his offer. "How is Charles taking this, keeping the secret all these years? We all owe him a debt of gratitude."

Before Matthew could answer, there was another knock at the screen door. It was unlatched and Addie called out.

"Come in."

She stood to greet Officer Murdock, the investigating officer who had been at the hospital.

"Mrs. Ducharme, again I am sorry for your loss." His gaze fell on Matthew. "May we speak in private for a few minutes?"

"Please join us for a cup of coffee. This is my stepson Matthew. We are partners of the winery now." Addie couldn't help deflecting her resentment.

The men took seats across from each other and Addie sat at the head of the table. Officer Murdock's eyes were on the platter of blueberry muffins in the middle. Addie nodded and laughed as Maria returned with three plates and a crock of butter.

"The death of your husband is looking like homicide. We won't know for sure, but early forensics lead in that direction. Do you know anyone who would wish any harm to Zach?"

Addie searched Matthew's face hoping to see shock and grief, but there was nothing.

He's going to play on the sidelines, I can already see it.

"Yes, I expected this," she said. "The field foremen told me he found a mechanism in the rubble. It may have caused the explosion."

"Well then, it's only a heads up for now. I'll keep you posted on developments. You'll notice my people working around the service huts. The crime scene will be restricted until the police tape is removed. If you recall anything suspicious, please call me."

The officer stood and passed a business card to Addie. He put his cup in the kitchen sink, nodded and let himself out the back door.

"Matthew, it was on my mind to tell you about Officer Murdock, but my head is a blur. Would you mind going through your father's desk drawer and sorting out the bills and whatever else is in there needing attention? That is where he kept all his secrets.

"Also, could you call Zach's sisters and brothers? The funeral will be the day after tomorrow."

Inner panic pinched Matthew in the gut. Contacting the brothers and sisters, his aunts and uncles, was something he didn't want to do. That would mean contacting Charles, whom he claimed to be his adoptive father.

"I can do that later, Addie. I see you're on your way somewhere. You always look lovely in that black dress. If you wish, I'd be obliged to take you into town." He had a calm reassurance, the same as Zach.

His patronizing is sickening.

"Thank you, Matt, that would be nice. I'll need a few minutes first.

"Matthew, do you remember your aunts and uncles and grandparents? I have only vague recollections of you as a boy."

Matthew squirmed. "No, I hardly ever met them. Charles and Evelyn were not sociable people." He glanced at the screen door like he needed an escape. His lips were pursed. "I'll step outside to smoke."

Addie watched his shadow outside, concerned that he had referred to his adoptive family with such disdain.

From the kitchen wall phone, Addie rang through to New York.

"This is Addie, I need to speak with Marion?"

A groggy voice finally came to the phone.

"Addie, you know I don't function before eight in the morning. Do you realize it's only 7:00 a.m.?"

"Marion, its Zach. There was an accident yesterday. He didn't make it through surgery. I'll give you more details about the tomorrow's funeral, but I need to get in touch with Rachel. Can you give me her number?"

"Addie, dear Addie. I am so sorry about Zach. Of course, anything you need. Are you suspecting murder?" Marion took a deep breath while she fumbled through papers.

"Thank you Marion. The funeral will be small, and let me know if you can come. I'm surprised to find you at home. I'll look forward to seeing you. How's Harold?"

"I assure you we're all fine. Can you hold for a minute?"

"I found it in Amy's jewelry box. Those girls always held secrets from me. Both of them dearly loved Uncle Zach."

"I believe this number is current. It's in Paris, and I'm not sure if you'll be able to reach her."

"It's worth a try, Marion."

Montmartre, Paris, France

Church bells pealed from the Basilica, echoing through Montmartre to St. Pierre, near the bottom of the hill. Thomas and Rachel York were in the loft, still reeling from Eloise's attack at the Harkness Detective Agency.

In France, they were still known strictly as their aliases Joseph and Emily Harkness, names given to them in witness protection when they had left Albany, New York.

Joseph said, "I'll never forget the site of Eloise staring down the barrel of her gun. My life flashed before my eyes."

"Thankfully, Madge had the guts to shoot Eloise in the back of the head, the instant the safety was released. In eerie slow motion, I saw her rise from her desk with a focused strength in her face that I never could have foreseen.

"From behind Eloise, Madge stealthily took a stance, aimed, and fired at the same second. Fortunately Eloise's back sense caused her to falter and her bullet, intended for me, went into the wall."

"My first reaction was that you had been shot; then I realized the blood spatter on your shirt was from Eloise." Emily added. "Thank the stars for Madge."

"When I saw you bent over me, I thought you were a heavenly angel."

"Well, I am an angel, Joseph."

The heroics of Madge Bitteridge didn't miss catching the lure of newspaper columnists. It made for a scandalous story. Emily had picked up a copy when she went for the morning pastries.

She stopped in her tracks when her eyes fell on the item on the bottom of the front page.

GUNSHOTS ROCK RUE EULER

The escape of a prisoner, Scott Marchand, led to an event on Tuesday at an unlikely detective agency on the brink of Blvd. Champs-Elysees. Eloise Marchand, had planned a deception to a secure South African diamonds, but when her plan failed, she turned her fury to the detectives.

The booty of fifty carats of blue diamonds was last known to be in the hands of Winston Metcalf, a London financier, who was killed by Scott Marchand.

Witnesses recount the bravery of Madge Bitteridge at the detective agency. The agency partners, Joseph and Emily Harkness, state that their relationship with Ms. Marchand was amicable and the incident unexpected.

"Madge clearly gets the credit she deserves." Emily tossed the pastry box and the newspaper beside Joseph.

"Joseph . . . you need to rest. The police suggested you see should a psychologist to talk about Eloise."

"Nah, all I need is you." He needed no convincing to put his arms around Emily.

In the business district of Paris, a local attorney also saw the news item of the Harkness Detective Agency. The front page included photos of both Joseph Harkness and Madge Bitteridge.

There's something familiar about this Harkness fellow.

The lawyer pondered over his desk before reaching into a file drawer. Shuffling through a mound of documents, he pulled out a photo of Thomas York from Albany, New York.

Hmm . . . Sanderson was looking for this one! Albeit time has passed but considering the time he's served in prison because of York, I'm certain he'll be interested.

Picking up his telephone, he made a call to Albany.

Below the Montmartre loft, Toby, the bloodhound was baying in the Paris florist shop. He objected to the drizzling weather of the last few days. In his rainy walks, his tail wagged less.

When Maria opened the flower shop in the mornings, Emily would take Toby for his runs through St. Pierre, climbing the one hundred and fifty steps and back again. The smells of the butcher shop and bakery always brought him to a halt.

Emily Harkness watched the rain run down her patio windows, and she hoped for a rainbow. The gray skies dampened her spirits—when she felt low, her memories of home, her sister, her parents back in New York State compelled her.

She wanted to go back to the States, to end their aliases, to take her real identity as Rachel again, and for Joseph to become Thomas York.

FOUR

Rachel was thirty years old, still slight, with striking blue eyes and long auburn hair held by a clip. During their stay in Paris, using her alias Emily, she was spirited yet demure. She flourished in their life of adventure as they took on detective cases, dallying with danger. With the love of her life, she travelled throughout Europe.

Thomas brought her a steaming mug of black coffee, a morning ritual. On the garden chair next to her, he touched a wayward strand tucking it behind her ear and kissed her forehead. He knew she was homesick.

"We've been in Paris for three years. I called Lieutenant Jamieson, and he said all the fiends connected to David Sanderson are safely behind bars for many years. He doesn't see any reason why it wouldn't safe for us to go back for a visit."

Thomas was a brawny six foot tall detective with trusting brown eyes, a strong jaw and golden brown wavy hair with a lock dangling over his forehead. He was strikingly handsome and a true romantic, always intuitive to Rachel. Faced with death once too often, they were deeply bonded to each other.

"We could take a visit back to the United States for a break. No one needs to know about the aliases we've been using, we can come back to them anytime.

"Madge has a tight hand at the detective agency, and the new chap brings in his own clients now. Madge feels vested in me since . . . since she saved my life." He paused for a deep breath.

"Madge is one in a million, that's for sure. Do you think we could leave the agency for a few months?" Rachel searched his face for an answer.

Thomas said, "My father's health is failing and I'd like to see him before long. He's moved back to New York to be near old friends. Eddie's passing struck him hard. Let's get an early start into the office and start making plans to go home."

Rachel's cell phone rang, the special number she had given to Amy, only for emergencies. Fearfully she looked up at Thomas, afraid something serious had happened to her family.

"Hello, can I speak to Rachel Redmond? It's her Aunt Addie."

Thomas handed the phone to Rachel. "Your Aunt Addie is asking for you."

Fond memories of Addie and Zach at the vineyards flooded her thoughts. Addie was her mother's elder sister; they were Cumberlands.

"Aunt Addie, how are you? It's been ages, and that's my fault, I'm so sorry."

"Sweetheart, Uncle Zach passed away during the night after an accident. I know without a doubt it was murder. I beg of you, Rachel, would you come for a stay and help me with this? I can cover all your expenses."

Rachel looked up at Thomas who had paused to await information.

"I'm so sorry about Uncle Zach. Do you have evidence that it was murder?"

"Yes, those were his last words to me—that it was murder."

Thomas gave Rachel a nod. Instinctively they were two of a kind.

"We'll be happy to come, Aunt Addie. My husband Thomas is also a detective and we've been talking the last few days of coming to the United States, and California sounds perfect. We can comfortably cover our own expenses. Are you safe where you are?"

"Yes, I'm fine, I have good people to rely on, but I need you to stay at the house. It's complicated. I'll send one of the men into San Francisco or Oakland to pick you up. The Oakland airport will be closer. The funeral's on Wednesday afternoon."

"We'll rent a car; we like to be independent that way. As we speak, Thomas is looking up flights. I love you, Aunt Addie."

Addie put down the phone, still with a troubled look.

Rachel relayed Addie's suspicion to Thomas. "Aunt Addie has never been one to overreact."

"Tell me more about the vineyards." Thomas asked.

"It is a wonderful place to be, with the warm California sun and gentle breeze. It's an enormous expanse of land south of a quaint town called Vallejo. The area is famous for their wines. The main house is majestic, with stone pillars at an imposing front. No one uses that door. The friendly door is off the kitchen.

"My sister and I used to play hide and seek in the back fields. The winery has been in the Ducharme family for one hundred years, right in the heart of the Napa Valley.

"There's a volcanic cave below the fields—I loved going down there; I still remember the musty smell from the barrels. And the Saturday night parties. Oh, I can feel the excitement right down to my toes. I wonder if they still hold those."

Thomas raised his brows and laughed. "I'm already looking forward to it."

"Uncle Zach told intriguing stories about the vine roots that were brought to America from orchards in France, transported across continents in burlap sacks to become the California crop. Here we are in France and the old Ducharme roots came from an ancient vineyard not far away.

"I wish you could have known my uncle; he had passion, courage and bravery, just like you. And a great sense of humor and humility."

"Addie is part of your family, so we will help her, whatever the circumstances. I'll get reservations to leave as soon as possible. I suppose you already have packed suitcases under the bed." Rachel couldn't help but laugh at the possibility. She had a reputation of preparedness with a weekender always ready.

Rachel said, "I'll let Madge know we'll be leaving Paris so quickly. She's learned to be a pretty good detective and likes being in charge."

"I couldn't find my old Thomas York passport. It's probably already expired. I'll travel as Joseph Harkness."

"Harkness it is for both of us. I need to run to the drugstore while you go to the office. Send Madge my love and reminder she can call me anytime."

Napa Valley, California

Matthew and Addie arrived at the funeral home in the town of Charron, a place where everyone knew each other. Receiving many condolences before she even stepped inside the funeral director's office, she felt prying eyes upon her. News had spread like wildfire.

Addie whispered, "Matthew, a murderer is somewhere in this town. Keep your eyes and ears open."

"I'm sharp as an axe."

The undertaker led them to a plush room with sofas and armchairs, with a fresh water jug and glasses on the fireplace mantle. Already several floral arrangements had arrived, but Zach had was not ready for viewing.

Details of the family's wishes were discussed. The director suggested that a collage of Zach's photos over the years would be appropriate. Visitors would be received the next afternoon and evening, then the ceremony would be at 11:00 a.m. the following day.

"Melissa can delve into the shoeboxes when she gets here today. I'd like to keep her busy. Everyone needs to find their own way to grieve and Melissa needs to be involved and feel close." Addie nudged Matthew with a smirk.

"I'll look forward to seeing her again," Matthew acknowledged with little enthusiasm.

"Well, I guess you are step brother and sister. I'm not sure how she'll react. Use your father's tact and lots of compliments. You'll need to escort her through the funeral service."

Finalizing arrangements, Addie selected a new stone from the online catalogue. Entirely new engravings were ordered for both Zach and herself. Her maiden name, Cumberland, would be inscribed as large as Ducharme, with her dates to be etched in the future.

"Ah, that feels better," she muttered, taking back control.

Last stop was the lawyer's office, where a Will in the possession of the lawyer was read. There weren't any real surprises—the letter had taken care of that.

Don't think for a minute Matthew Ducharme that you'll inherit Zach's estate.

FIVE

Thomas and Rachel picked up the rental at San Francisco airport for the drive to Vallejo. Rachel was familiar with the trek to the Ducharme Estate & Winery, passing other vineyards along the route. They arrived into a tropical world, a long way from France.

Addie ran out from the house as they pulled through the gate.

"I'm so glad to see you, Rachel . . ." After a meaningful embrace, she turned to Thomas. "I haven't met this handsome fellow of yours."

"Aunt Addie, this is Thomas, and yes I agree he is handsome."

His face flushed, but he was quick to plant his feet. "Let us know what you need us to do and we'll start with the clues you have. I'd like to be up-to-date before the funeral. The guilty one often returns to watch the family suffer."

"You have free reign over anything here on the estate, Thomas. I'm glad you came all the way from France." She teased, "After all, you are related to the Cumberlands by marriage."

"I'll remember that."

"Leave your bags here. One of the lads will take them up to your room. You'll be in the same room, Rachel, where you and Amy spent summer vacations."

"That's thoughtful, Aunt Addie."

"Come, let's sit at the kitchen table, we need to discuss."

Maria was working in the kitchen and brought mugs and coffee to them along with a plate of warm, buttered banana bread.

"First, you must meet my Maria. She's my right hand—she digs in and takes over without my asking. Maria has been with us ten years, almost like a daughter to us."

"It's a pleasure to meet you, Maria," they chimed.

"Miss Addie is too kind." Maria blended back into her kitchen duties with an ear open to the discussions. She had learned much in this way while listening in English and speaking in Spanish.

Addie said, "I've had a shock after Zach died. He left a letter for me, introducing me to a son that he supposedly had before we were married. Zach claimed to be young and not able to raise a child on his own—you see his wife died in childbirth. His brother's family was kind enough to raise Matthew as their own.

"But I'm only hearing this is a letter after almost forty years. It is understandable that I should be somewhat annoyed at my Zach. When I get to Heaven, we'll be having a long discussion."

She took a sip of coffee and looked into the cup.

I should have told them the truth. I should have told them outright about Zach's theory.

Rachel and Thomas smiled at the spunk Addie exuded.

"I'm sorry, Aunt Addie," Rachel said.

Addie forced a smile. "No sense in being sorry. Matthew and I actually get along well; Zach left half of the family winery to each of us. Matthew has been a welcome support in these last few days."

"Aunt Addie, when you told us about Matthew, I detected some hesitation. What you said about his birth story, do you believe that to be the truth?"

"Thomas you are wise and perceptive, but let's have some faith and give Matthew a chance to prove himself."

Rachel recounted, "I remember Matthew vaguely. There was a family event when I was a child, perhaps one of the Saturday night affairs; all the kids played hide and seek. I found Matthew, out of bounds, hiding in the wine caves. Will Charles and Evelyn be at the funeral?"

Ah ha! I thought he seemed familiar about the house without even a tour. He knew exactly where Zach's desk was.

Addie toyed with the thought.

Thomas prodded with his diplomatic way. "Aunt Addie, tell me about the clues. It's better to get onto the trail before it gets too cold."

"I agree, Thomas. You should talk to Jonas, our field foreman. He found the detonator in the rubble and the police have it now. You should also ask Officer Murdock in Charron about the forensic investigation."

Thomas stood up tall. "That will be a good start. Have you personally noticed anything or anybody peculiar?"

"Matthew and I have been at the lawyer's office. I'm not sure why he was so keen to join me. I'll give the lawyer authorization to talk to you about the Will. One more thing, Thomas, the lawyer had the Will from Zach's desk drawer; I didn't give it to him. Maybe you could check with Matthew."

Addie stopped and bit her lip but it was too late. Thomas picked up on her hint.

"Sure, I can follow up. Any strange people in the vineyards in recent months?"

"Talk to Jonas. An incident a few months back got Zach pretty riled; something to do with one of the neighboring wineries. He filed a police report and applied for a restraining order as a result. The police can give you a copy."

The screen door opened and Matthew let himself in. He smiled warmly at his step-mother. "Hello, Addie, I heard you were looking for me."

Addie stood and gave him a ceremonial hug, then turned to Rachel and Thomas.

"This is my step-son, Matthew. Anything we discuss shall be kept between the four of us. Matthew is helping to delve into the state of affairs at the winery." She gave a wink to Thomas.

Thomas and Rachel stood "It's a pleasure to meet you."

Addie turned to Matthew. "I'm sorry I didn't think of it sooner, but the old library was remodeled into a lovely ensuite a few years back. Would you like to move into it? It's in the extension?"

"Thanks, Addie. Tomorrow, after the funeral."

The ceremony was a solemn affair in the chapel. Rachel consoled the heart-broken Melissa. Thomas stuck to Addie's side, like a bodyguard, observing visitors and getting introductions.

Melissa read a poem recitation of 'Look for me in Rainbows'. At times her voice broke, but she regained her composure.

Time for me to go now, I won't say goodbye.
Look for me in rainbows, way up in the sky.

In the morning sunrise when all the world is new
Just look for me and love me, as you know I loved you.

In the evening sunset, when all the world is through
Just look for me and love me, and I'll be close to you.

It won't be forever, the day will come and then
My loving arms will hold you, when we meet again.
Every waking moment, and all your whole life through
Just look for me and love me, as you know I loved you
Just wish me to be near you
And I'll be there with you.

Matthew read from Isaiah, "Fear not, for I am with you", and the organist played "Nearer my God" and "Be Still my Soul". The building silenced with the tearful Eulogy by Addie. Guests were invited back to the estate for a light reception.

"Mom, did Matthew's parents come? Uncle Charles?" Melissa asked.

"No I didn't see them. They never were close, but you'd think Zach's own brother would attend."

Under the late afternoon sun, the family arrived back at the main house where many locals wandered the back lawns.

Fatigue was wearing on them all from forced smiles at the veranda reception. Melissa envisioned permanent laugh lines imbedded in her cheeks.

Maria and her sister primped finger sandwiches and cakes and kept the coffee pots full. Melissa was quick to claim Addie's rocker on the porch and looked upon the scene as if she were in a faraway place. As expected, most of the village of Charron passed through the veranda offering condolences to Addie, Melissa, Matthew, Rachel and Jonas.

Cars and pickups lined the driveway and boulevard, and with the excitement, even a discreet visit by Gregoire

Delacroix went unnoticed until Thomas saw him approach Jonas. No-one else noticed the confrontation by the road.

Thomas watched the conversation first from a distance. Delacroix was six inches taller than Jonas, but Jonas had no fear of him. He put his hand on Gregoire's chest to push him away, shouting close to his face. Stepping closer, Thomas could hear them.

"Delacroix, you have some nerve showing up here. Respect Mrs. Ducharme and leave immediately."

"Let bygones be bygones, lad". He pushed Jonas's hand away to barge by toward the house. "The restraining order died with old Zach."

Thomas came within feet of the two men.

"Jonas, do you need help here? I'm excellent at a good karate chop to the neck that will have him on his knees in an instant."

Delacroix huffed then spat at Jonas.

"Watch yourself, both of you. I'll be back. Tell the lady of the house, I was here."

"If you come back, you'll be facing another restraining order, Gregoire."

Gravel flew as he tore onto the road. Addie saw it all from the house.

Three Months before Zach's Death

In the back field in the spring, an incident had escalated into a fight between Zach and Gregoire, unbeknownst to Addie.

Infuriated at the blatant thievery of the Delacroix family, Zach picked up the sack and asked Jonas to find the planting supervisor.

Jonas gave a shrill whistle twice that was meant for Cole and in minutes, the lad was running toward them. Zach was already in the truck. Cole jumped in the other side and they headed toward Charron.

Zach was in a rage and didn't speak for the first ten minutes, stepping on the gas recklessly. Cole sensed that a battle was brewing and looked out the window in silence.

"Cole, you're in charge of the planting stocks. Have you seen cuttings like these on the ground when you do your morning walkabouts? Have you ever seen strange vehicles or men in the back fields?"

"I did notice the cuttings this morning. I was about to go to find you when you called me, Mr. Ducharme. There was one other strange event some weeks ago. It was time to go for dinner and I was taking a count. Rocky was missing.

"I called for him and then saw him bending low on one knee talking to another man. I'd never seen the man before and I didn't have a clear look at his face. As I came toward Rocky, the man ran into the field.

"Rocky lied to me. I can tell when my men lie. I see deceit in their eyes."

"Why didn't you let me know about this?"

"Rocky told me it was his brother coming to tell him that his mother had taken ill, and he should go to the house. I chose to believe him, but I now take extra care to watch him at the end of the day. I'm sorry, Mr. Ducharme, that I gave him a pass."

"What's done is done. We're going to speak directly with Gregoire Delacroix with this evidence in hand. In the past, he has made me several generous offers for us to sell the estate. But he had a broiling resentment towards us since the day I paid a chunk of his mortgage. I didn't want anything in return. We had a bumper crop that year, and it seemed like the right thing to do.

"The man was about to lose his home. His wines have not done well in competitions and he was desperate to improve his crop. I am a man of God, but to love they neighbor when it's Gregoire Delacroix is a test.

"Obviously, his plan includes stealing cuttings from our Bordeaux stock. I wouldn't put it past him to dig up some of our roots. Roots my grandfather brought from the family estate in France, a hundred years ago—strong old roots. This is a travesty. An indignity to my family name."

I shouldn't feel shame preserving our heritage.

"What are we going to do when we see Mr. Delacroix?" Cole asked.

"First, I want all the cuttings back. I'll threaten charges against him for trespassing, theft and vandalism. If I have to, I'll get a restraining order. The outcome depends on how he intends to resolve this."

"I guess he probably doesn't know we are on to him, so you have the upper hand."

"Here we are, it's just ahead." Zach skidded to a stop at the end of the Delacroix vineyard gates.

The oldest Delacroix son appeared from the front tasting room and shop. He recognized Zach immediately.

"What can I do for you Mr. Ducharme? Are you reconsidering our offer to buy you out?" The lad stuck out his chest with his new found assertiveness and arrogance.

"Actually, Lane, I've come to see your father. Is he here?"

Lane stood with his arms crossed over his chest, trying to anticipate his next move. His eyes shifted to Cole and in that moment they both knew; he had been the stranger talking to Rocky in the back field. Lane behaved like a deer in the headlights, frozen, but then murmured something and left to the main house.

"Did you catch what he said, Cole?"

"He said he'd be back in a minute. You saw that he recognized me from the night of his trespass."

Ten minutes later, Gregoire Delacroix appeared at the front entrance to the main house. He stopped to watch the two, then walked toward them.

"Hello, old boy! Have you come to negotiate? Come on in, we can sit down and talk this over." Gregoire had already turned and was walking ahead of them to a tasting room, heavy with oak barrel and wine aromas.

He turned to Cole. "What's your name kid? Are you learning the ropes from old Zach?"

"No need to know my name. I'm the field foreman that checks for stock damage in the back fields." He fixed his sight directly on Delacroix's shifting eyes.

"Well, Zach, if this is your back-up man, you've got some worrying to do?"

"Cole is a fine foreman, you'll see he doesn't miss much."

Zach nodded to Cole to bring out the bag.

"It would seem, someone from your vineyard has been trespassing on my property in the night. In fact, he dropped this sack of cuttings from my vines. He was kind enough to leave his calling card—see 'Delacroix' written on the burlap. I've a good mind to call the police and have you charged."

Delacroix was on his feet, with his face flushed purple. Glaring at each of them, he pounded his fist on the table.

"I dare you to accuse me of such a thing. My bags are everywhere, anybody could have left that. I know nothing about such a fabrication. You have called me a thief."

Cole spoke up. "Mr. Delacroix, I'm witness to your son, Lane, trespassing about three weeks ago in a discussion with our man Rocky. Shall we ask Rocky to explain in detail what transpired?" Cole was realizing he was a kingpin and stood his ground.

The shop was empty. Gregoire walked behind the sales counter near the till. Reaching below he pulled a shotgun, leveling it at Cole's head.

"You have no right to come here and accuse me of thievery. Get out of here. And don't step on my land again or I'll have a bullet waiting."

Enraged, Zach and Cole stormed out of the wine shop and spit gravel veering onto the road. He drove directly to the local police department.

Gregoire stood pondering the confrontation.

I shouldn't have been so harsh to my neighbor. I have to wonder what Lane has been up to. Sounds like he's got a scheme going that he doesn't want me to know about. I suppose it is possible that the father doesn't know what the son is doing.

SIX

The morning after the funeral, Thomas and Rachel rose at seven to drive to Charron.

At the police station, Officer Murdock wasn't available, but another officer took them to a desk to discuss the progress. Two items were on their agenda, the restraining order and the investigation of sabotage to Zach's tractor

The officer leafed through the file and looked up at Thomas.

"From talking to the field supervisors, we found a consensus that there was suspicious nighttime activity on the property. A broken fence provided access in the back quarter and tire tracks crossed over from the Delacroix side. One of the workers, Rocky, was reluctant to talk to us—he refused, in fact. Possibility he's an inside man.

"We've have taken imprints to compare to the Delacroix trucks. There's been bad blood between them since the day Mr. Ducharme filed his complaint three months ago."

Rachel pressed, "Were any fingerprints found on the tractor device?"

"Jonas claims he didn't disturb any clues when he picked up the detonator. We found a half print matching Jonas and also two others. Rocky has been cleared and Mr. Delacroix is refusing to co-operate. We are looking for his son, Lane, to answer some questions."

"May I suggest that the piece with the fingerprints be sent to the San Francisco lab where they might have more accurate equipment?" Thomas urged.

"Slow down, Mr. York, we might be slow, but we have a reputation of being accurate."

"Certainly, Sir, I meant no offence. My apologies." Thomas's face flushed for an instant.

Rachel said, "Officer, I see we've taken quite a bit of your time. We'd appreciate being kept up to date. Addie has asked us to help and we're grateful for your assistance."

"Addie is a dear lady. Anything to help her."

The guest bedroom that Thomas and Rachel were using faced the fields with a panoramic view, with a telescope on a tripod in the center window. Peering through the powerful lens, Thomas could see close up details of the rear service area.

"Rachel, look through this. I wonder who frequented this room and the telescope."

"I'll ask Addie and Maria. Also I'd like to have a long chat with Maria on the veranda. It looks like I'll be peeling potatoes this afternoon."

"Great," Thomas said. "It is often the ones that blend into the wallpaper, that know the most."

"Speaking of wallpaper, I always wondered why this room was never painted nor the wallpaper changed. When I was a little girl, I played there by the window pulling little strips of paper from the wall. One morning, Uncle Zach was passing by and told me in no uncertain terms that I shouldn't touch the wallpaper. He said it was as valuable as an heirloom.

"He was stern enough that Amy and I never touched it again. We made fun of the wallpaper and called this bedroom the Heirloom, but never when Uncle Zach was around.

"Interesting," Thomas said.

Rachel gave him a peck on the cheek. "I'll spend the afternoon with Addie and Maria, so I'll see you around dinner time."

"I'll be in the back fields to chat with the supervisors and check the broken fence."

"Perhaps you could spend a little time with Matthew too."

Her eye sparkled with mischief. "I don't suppose I could slide down the rail?" She flashed a teasing smile at Thomas and descended the stairs in a ladylike manner.

The telephone rang in the front hall, causing a clatter of feet. A soft female voice answered, and Rachel thought it sounded like Maria. She heard only a few excited words in Spanish, then the phone was slammed down.

If Addie trusts her, so should I.

On Sunday morning, the vineyard was quiet. Crop workers were at home and it was peaceful. Addie made a cup of Earl Grey intending to relax on the veranda. The row of lilacs at the far end of the porch were dancing with the wind, and she could taste the fragrance.

Ah, a nice morning to try to enjoy nature.

The grape vineyards had their own seasons. April showers had long passed and it was time to retie the vines to the wires and replace old posts and twine. Mowing was overdue between the rows across the Ducharme Estate. Weeds were a year round challenge but mowing helped to keep the seeds from spreading.

Addie was impressed how Matthew started to pour himself into the business. He oversaw the vineyard preparations for the best blossoming grape leaves and the sweetest grapes. She was happy that Matthew and Jonas were inseparable during most days, and particularly astounded how a forgotten son, the son of a mechanic, would know so much about grapes.

But her suspicions remained.

The son of a mechanic! Someone with a mechanical advantage was responsible for the bomb on the tractor.

Since Zach's passing, his murder had taken many twists and turns. Addie felt an evilness hanging over the back fields, and knew that the familiar serenity of the vineyard was gone.

Opening the kitchen door to the veranda, Addie was aghast. On her favorite rocker was a tiny sparrow with its neck broken and a note attached to a rock. She felt humiliation, fear, disgust and anger all in the moment.

She screamed out. "Matthew! Thomas!"

Matthew had been in the front garage polishing a pair of vintage Harleys. He and Thomas could take a spin on later.

Coming out, he looked at Addie's horrified face, and Thomas burst through the kitchen door seconds later.

Matthew cupped the bird in his hands and removed it leaving the note on the chair. He gave Thomas a nod, and the note was quickly intercepted.

"Come on, Aunt Addie, let's have our morning coffee in the kitchen." Thomas touched her elbow and led her back into the house. Matthew, Thomas and Rachel joined her at the breakfast table.

"Maria, will you please warm up those sweet buns for us." Addie asked without looking at her. "I was already for a nice peaceful morning, then this disgusting matter ruined the day."

Thomas was attentive to the current circumstances, but still had room for buns. Nobody spoke a word, waiting for Addie to compose herself.

"Matt, will you read the note to us."

The paper was unfolded and stretched on the table. All that it said was 'SELL'.

Thomas said, "I'm going to call Officer Murdock. This might be part of the murder investigation."

"Who would be so bold to do this?" Rachel asked. "Someone uninvited was here on the veranda. It's a blatant violation, although it sounds more like a warning than a harmful threat."

"I've been concerned about the broken fences in the back quarter. Thomas, would you mind helping me to reinforce the fence." Matthew said. "I bought a video system to install to catch the culprits red handed?"

"Sure, Matthew, one more bun and I'm ready." Thomas tried levity, but thought Matthew seemed too eager.

Rachel reached to Addie's hands. "Aunt Addie, let's go down to the caves sometime today?" She thought it would be a good distraction, but she also wanted to inspect the walls.

"Sounds like a good idea."

Addie paused and turned to Maria.

"Maria, isn't this your day off? You should be home with your family enjoying the outdoors."

Maria looked embarrassed.

"I forgot, Ma'am. I'll leave once the breakfast things are put away. You are in good company, I see."

Addie knew that Maria was always eager to listen in on kitchen secrets, but now with a house full of guests, she was pushing it too far.

Thomas and Matthew were already in the back quarter, when an older pickup truck pulled into the drive. Maria called from the backdoor to warn Addie.

The man was ruddy and poorly groomed with stale cigarette odors and ignored body hygiene on his clothing. Chewing a soggy cigar, he extended his hand to Addie.

Wiping her hands in her apron, she avoided the gesture.

"I'm sorry, I don't believe I know you," she said sternly.

"No, I don't believe you do, but we need to have a wee chat."

"Right here will be fine." Addie looked to the house hoping to see Rachel.

"I suppose I have no reason to expect hospitality. You see, I'm an old acquaintance of Zach."

"And you are?"

"In prison they called me Dex but now that I am ready for the good life, you can call me Kincaid. I had a deal with Zach."

Rachel peered out the kitchen door, unsure if she should intrude on Addie's discussion with the man. Addie caught her eye and signaled for her to join her.

"Zach was holding an old box for me. I've come for it."

"I have no idea what you are talking about."

"Addie, is this man harassing you?" Rachel interjected.

"Yes, he is."

"That's okay Ma'am, it's a nice Sunday—a day of rest. I'll be back in a few days; remember the box is mine. Do I need to enlighten you about an old bank robbery during Carnival?"

Addie gasped.

"Ah ha, I see you know what I mean."

The stranger hobbled back to his pickup and disappeared in the direction of Charron.

Sunday night dinner would be at a local Steak House, a break from the disturbances of the day and a chance to catch up. The restaurant had plush red velvet arm chairs and a private booth braced with railway ties.

"Matt, when you went through your Zach's desk, was there anything odd?" Addie asked.

"Maybe a key, or a note with an odd description?" Rachel added.

"Well, Addie, I was going to go over some things with you and found this key in a small envelope. It looked like it's for a cash box. The date written in pencil is 1967, on fragments of deteriorated pieces of newspaper. They began to flake into pieces when I tried to tap it out, so I thought it best left alone. It looked like more than one article."

Thomas said, "That is worth further investigation. I can collect the pieces and photograph them, then reconstruct it so it's readable. Since Zach had it with his secret papers, this might be significant. That was before you were married, wasn't it, Addie?"

"Five years before we were married. Never a word of anything before our wedding. Zach's beginning to sound paranoid about secrets. Nonetheless, he was an honest caring man who couldn't be involved in anything illegal."

Rachel said, "Zach would have been in his late teens and living on the estate. If I were to hide a box somewhere there, I would look behind the racks in the wine cellar or in the caves. In the movies, the culprits always searched in the most preserved places."

"There you go—your sleuthing mind is in full swing. Watching too many mystery movies." Thomas teased but added, "Tomorrow, we check the caves."

Addie said, "How did your work in the back quarter go? Perhaps I'll take a tractor ride myself in the morning and have a look at that fence you boys fixed."

"Hey, Addie, it's a big job. Why don't you wait another day or two?" Matthew winked at his step-mom.

"Matthew, if we are taking stock of unwanted visitors, we now have two of them threatening to return in a few days—Delacroix and Kincaid," Thomas said, then quipped, "Another security camera on the driveway and the house might be a deterrent."

Addie said, "Go ahead with that Matthew. I'll take you into the bank with me tomorrow and put you on the bank account. You must be accumulating some expenses belonging to the winery. Sorry I didn't think of that sooner. You must remind me when I overlook details."

Matthew was distracted at the impending access to the Ducharme bank accounts, but tried not to show his elation. "Steaks are here folks, let's enjoy this dinner."

SEVEN

Thomas and Rachel stayed up late to scrutinize Zach's desk drawer. Besides the envelope with the key and scraps of newspaper, there was another letter from the same time period. It was threatening, demanding that Zach secure the dole. It was signed by Dex.

Another note had been torn into four quarters and pushed into the back drawer crevice where it got stuck. It was from last year, warning Zach that Dex would be coming, and that it all better add up to 80,000 Brazilian cruzeiros.

A legal size envelope in the drawer was marked 'Offer'. Thomas pulled out the document. It was from Gregoire Delacroix approximately six months ago. The offer was for the entire vineyard, winery, and estate manor for one million dollars, a fraction of the present value.

Thomas didn't need to find how Zach reacted to the Offer. He knew the family ties to the estate could never be put up for sale. The land was a prized inheritance for generations to come.

Why did he even keep such a ridiculous offer?

Shreds of the newspapers were coming together. Thomas had photographed all the pieces and printed it. Rachel cut out each piece like a jigsaw puzzle and placed them together. The newspaper articles were starting to tell a story.

One was of The Great Train robbery in England in 1963. The next items were from a Brazilian newspaper; one in Portuguese and the other in English, both from The Rio News in Brazil in April, 1967.

"The common thread here, Thomas, is they are all bank robberies. I won't believe Uncle Zach was part of a robbery gang. It's too preposterous," Rachel blurted.

Thomas was absorbed with a magnifying glass.

Rachel mused, "It appears to be a matter of interest, or inspiration. Aunt Addie said Zach was born in 1951 so he'd be sixteen years old at this time. A kid out of high school wanting to see the world. Must have been scared silly all on his own."

"Rachel, did you see a passport in the drawer?"

"I'll have a look."

She found a small stack of personal papers, driver's license, birth certificate, and passport held together by a disintegrating elastic.

"Here it is," Rachel replied. "It expired many years ago, but it does have a Brazilian exit stamp from 1967. Only one trip, with a stapled attachment indicating his entry papers were missing. This is an Exit Appeal stamped by the American Embassy."

"Keep looking for anything else. Anything coinciding."

Shortly after midnight, Thomas and Rachel were interrupted by the glare of the motion detector lights in the driveway, and the German shepherds barking.

Within seconds, Addie's cries came from her bedroom as her window glass splintered.

Thomas took off out the back door, and Rachel raced upstairs. Addie was standing in the hall, holding a rock with paper wrapped around it and blood on her feet.

As Thomas turned the corner of the house, a red Silverado pickup sped past, but he got a partial license plate through the dust. With a flashlight, he followed the intruder's muddy footsteps to the back lawn.

The person knew Addie's window. Looks like inside information!

The commotion drew Matthew outside. Thomas noticed that Matthew was dressed like he'd come from the bar, and a bruise on his cheekbone was testament. Stepping closer, Thomas smelled the liquor.

"Will the footprints be valid evidence for the police?" Matthew asked with a moderate slur.

Thomas crouched to feel the print. "This one here is pretty good. I can take a photo but how do we make a cast of it? If we leave it until morning, it will blend into the dew."

Addie joined the inspection. "I have plaster of Paris in the garage, will that do, Thomas? Matthew and Thomas, you guys should have a look at the rock. Rachel and I are going upstairs. Goodnight."

Officer Murdock arrived at the winery at nine the next morning, with another detective.

"Addie, could I talk to you and Matthew for a few minutes?"

"Absolutely, I have a few things on my mind." Matthew heard them from the kitchen and took a seat.

"We've confirmed a fingerprint on the timing mechanism of your husband's truck. It belongs to the Delacroix boy, Lane. We'll send a warrant this morning. If his father put him up to it, there's nothing we can do unless the boy cops up.

After a few days in the clink, Lane will realize he'll be going away for most of his life, so he might turn on his Dad. The station will let you know when a date is set for trial."

Addie said, "It still leaves a situation with the Delacroix people trespassing and tampering with our grapes. Did Rocky ever come clean with the confrontation in the back quarter? There's no real damage to the vines, but it's the principle."

Officer Murdock was sitting at the table writing notes.

"I totally understand. But Rocky has disappeared. His mug shot is in the system, whenever he comes back to town. I'll follow-up with Jonas. Rocky must have given some indication of his involvement. My partner here is going to your back field today to talk to the men once more."

"You're free to talk to anyone working on the vineyards."

Matthew joined the conversation.

"Officer Murdock, we've had night visitors. The first one left a sparrow with a broken neck broken on Addie's rocker, telling her to sell. Then last night, he drove a red Silverado and threw a rock through Addie's window. It would have to be someone who knew where Addie slept. Here's the note."

"I'll take it and see if there's a chance of a fingerprint. Too bad you handled it without a tissue, Matthew. Maybe we'll get a match with the tire grid."

Matthew said, "For certain, it's the same person."

Thomas came in as Officer Murdock stood to leave.

"Hello, I saw your cruiser in the driveway and went to retrieve the security video of last night's intruder. Can you stay for a minute and I'll put it on my cell?"

"Go ahead."

"The intruder wore a balaclava, but his build was a sure match for the man claiming to be Dex." Thomas glanced at Matthew as he spoke.

"Do you know where we can find this Dexter fellow?"

"We don't, but we'll be more vigilant when he's back."

EIGHT

Rio de Janiero, Brazil, March 1967

Zachary Ducharme had finished his last high school semester, ready for a summer of adventure. He had two weeks before it was time to apply herbicide and the pre-post emergent. It was guaranteed to take more than a week.

His parents had given in to his relentless begging to go to Carnival in Brazil, right before Easter. Many conditions came with the plane ticket—no drinking, don't hook up with strangers, respect your curfew and avoid those Latino girls using their wiles to take your money.

His father demanded, "Remember to call your mother collect every other morning."

"Of course, Papa, we've talked about this many times."

Zach had surpassed his father in height—over six feet and growing. With raging hormones, he was a restless spirit. His mother saw him as a tall, strong, muscular, clean-shaven young man who would one day take over the vineyard and raise a family of his own. All her hopes rested on Zach.

Ma's worries were in her brow. "We'd be happier if you went with a friend. Traveling alone makes you a target for those drug people."

"I promise, Ma, when I get there I'll check in directly with the American Embassy. I'll stay where they recommend."

One heavy duffle was loaded into the trunk of the car. Ma had put on her Sunday hat for the ride to the airport. She chattered all the way, mostly with more rules and suggestions.

Deplaning at the Santo Dumas terminal in Rio de Janeiro after a long flight, Zach pushed through the crowds to the conveyor belt for his luggage. His backpack clearly identified his nationality with the bold luggage tag displaying the Stars and Stripes.

"Hey, Americano!" A fair-haired boy called from the other side of the circulating suitcases.

Feeling awkward at the loud announcement, he pointed to himself to be sure that he was being called. Other passengers were looking at him.

"Come here, over here." The boy gestured for Zach to make his way to the other side.

"Hey, man, it's nice to see a comrade. I'm an American myself—I've come to see the Carnival. Are you looking for a travel partner, kid?"

"Me too, but I'm checking in with the American Embassy as soon as I leave the airport."

"Naw, that's not necessary. Come with me, I have some friends with lots of room. You can stay with us." Zach received a friendly slap on the back and wasn't sure if there had been pressure against his side.

Zachary was burdened by his promise to his parents and the temptation of his new friend. He couldn't let his mother down. She'd harped relentlessly for the past week.

"I'll come with you, but I insist on going to the Embassy first. I still don't have my luggage."

"Suit yourself kid; I was only trying to help you out. You're on your own then." The young stranger picked up his duffle and blended into the lines of passengers waiting to clear customs.

Most of the luggage for his Los Angeles flight had cleared. With one last beep, a group of straggler bags were dumped in front of him.

Zach picked up his duffle, marked with a green neon sticker, and stood in the security lane which had already thinned out. The American was nowhere in sight.

Two Portuguese policemen stood against the wall watching, and making Zach uncomfortable as he edged forward. Two more passengers were in front of him.

Before he reached the passport desk, the two policemen came over and began speaking in Portuguese. One took him by the arm leading him to a small unventilated office out of sight of the waiting room.

"Americano, come this way."

"What did I do? I haven't cleared customs yet," Zach said.

"Quiet! We have rescued you from a nasty search. The American that spoke to you, put a packet of cocaine in your pocket. In Brazil that is a long prison term and you won't like our prisons. This neon tag has marked you." Suddenly, his Portuguese became clear English.

"I don't understand. I need to call the American Embassy."

"Don't make a scene or we can't help you!"

"Sit down," the other said.

Zach sat on the edge of the metal chair with perspiration dripping from his forehead and his fists clenched.

"From customs point of view, you should be dragged away for smuggling drugs. From our point of view, we could use the help of an American. It is your choice. He looked down at the passport in his hand. ". . . Zachary Ducharme."

"I'd like to call my parents."

The two men laughed and shook their heads with pity.

"I understand, and no I don't want to go to a Brazilian prison. The second choice, I'm not clear about."

"Ah, it is the second choice then. You'll come with us. It is important we have the help of an American with a passport who can easily leave the country. We have an enormous task and several other people to help. The drive to a town where we have our base is many hours' drive from Rio."

"For appearance sake, we will handcuff you and take you through the back halls where we have transportation waiting. Don't speak to anyone along the way."

The other gripped his arm and forced him toward the door. "Keep walking."

A faded green army vehicle was at the curb, with a canvas tarp tied over the open back, stacked with crates and sacks. Zachary climbed in with his duffle. He was still cuffed and they shoved him under the tarp.

Passing through a security checkpoint, both Portuguese men spoke their native language, joking with the guard. It was afternoon and the sun was burning the tarp, like a furnace for Zach, without water.

He called through an opening. "Sir, it's hot and I'm thirsty."

A warm bottle of water was passed to him and they opened the tarp to create a window space of air. Feeling dehydrated, he rested his head on the side rail with his face to the breeze. He imagined freedom but couldn't see a way.

Three hours later, they arrived at a lush estate in the quaint town of Santos del Mer. The iron gates were opened by remote and two gardeners came to speak to the driver.

The head man pointed to the side of the house. "Park your truck in the lane and leave the boy with me."

Zachary voluntarily climbed out of the back and his handcuffs were removed.

Directed into the mansion through the front doors and marble hall, his eyes were wide with awe at the opulence in the living room and the long dining room. The furniture was luxurious and still covered in plastic wrap.

"Follow me." The gardener led him down to the lower level where eight men were working in a tunnel. An elevator sized door had been broken through in the basement. They looked at him and returned to their work.

"Sit here, Zachary. I'll explain our mission to you and how important you will be in our success. Martine will prepare you a good lunch. Perhaps you'd like a shower later before your shift begins. You'll be in the tunnel for six hours before you come back out to rest."

"What is the objective of the tunnel?"

"Not too many questions. It will become clear to you in time. We have been working for almost two months and need one more month before we arrive at the Banco Centrale. That's quite enough for now."

"I promised my parents that I would call to let them know that I arrived safely. May I please telephone them? If they don't hear from me, they will set off alarm bells with the Embassy. I can't stay for a month, I'm due back next week."

His Portuguese hostage taker was in charge and shook his head. "Not yet. We'll talk about it again later."

Martine brought a hearty bowl of black bean stew with a corn tortilla. Zachary ate without looking up; it was his first meal since San Francisco. He was still hungry when Martine collected the bowl and wine cup, and she was pleased that his bowl was wiped clean.

"I have acarajé in the kitchen. They are cold but you can have a few." Zach was confused but polite in his single nod. "They are balls made with deep fried shrimp, black-eyed peas, and onions. They are especially tasty. Would you like to try them?"

"Yes, Ma'am. The stew was delicious."

The Portuguese policeman came back to collect him for the job. "Are you ready, my friend?" he asked.

"I suppose, Sir. What I am to do?"

"You can call me Kane. Take this lantern and follow the rope until you come to some other men. They will teach you how to pass. Roberto will show you."

Zach didn't know where he was and had no means of escape. Descending into the earth put his stomach in knots. For twenty minutes, he forged through the dark cave with his lantern, and a bottle of water attached to his belt.

The tunnel was well fortified with plastic lining and stud posts with a double metal track running through the middle. Buckets of earth were loaded onto a rolling dolly and sent along the track to the basement. The month passed quickly, with Zach digging and filling pails with dirt.

He stopped as Roberto dumped a full pail on him at the alcove. Before he could turn, a burly man climbed toward him, shoving him to the ground for attention and intimidation.

Zach shouted, "What the heck are you doing?"

"Hey, boy, watch your tongue! I'm Dex, show me respect. I'll be checking on quality performance." The man's anger turned to an ironic laugh.

"Sorry, Dex. I'm Zach."

"Yeah, I know. Listen up Zach." He took a swig of beer. "In the evenings open your ears to the talk that goes on rehearsing the robbery. You and I can make a deal. In here is the best privacy. I'll be meeting up with you again."

He swallowed another mouthful of beer.

"The way my plan stands now, you will be staged as a customer in the bank carrying a briefcase. During the kafuffle, you'll make your way into the vault. A brown bag will be waiting for you to stash into your briefcase. Take it and scurry back to the house. My cousin will have a produce truck nearby for you to hop a ride to Rio.

"Get directly out of Brazil, and I will find you in California later—I know your address. With the numbers involved, there are sure to be arrests. Keep your head under the radar and you will be thought of as a scared rabbit. But if you do not join my double-cross, you'll get a bullet in the back of the head when you leave the vault. It's just the two of us. The other plan that Kane has for you is impossible. You wouldn't make it out of the bank alive."

"I'll keep my ears open at night," he agreed.

Zach had a new level of fear and adrenaline.

Trucks came and went during the night from the back garage door, with the watchmen confident the neighbors' curiosity wouldn't be peaked. Buckets of earth were dumped into the hold until each truck heaved under the weight.

Sleeping bags were spread in rows on the main floor in a room that could have been a library. Zach's nightly routine from the tunnel was always mechanical. Simply to shower, eat Martine's supper and take his aching muscles to bed.

But tonight he took extra time to eavesdrop. He listened to Kane talking with Roberto and Dex about the vault details, and about photos of the interior that he'd stolen from the security company.

Dex was right. In the morning Zach was much smarter, but bags showed under his eyes.

Ten days later the target date arrived and they were ready. All it needed was a tap through to the vault. Celebrations with beer and special paella were created by Martine, with shrimp, sausage, chicken, mussels, rice and beans, a welcome levity for the industrious gang.

Dex gave Zach a wink, and handed him a bottle of Skol, his first as a minor.

"Zach, Martine's brother will take you to the Banco Central at 8:00 a.m. You'll be one of the first customers to enter when the doors open. Be sure not to look at security cameras, or at any of the men; keep your head out of view. The boys will burst through from the vault at precisely 8:10 a.m., after the manager has unlocked the vault. You know what to do after that, right?" Dex slapped him on the back hard enough to know the meaning.

Voices murmured throughout the night as anticipation became anxiety. Zach heard something Dex hadn't mentioned and wondered if it was a deliberate trap. But common sense told him it wasn't, it was part of Kane's plan all along. With Dexter's secret plan, Zach would escape back through the tunnel to the house.

Zach thought about all the consequences and mostly how he could get out alive.

I'm on my own. I can't trust any of them!

He shuffled closer to Kane to listen to that plan.

Kane was whispering to Roberto. "As soon as we clear the vault, you will detonate the setting in the tunnel. They are set at spaced intervals to blast the tunnel back into the earth without creating a crater above ground. It will take them a year to find the house."

Roberto nodded. "I'll give the gang five minutes to exit the vault and get into the bank. I'll set the timer for five minutes after I follow you."

Zach's heart was pounding while he made desperate calculations.

Ten minutes max. I won't have a second to spare.

He'd have no choice but to race through the tunnel ahead of the detonations. The briefcase was going to weigh him down. Inventing scenarios of how he could stash the goods on his body, his mind didn't rest.

I'm counting on the luge track in the tunnel to save my life.

Morning came too quickly. After his shower, Zach dressed in the clothes laid out. All the clothing went through Martine, checking pockets and shoes. Beside the clean clothes were his backpack and passport that Dex had returned. He emptied the backpack and strapped it on.

Kane called up the stairs. "Zach, it's time to come down. Enrique is here early."

A glass of mango juice and a sandwich were on the kitchen counter for him.

"I'm ready, Enrique."

At the road, an old Harley motorcycle waited for him. He climbed on the back.

I'm not sure this thing will make it to town.

The banco doors opened precisely at eight with half a dozen customers surging through. Zach sidled to a nearby restroom, then emerged into the main bank. When it was clear, he took a place at the end of the customer line, where he was less obvious. A nerve twitched on his face.

The plan was for Zach to trip over his briefcase and create a deterrent for the men coming out of the tunnel from the basement floor. Kane entered the main floor quietly and surprised the Manager as he opened the vault doors. Kane smashed the man's head on the steel vault and dropped him to the ground out of sight.

Anxiety overcame Zach. He checked his watch every minute. Soon they would notice the Manager was missing.

I can do this!

The troop of robbers wore masks and fired into mid-air, beginning the chaos. Kane led the four gunmen past where

Zach stood. Recovering from his fall and distraction, Zach stepped slowly. He inched to the side and then around the thieves and backward down the stairs into the vault past Roberto. The gang didn't see him leave.

That's Dex's bag. So far so good.

Dumping Dex's contents of currency and jewels into his backpack, Zach was the only one left in the basement. He could tell from the sounds that there wasn't a clean escape upstairs for the bandits, but he stayed focused on his plan.

Sirens blared and the volley of rat-a-tat-tat gunfire now inside the building was relentless. Zach's breathing was rapid. With a thrust of adrenaline, he crawled into the tunnel easing himself onto the sliding luge platform on the track, always counting out loud.

At the sound of Robert's voice, he glanced back a final time. Roberto was screaming Zach's name into the darkness, yelling for him to return. With the strength of both arms, he pushed to propel the luge into the tunnel.

Travelling a third of the distance in the first five minutes, he heard a harrowing crash behind him, and a grey dust cloud surged through the tunnel. The track turned sharply every hundred feet, jolting Zach along the two mile track, but he held on with confidence built up from his familiarity with the route.

Zach's pace accelerated, but as the explosions got closer and the suffocating cloud almost upon him, he pulled his shirt over his nose and mouth, and gasped for breath. His eyes squinted into the clear tunnel.

His imagination called out to him. "Zach!" He heard it and shook his head as it broke the solitude; it was impossible, a delusion. Then again, "Zach!"

He couldn't take a chance of slowing, but someone was behind him. Another implosion echoed through the smoke and he felt hands grabbing at his ankles. The weight of the earth was heavy on his legs and struggling would be futile.

NINE

Light from the garage was filtering ahead in the final stretch. Zach pulled his legs forward and snapped them with a frog kick, knocking the assailant from the dolly, and releasing his own feet from the man's grip.

A final explosion shook the tunnel, crashing the dirt and boards around him. Zach had reached the end and could breathe the fresh air, but his body was partially entombed except for his head and forearms. Nothing was behind him other than soil, and surely his pursuer had suffocated.

I'm guessing it was Roberto.

Clawing with his fingers, the soil eased until he moved his arms; then his legs wrenched, giving him leverage. There were moments when Zach thought he was doomed to die, and it took more than an hour to break free.

He pulled himself out onto the floor of the house, and stayed still to allow his lungs to expand and breathe deeply.

I am a Ducharme with strength and courage. I can keep going. I will.

Zach carefully checked for life in the house, but it was totally empty. It echoed without the furniture, and all signs of habitation were gone. Appliances, sinks and doorknobs had been polished clean and he was careful to avoid leaving new fingerprints.

He showered quickly and changed to his own clothes from his backpack. He packed a layer of currency into its lining, then ripping a small opening in his leather jacket, he padded that with bills.

All that was left in the briefcase was a handful of jewelry. He stuffed some into the toes of his shoes and the few remaining diamonds went into a waist safe under his shirt.

The fruit wagon was waiting at the corner, as Dexter planned.

"Obrigado!" Zach greeted the wagon driver and settled in for a slow trudge to Rio, glad to breathe the fresh air but weak from his struggle with death.

The secondary roads were bumpy and tedious, but the '52 Chevrolet stake truck kept a steady pace through the farmland. Twice in the three hour trip, they stopped to rest the truck and add water and coolant to the radiator. Sitting with the driver, Zach maintained small talk in Portuguese that he'd learned from the boys at the casa.

Zach knew in his heart that his parents had contacted the American Embassy and police. With no word from him in over a month, they would have feared the worst.

Nervous that he'd be tagged by the American Embassy, Zach anticipated a challenge at Rio customs and airport security. He knew the border guards could assert their authority without provocation, as he had no stamp of entry. His only hope would be an appeal to the American Embassy for a visa to pass.

A few miles into the city of Rio, the wagon driver stopped at a service station.

"I can't take you further, Zach. These roads are closed for Carnival parades and parties today. But you can rent a motorcycle from my friend who owns this gas station. Or I'll ask if he can spare an old bicycle."

Blocks from Copacabana beach, Zach wound in and out on the bike through reveling locals and tourists, toward the downtown embassies. He had no choice but to wear his padded leather jacket in the heat of high noon.

At a pay phone, he made two calls; the first to the American Embassy to confirm that he was safe and still in Brazil, and the second to his parents.

In the imposing American Embassy, he insisted on waiting for an interview. The questioning on his past whereabouts was tense, but they accepted his story of staying with friends to attend Carnival. By late afternoon, as the Embassy employees were ready to party at the beaches, he walked to the street with a prized entry card.

Kane had left Zach's original papers and US currency intact and he had enough cash for a taxi. The cab maneuvered back streets to avoid the parade from the Ipanema shoreline. They jammed and jostled through the traffic circles and within an hour they could see the airport signs.

A new wave of panic was on his mind, fearing both a pat down at security and a red flag from the entry stamp missing on his passport.

Zach purchased his ticket on the evening flight to San Francisco, and passed through Brazilian security without suspicion. The screener asked about his leather jacket, and Zach joked that he couldn't fit it into his luggage.

Landing at SFO, his backpack was pulled aside for a drug search, however a search dog gave him a pass.

TEN

Napa Valley, February 2012 (2 years before)

Zach collected a postal special delivery requiring his signature in Charron. The contents gave him an unexpected jolt.

> *Zach,*
> *I am out of prison. Meeting up with you there has given me a goal to get to America. You will remember, half the booty is mine. Be warned, I am coming for it.*
> *Dex*

Zach noted the date and return address, then folded the letter into small squares and stuck it in the back of his wallet. A cell phone number was on the bottom corner in pencil.

Rushing through the back kitchen door, he saw Addie.

"How's my girl?" Zach gave her a hasty kiss on the cheek. "I'm going down to make a count of the last batch of Beaujolais."

"Suit yourself, but lunch will be ready in an hour."

Calling the cell phone, a husky aggravated voice answered.

"Zach, I've been waiting. You still got the goods?"

His heart pounded. "I have them securely hidden in my wine caves, the sooner I can be rid of them, the better. The whole lot is yours—I don't want any part of it. I was a hostage, not your partner."

Dex lightened up. "How be we share a drink? You got a local pub, that way I don't have to take a chance on meeting the Missus."

"Sure. How close are you to Charron?"

"A half day's drive."

"Meet me at the Rusty Nail. South of Charron in the town of Ascot, not much there but a pub."

"I won't miss it."

The face was unrecognizable, but the years quickly washed away when they stood across the room from each other at the Rusty Nail.

"Still want your beer, or try something stronger like Whiskey?" Zach asked.

"Corona with some pucker."

Zach returned with two drinks, deliberately avoiding eye contact with the bartender.

Dex took a long gulp.

"Where's the goods?"

"I couldn't bring it today, but it hasn't been touched in all those years. I need a decoy, to give me time in the wine caves to retrieve it. Where are you staying?"

"There's a fleabag motel up the road, called Sunset Slumber." Dexter leaned across the table and yanked Zach by the collar. "I'll give you forty-eight hours and no more."

Dex lingered over another beer after Zach departed.

A tall man in a straw fedora had been sitting at the table behind. For the last two weeks, he'd been tailing Zach. He stood and approached Dex.

"I overheard your conversation. Sounds like you have business with Zach Ducharme."

The man stood calmly as Dex's face turned red with rage.

"How dare you."

"No, no, Dex. I would like to offer my assistance to recover your debt."

They stared at one another, before the stranger spoke. His voice had a slow drone.

"Zachary Ducharme has become a stubborn obstacle and I assure you I can make matters easier for you. Those vineyards are like the back of my hand. Can I buy one more round?"

Napa Valley, present day

Thomas and Rachel sat across the desk from Addie's lawyer.

"We have an Offer to Purchase for $1.5 million by a numbered company. My search shows that the company is registered to Lane Delacroix. But an odd situation arose in the process. Shares of the Delacroix estate were recently given to a man I've never heard of, Dexter Kincaid."

Rachel gasped.

"I smell a rat," Thomas exclaimed.

"Excuse me?" The lawyer's face was sullen.

"Dexter Kincaid has been harassing Addie, by throwing a rock through her bedroom window and trespassing."

"Have the police been notified."

"Oh, yes," Rachel said. "Officer Murdock has the details."

The lawyer asked, "Why do you think this man is mixed up with the Delacroix estate?"

Thomas said, "Zach Ducharme was a quiet man keeping his secrets in his desk drawer. From our research of restored papers, his past as a possible hostage in Brazil has come around to haunt him. There was also an envelope marked '1967' with a key inside.

"The article says that all the bank robbers were accounted for, with four dead and four incarcerated. There was mention of a missing customer that disappeared during the melee."

"Mr. York, are you suggesting that Zach was the missing customer and is somehow involved?"

"That's a possibility. During the heist, Zach life's was constantly under threat. The four men that went to prison were serving terms of up to forty-two years. If you calculate from 1967 to now, it's feasible."

"How do you know about all this?" The lawyer retreated. "You have entered a realm of suspicion I cannot tread into. All I can help you with are matters relating to the Will and the Offer of Sale."

Rachel stood up.

"We didn't fully introduce our background. My husband is Thomas York, and I am Rachel Redmond, we're detectives. We were invited here by Addie to solve her husband's murder. You're aware that the explosion was not accidental, but rather intentional murder."

The lawyer's eyes widened.

"I'm sorry," he said. "I didn't know it was murder."

Addie was on the veranda when they drove in, eager to hear about the meeting with the lawyer.

"How did it go?"

Rachel said, "Reasonably well. We learned that Dexter has a share in the Delacroix property."

Thomas looked Addie in the eye. "We need to agree on a solid story to protect Zach's reputation. If tongues wag around town, there will be a lot of guessing and fabrication."

Addie was ready to face the fact that it was close to becoming both news and gossip.

"We'd already been married a number of years when Zach told be about the robbery. I was aghast."

Thomas said, "Zach needs the truth told, in his memory. As a mere teenager out of high school, he was coerced into an armed gang of thieves, planning a heist of a Brazilian bank. He was kidnapped and forbidden contact with his family. Followed by threats against his life and his family, he returned to California with a small booty to be recovered by the thieves."

"Thomas, that's about right. From here on, we will all stick to the story, with no deviations," Addie stated firmly. "I don't see any reason to say more."

"What story does Matthew have?" Rachel asked.

"I'll talk to him. And Rachel, we should see for ourselves at the Land Registry office about the titles on the Ducharme estate and the Delacroix estates."

"That's good," Rachel said, "we need valid proof of the geological ownership of the wine caves and volcanic lava more than six feet under. They may be under ancient crown leases. I did research about these volcanic caves.

"The lava tunnels are in deep embedded caverns extending in underground creeks. The enriched soil is volcanically enhanced producing the highest quality grapes and unique wines that have become the trademark of your estate."

"Are you saying this volcanic lava is all over the Ducharme property?" Thomas asked.

"No, but it is definitely under the west fields. The long tunnels were originally a flow route on long distances, but the caverns don't seem to have an open root system."

"Wouldn't it seem likely that the Delacroix land would also benefit from the lava?"

"They run in veins, it could impact them."

Thomas said, "Perhaps Gregoire and his boys don't know, if they've never surveyed their land below the surface. There might not be any reason for their jealousy of Zach's crops—they may have had the same opportunity."

Rachel nodded. "We'll see when the last land survey was taken."

At the registry office, the original purchase of the Ducharme estate from the United States government was dated July 1880, with the land description amounting to one half hectare of unturned agricultural land, equal to about four sections.

The taxation rolls of the early 1900's indicated that fifty percent of the land was fertile, turned agricultural land and used for the purpose of a vineyard. A small strip on the frontage was designated for residential and commercial use.

"I assume the Ducharmes had to clear the land by hand and oxen. I find it admirable that a large family would pull together and accomplish fifty percent clearing of so much land."

"Those were the days when folks worked from dawn to dusk seven days a week, and struggled to feed their families. I'd be interested when their first wine was produced."

Rachel reviewed the county census records for 1970, when Zachary would have been on the estate. She printed copies of the document for each of them to review, listing residents of the estate first, and workers in the field camp.

DUCHARME, Francois, Head of Household, 45 yrs.
CHEVALLIER, Margaret-Louise, Wife, 42 yrs.
DUCHARME, Antoinette, Daughter, 22 yrs.
DUCHARME, Zachary, Son, 20 yrs.

DUCHARME, Celia, Daughter, 19 yrs.
DUCHARME, Pierre, Son, 18 yrs.
DUCHARME, Marie-Louise, Daughter, 17 yrs.
DUCHARME, Robert, Son, 16 yrs.
DUCHARME, Jacob, Widower, 79 yrs.
BAPTISTE, Jean, Cousin, 26 yrs.
ESTABAR, Maria, Kitchen help, 23 yrs.
WILKES, David, Foreman, 24 yrs.
HANSON, Nathan, Foreman, 27 yrs.
WALKER, Edward, Foreman, 19 yrs.
DAVIS, Jeremy, Foreman, 22 yrs.

"A further list documented family members of the foremen residences at the field camp, representing a cluster of eight cottages in an open area accessed from a lane at the east boundary of the estate."

Rachel pulled a pen and notepad from her bag to draw a property sketch.

"Next to the cottages is a garage. An upper level has been converted to a bunk house, with several rooms lined with bunk beds."

"Can we stroll through it when we get back? Charles must have left before the Census."

Rachel said, "This accounts for the period a few years after the Brazilian caper. Zachary's brother Pierre was two years younger. I wonder if Zach revealed his secrets to him."

"Not likely. Zach tried to conceal that part of his life."

"Thomas, look! The list of residents in the village is lengthy but here . . ." Rachel pointed to an entry for the spouse of Nathan Hanson.

"Caliste Delacroix!"

"There are two ways to look at this," Thomas said. "Either she never revealed her maiden name to the Ducharmes, or the two estates had a congenial relationship forty years ago."

"Frankly, I still have suspicions about Matthew. We don't know much about him, like how he suddenly arrived."

Rachel said, "You're right. Jonas was unable to locate a current listing for him in Addie's address book. Yet he turned up the day after Zach's death, knowing exactly what the Will stated."

Driving into the estate lane, they found Addie sobbing on the back lawn.

Rachel ran from the car. "Addie, what happened?"

Addie pointed at her laundry line and struggled to get up. On Fridays, Addie washed the linens in her machine, but instead of using the dryer, she always hung them to dry in the California sun.

"Someone is threatening me. They've spray painted the words 'You Owe Me' on my clean linens. I don't care about the linens, it's the constant threats. Is my life in danger next?"

Rachel looked up. "Thomas, do the security cameras cover this area of the lawn?"

Thomas helped Addie to a chair.

"Rachel, could you make a cup of tea for Addie inside?" Before the two women reached the kitchen door, Thomas called out to Addie.

"One more thing. Have you seen Matthew this morning?"

She called back, "I saw him going into the back field with Jonas. I don't know if he returned, but he wasn't in for lunch."

Thomas surveyed the scene and lowered the linen evidence for the police.

I don't trust Matthew, I know he's involved with this whole mess.

ELEVEN

Thomas stretched his hand into the eaves trough above the workshop for the security room key. He unlocked the weathered door to the corner alcove and switched on the hanging light bulb. The monitor and recording machine were on a high shelf with two boxes of discs filed by date.

Jonas and Zach were the only ones with known access to the room to remove or back up the discs.

Thomas took out the latest one and inserted it. He fast forwarded to when Matthew went to the fields, and started the action with Addie hanging her sheets. Stopping at intervals to watch for potential shadows, nothing moved except a cat and a pair of wandering goats.

Scrutinizing the frames, as Maria walked to the garden to pick a few tomatoes, he returned to the house.

At 11:35 a.m. there new was activity. Jonas knocked and waited at the back kitchen door for over three minutes before Maria responded. She handed him the lunch hamper and jugs and he returned to the field truck, stowed the hamper, and drove into the lane.

As soon as Jonas had gone, a new figure moved along the west side of the garage, then waited under the gigantic magnolia tree. Then a second man walked from the direction of the road and met with the man in the shadows. He was tall with a straw cowboy hat.

Pulling a handkerchief over his face so the camera couldn't get a clear look, he removed a can of spray paint from a bag. The first man was still at the magnolia.

He obviously is aware of the cameras. No one outside the house knows about them other than Jonas. Matthew is the problem.

The first man stayed at the magnolia, but the second strode with confidence over the knoll of the back lawn toward the laundry line. He was on the opposite side of the sheets, with only his feet and hat visible while the deed occurred.

Returning to the tree, he tossed the spray can to the first man still concealed by the shadows, then walked down the driveway. Moments later, a truck engine roared away toward Charron.

Thomas kept his focus on the first man, trying to find a detail he could match. The shadow remained, watching the sheets until Addie came out the back door to retrieve her laundry at the platform at the end of the veranda.

Switching to a different disc vantage from the back of the house, Thomas could now view the entire width of the property, including the garage. Slowly he watched the frames for anything to change. He noted each vehicle and accounted for the usual ones from the main house, and the foremen. Nothing was unusual.

In the corner of his eye, he saw a slight movement at the back of the garage. Walking nonchalantly, the man came to empty space and then disintegrated into the rows of grapes.

Preposterous! Is it someone at the estate focused on distressing Addie? They stood and watched her suffering and pleading for help.

Matthew came in as Thomas was locking the security room and the garage doors. Zach's two motorcycles were harbored inside, along with a broken down vineyard truck.

"Hey, Thomas, you missed a commotion."

"No, Matthew, I didn't."

"Has something upset you?"

"Of course, aren't you upset that someone is harassing Addie. I don't understand why. She has no intention of selling the winery."

"That's not an absolute, Thomas. I am now part owner too. I have a say."

"You're crazy to have such a thought. The winery has been the passion of the Ducharme family for years. Addie doesn't know any other life but this. Zach's memory is around every corner."

"Well, Thomas, I really didn't ask your opinion. I can make my own decisions."

Matthew face bristled with tension as he turned and went into the house. Thomas watched him go, and decided to blow off a little steam. He headed on foot toward the second service house.

"Hello, Thomas!" Jonas was pruning nearby and dropped his hardware to speak with him.

"Hi, Jonas, I didn't mean to disturb you, I needed a walk. It's peaceful back here, with a scenic view of the main house."

"You never disturb me." Jonas said. "I'm always glad to see a friendly face." He displayed a fine row of pearly white teeth.

"Can I talk to you?"

"Sure! What's up?"

"Did you hear about Addie's sheets? Have you seen anyone at the back of the house a few hours ago?"

"Oh, no. I wondered what the raucous was about. I'm afraid, I keep my head down. I get absorbed in perfecting the vines. Sounds are different though and I did hear the garage door slam about three o'clock."

"It's a shame someone would agonize such a delightful woman. You know she is determined not to sell."

"I would hope not. Zach and Addie both loved this place. We are like one big family here. Before Zach died, we used to spend time after dinner discussing the smallest of events in the fields. They both had a great sense of humor. Addie deserves to be taken seriously. She is smart and will manage the winery, as well or better than Zach."

"I'm sure she would appreciate your confidence. One more thing, Jonas. Has anyone approached you in the last year about working elsewhere?"

Jonas's eyes went to the ground and his feet shuffled in the dust.

"I turned them away flat. One time working in the far west corner, a man came through the lanes to find me. I've told him to stay off Ducharme land, or I would see that he is charged with trespassing."

"Thanks, Jonas, you're a good man. Did you recognize him at all?"

Jonas looked to the ground, and Thomas gave him a pat on the back.

As Thomas turned toward the house, Jonas called. "I don't like to incriminate an innocent person, but I'm sure it was one of the Delacroix boys. They both look a lot alike so it's hard to tell."

"I can see your dilemma."

"Thomas! You know things aren't right, don't you?"

"If you have something direct to say, say it, Jonas."

"It's about Matthew. But I'm afraid I'm not showing respect to my employer. Matthew is now a full partner of the winery. I'd sell my false teeth, if it wasn't him I saw with a bad dude at the Rusty Nail near Ascot, shortly after Zach died."

"Are you positive?"

"I was picking up a case of beer for our Saturday night barbeque, and I happened through the bar. It was only for a second."

"Think hard, Jonas. Have you seen the man around here in the last year?"

"I can't be sure. The straw hat that he wore at the pub—I did see one like it in the worker's village. It has a red feather in the band, and no red birds are in this part of the Napa."

Thomas felt he was onto something. "What drew your attention to him?"

"He was talking with Nathan Hanson. Nathan is retired now, but he stops in from time to time. I've seen Nathan talking with Lane Delacroix once or twice."

"Why does he do that?"

"Being friendly, I thought."

Thomas said, "I did some checking up on the workers and found there was a Caliste Delacroix married to Nathan Hanson. Were you aware of that, Jonas?"

"My goodness! That shakes the cobwebs loose. There was some sort of incident with Caliste way back. Whatever it was passed, and the Hansons continued to live on the estate through several generations. They were set up by Zach and took a retirement cottage in Charron, but a few of their boys are around." The two men looked at each other realizing it was a piece of the puzzle.

"This is such a huge piece of land, it's difficult to keep track of people throughout the day. On the low down, will you keep an eye on Matthew?"

"Sure!" He held out his hand. "Glad to help."

TWELVE

Remote Island off the coast of Normandy, present day

Streteched out on a cot in a dark stone-walled room, Daniel Boisvert's shoulder length locks were drenched in sweat from fever. He had grown an uncomfortable beard.

A man in a long religious robe knelt beside him.

"He's been in and out of a coma for the last week. Perhaps it's time to bring a doctor from the village."

"No. There can be no sign of him ever being here."

"The Tylenol for fever hasn't made any difference. I've kept him hydrated through intravenous and added a drop of morphine when he appears to be near convolutions. What else do you expect me to do?"

"He must remain alive."

The inquisitor turned his back locking the door behind him, then climbed a ladder at the end of the hall. Opening a dormer, he emerged into sunshine and embarked on a rowboat tethered to the dock. The surf rolled in crashing against boulders, then trickling back onto a white beach.

Napa Valley, California

Rachel and Addie were having coffee when Thomas walked in.

"Hello, Thomas. Rachel tells me you've been out around town doing some sleuthing."

Thomas bent over Addie and kissed her forehead.

"You are stuck with us for a few more weeks. Any objections?"

"I love the company. I'm not ready to sleep again in a stark quiet house."

Rachel said, "Thomas, I was waiting for you to come in before I told Addie about our discovery."

"Discovery? Oh good." Addie laughed and rubbed her hands together as if she was about to hear an old mountain legend.

"Rachel, you tell the story," Thomas prodded.

"We wanted to affirm, from the 1970 Census, who lived in the Ducharme estate at the time Zach was about twenty years old. The newspaper articles we found were from that period."

"I would like to see that. It would be close to the time we were married."

Holding the copy of the census in her hand, Addie perused and mouthed each name softly.

"Poor Grandfather Jacob was a widower. There was an older brother, Charles, who I see must have left home before the census. I wasn't sure what took place between Jacob Sr. and Charles, but it caused Charles to leave. There was a strain in the family and I didn't see Charles much, so I wasn't surprised when they got Matthew."

Rachel said, "Of particular interest, was the list of residents in the compound."

"Oh, yes," Addie reminisced. "On Saturday nights, we all went to the worker's village for a pig roast barbeque and corn husking. We'd sing and dance long into the night; they were grand old times. I wonder why that stopped. Perhaps I'll ask Jonas to take me back there on Saturday."

"Addie, do you remember one of the girls in the village, Caliste Delacroix?' Rachel asked. "She was married to Nathan Hanson."

"Goodness gracious! I didn't know a Delacroix worked here. I wonder if any more Hanson descendants are still workers. The commotion about Charles had something to do with Caliste."

Thomas said, "I'll get a current list of workers from Jonas to look for connections to your neighbors."

Rachel stood up to change the tension. "I'm going to get us fresh coffee and some of those currant scones that Maria pulled out of the oven."

"Thanks, Rachel, but maybe a cup of tea instead. Chamomile will settle my nerves. Oh dear, I am asking you to make me tea; I'm supposed to be the hostess."

"Aunt Addie, we are family. Stay where you are. Besides, I miss fidgeting in the kitchen."

"Thomas, you really picked a good one," Addie winked.

"I tell myself that every morning."

Matthew came in as Rachel laid out the scones. He took a chair at the table and avoided eye contact with Thomas.

"Are any sandwiches left from lunch? I got working in the back fields and forgot to meet up with the lunch wagon."

Rachel said, "Sorry, Matthew, the lunch basket is empty. How about some fresh scones for now? Supper will be another hour and a half."

"Fair enough. What's the topic of conversation here?"

This time, Thomas gave Matthew a knowing glance, lasting an awkward amount of time. Addie noticed.

Thomas asked, "What were you so absorbed in that you forgot lunch? Didn't you hear the noon bell? I wonder if anyone else back there got forgotten. It would be pretty rough working through the afternoon with nothing in your stomach." Thomas inflected a taste of irony.

Matthew shot back in a flash. "Only a Ducharme would understand."

"Please boys, we need to get along," Rachel said.

"Well folks, I must adjourn for now. The tea hit the spot." Addie rose to tie her apron and pulled out an assortment of pots and pans.

"Aunt Addie, I'll help with supper. This is Maria's night off."

Matthew didn't move and asked for seconds.

"I guess I am the only genuine Ducharme here, anyway. What was your maiden name again, Addie?" Matthew's pointed sarcasm shocked Addie. She didn't turn her back, but Rachel could see she was biting her lip.

After dinner, Thomas excused himself. He called Addie aside.

"I need to examine Zach's desk again. There must be a major clue we've overlooked. From what I've heard about Zach and his devotion to the winery, there must be something we haven't found."

"What are you thinking, Thomas?" Addie was surprised.

Thomas said, "You understand what I'm thinking, don't you? Zach's character should not be in question. Someone is purposely tainting his memory and legacy."

"Yes, yes. You're right."

"Addie, if you wangle an invitation from Jonas to the workers compound on Saturday night, Rachel and I would like to join you. Sometimes, the stories from another generation are enlightening."

"Now, you've gone and ruined the romance of my evening." Addie chided and broke into a big smile. Then a blush.

At Zach's desk, Thomas went directly to the task.

Yes, the newspapers are still here but Matthew took the original Will to the lawyer, this is only a copy.

He held the Will up to the desk lamp to compare Zach's signature to another document.

It looks the same. Matthew is the only one to benefit from a forged Will or Offer of Purchase. The ages on the census could indicate that Zach's older brother Charles is Matthew's real father. Odd that he didn't attend the funeral. Addie said there was bad blood with one of the brothers years ago, but at a funeral he could let bygones be bygones.

Napa Valley April 1967

Zachary's parents met his arrival from Brazil at the San Francisco airport. They intended to scold him, but instead they were overjoyed that he was back and safe.

They could see he had been through some kind of trauma, as he wanted time by himself. Back a few days, he regained his appetite and routine, and asked if he could work in the wine cellars.

With a chisel, he notched a cleft in the corner of the cave wall behind the oldest of the wine racks, a place where no one would look. There was a natural fissure and a tight squeeze, and he emerged with vintage dust across his backside. He took several more hours sweeping and covering his tracks.

Two nights later, he went alone with a tin box containing the small amount of jewelry taken from the Brazilian vault.

Reaching into the crevice, he locked the box and placed it as far as it would go.

He slipped the key into his pocket in a brown envelope. He surveyed the area.

Odd that there's a draft from the crevice.

He walked back to the house in the darkness and to his bedroom over the vineyard. Since he was a child the telescope had been there, and whenever he couldn't sleep, he had spent hours searching the fields.

On the third day back, Zach went into Charron to the hardware store. Without telling his parents, he ordered new wallpaper for his bedroom. Secured in the trunk of his car, he waited until the house was quiet and his family asleep.

The wallpaper was smuggled up to his bedroom and tucked into the space behind his closet, a typical farmhouse pattern with colors of flowers and cherubs.

Napa Valley, present day

Thomas examined each scrap of paper in Zach's desk as if it could be the missing piece.

From previous experience, he emptied and removed the entire middle drawer. Turning it over, he found a letter size manila envelope taped with duct tape and a notation 'In the event of my death'.

Another Will.

The first thing he checked was the date, signed on the first anniversary of Addie and Zach's wedding.

I think the Will discovered earlier was dated about a month before Zach's death. No point in causing Addie undue alarm.

Rachel tiptoed from behind Thomas. Her arms reached about his waist and she nuzzled a warm kiss against the nape of his neck.

"It's time for bed!"

"Sorry, Rachel, I'm on the track of some significant evidence. You go ahead and I'll come along in a bit."

Her heart sank with disappointment. Thomas had been so focused on finding clues that they were missing time together.

"Perhaps if I give you a hand, we can go up sooner." Rachel rubbed his back and planted another slow one.

He slipped his hand to clasp hers and swung around pulling her onto his lap. She was eager for his closeness and their passion was reunited.

Thomas woke awake again at 2:00 a.m. He unlocked his iPad and opened to Google. The blue glow shone across the room and Rachel opened her eyes.

"What is it, Thomas?"

"I'm afraid to utter my worst thoughts, Rachel."

"I'm your confidant, surely you can tell me."

"I don't think that Zach's murder was an isolated incident. I believe it was months in the planning. A bond building between Matthew and Addie. She has given him full reign of the winery without a single question. My theory is that the uncle that raised Matthew would have been the older brother, Charles; that would explain a family resemblance."

"What are you getting at?"

"This afternoon . . . the incident with Addie's sheets. I reviewed the security tape, watching for shadows. Then I talked with Jonas to see if he saw or heard anything. The one thing that drew his attention was the garage door closing. The only people with garage keys are Addie, Matthew and myself."

"And it wasn't you or Addie."

"Have you noticed anything suspicious?"

"In my chat with Maria a few days ago, she blushed when I talked about Matthew."

Thomas said. "Unfortunately, then Maria's truths could be tainted."

"I'll take it with a grain of salt. Still, she has a history here."

"Yeah, stay close. Jonas is solid, but see what you learn."

Rachel rolled over and talked with her eyelids closed. "Sure. So what needs doing?"

The next evening, Thomas and Rachel returned to the desk.

"Matthew has collected all the bills and paid them from the business account. I'll ask Addie if I can look at the bank statement."

"You know you could be wrong, Thomas."

He nodded. "That nags at me too."

Continuing the examination, they emptied and checked the bottom of each drawer.

Rachel said, "It must be the same desk Zach's father and grandfather used. Dove tailed grooving and solid French pine. I'll bet it was handmade here on the farm."

"You always notice the little things. That's what makes us such a good team."

"Well, Thomas, you're right about the little things. Here in the bottom right drawer. A small piece of paper is tucked into the corner joints."

Thomas leaned over as Rachel unfolded it. They both stood and Rachel took it to the desk lamp. The writing in pencil was faded with age.

Addie,
CAVE 6. 4th North at 3rd East.
The Adelaide Window
An eternal historic treasure
Use it well.
Love you forever.
Zach

"Addie must know what this means," Rachel sighed.

"Operating the winery involves a lot of workers, and it could be someone on the estate. I wonder how long the Ducharme/Delacroix feud has gone on. The note was placed there within the last forty years."

"Rachel, I found a contradictory Will leaving the entire winery to Addie. There's a bonus provision to the workers of the estate and a trust fund for Melissa.

"Also, the signature on the current will appears to be traced."

"You're kidding, Thomas."

"Regardless, Addie is a generous soul. If Matthew really is Zach's son, she wouldn't change anything."

Thomas paused, ready to say something, but changed his mind.

"I saw that, Thomas York. What is it?"

Thomas relayed his encounter with Jonas and the conversation about Matthew. "We'll uncover the truth, but it takes time."

"Perhaps."

"Time to get shut eye. I suspect the sandman is going to have trouble getting through all the new stuff we found."

Turning out the light, they heard a noise in the upper landing. "Who's that?" Rachel whispered.

He put his finger to his lips. "The only person upstairs is Addie."

The staircase creaked as Thomas and Rachel maneuvered each step. Thomas gripped Rachel's arm.

"Don't move. There's a glimmer of a flashlight moving around in our bedroom. You stay here."

Thomas didn't wait for Rachel's answer, and took soft steps to the door. The flashlight went out. Thomas wasn't armed and realized his vulnerability. He slowly opened the door and turned on the light. The room was empty.

THIRTEEN

Thomas was up at sunrise preparing to talk with Jonas again.

"Last night, Rachel, did you notice anything different about the room?" he said. "Anything missing when we came back?"

"Yes. But I can't put my finger on it."

"Do you remember the tapestry rug in the middle of the room? It's gone."

"But why?"

"We'll find that out," he said. "Rachel, I'll be in the back fields for the morning to check for vandalism; then talk again to some workers. A few Mexicans are still learning English. I made the mistake of bypassing them with my questions. Jonas can help me interpret."

"I'll talk with Maria," Rachel said, "then a few of the female workers. Women have the advantage, when it comes to secrets—they love to gossip, but of course so do men. I'll talk to Addie about last night's intruder?"

"Don't worry her about the flashlight in our room there's no urgency. See if the CAVE 6 note makes sense. You're the best person to do it."

Thomas first encountered Cole and three supervisors, Enrique, Manny and Chavez, all of them showing grief. Each had worked on the Ducharme estate for more than ten years, to be have been appointed as a field foreman. There were no hints of animosity toward anyone at the winery. A worker Trevor was in earshot.

When Thomas inquired about the missing Rocky, several evasive eyes stared to the ground. He pushed further.

"Has anyone ever been offered financial reward to assist the Delacroix gang trespassing in our fields?"

No one volunteered a reply, but a few showed guilt. He thanked them and started to leave, but stopped and went back.

"Manny and Trevor! Please stay a moment. I want to talk with you."

Trevor's eyes were wild, and he glanced at Manny for direction. Manny put his hand firmly on his worker's arm, reassuring him.

"It is okay, Trevor. It's time to tell the truth."

Thomas looked kindly at the two men. "I assure you of no repercussions, if you give me information regarding any person stealing slips, digging up roots, or trespassing."

"Sir," Manny started. "Thomas, we are so sorry. At first it seemed harmless, a fifty dollar bill. Then they became evil and threatened to harm our families if we didn't co-operate. It sounded simple enough to look the other way."

"What were you asked to do?"

Manny was ashamed, but continued.

"We were asked to leave an opening in the back fields and move away from the west corner."

Trevor stepped forward to speak. "One day, I refused to help and they beat me to a pulp. Manny found me."

"Trevor's eyes were swollen shut," Manny said, "and his face was black and blue. They had guns, and we only had shovels and rakes."

"Do you know the names of any of them?" Thomas prompted.

"Lane Delacroix, several times; one of the Hansons, once; and Rocky was a pawn in their hand. Also men on his truck, who I didn't know by name. Maybe the other Delacroix son, but I can't be sure."

"Next time you need fifty bucks, come and find me; but if fifty bucks is the cost of your loyalty, pack your bags. Tell me now, will you be loyal?"

Manny and Trevor were close to tears. Manny's voice shook. "Yes, Thomas."

Trevor didn't hesitate. "I promise too, sir."

"Good. I will not discuss this with Addie, if I can be assured of your trust. Foremost, you will alert me or Jonas, anytime you see any trucks or trespassers. Understand? Only a phone call away! One call! We will protect you."

The man from the bar in Charron met again with Kincaid.

"I'm getting anxious for what's due to me," Dex mumbled begrudgingly.

Kincade said, "With Zach gone, it's not easy to find where the cache is hidden, but I am as determined as a fox. I have access that you will never have, you have to rely on me."

"What was your point of riding in on a black horse, if you didn't know where my treasure was?" Dex gathered as much saliva as he could, and spit it on the ground.

Kincade remained calm. "You have your advantage and I have mine. I've cozied up with Lane Delacroix. He's a calculating man determined to take over the Ducharme estate. I have my ways. Let's say there are a lot of loopholes in the adage that good fences build good neighbors. It can also be the opposite."

"Delacroix is indebted to me for a special service that I have no reason to mention to you."

"Did you kill Zachary Ducharme?" Kincade inquired.

"No comment." Dex displayed an evilness that shocked his partner. "Are you interested in the scenario that you and I could be neighbors, blending two magnificent wineries? Let's presume I have an investment."

"You're all talk! I'll get into the wine caves tonight. If I were to own this place, that's exactly where the cache would be. He was only a seventeen year old kid."

"This is your last chance though," Dex said. "I can't leave loose ends around or I'm a bagged duck."

"Ponder over the value of what I can offer you. Then compare it to anything you can do for me, Dexter. It's pretty much a no win for you. And I'm sure your parole officer would be interested in the threats to the Ducharmes."

Saturday afternoon, the workers had been brought up from the fields early for the weekend. Jonas took a shower and cleaned up. He lived in the bunkhouse for single men, in the village.

Knocking on the back door of the main house, Jonas was dressed in a crisp plaid shirt, a black leather roper's hat and a silver belt buckle. A whiff of Old Spice announced his entrance.

Rachel opened the door.

"What's the formality, Jonas? You can always come in. The door is never locked for you."

"I've come to take Addie to the barbeque. Are you and Thomas going to join us? I promise you, it will be the best time you've had since you came to California."

"Yes, thank you. I'm wearing jeans, should I change into a skirt, Jonas?"

"No, no, it's casual. Addie, is the boss, so I thought I should be respectful."

Rachel winked. "You're a really good guy, Jonas."

Addie heard the voices, and the clatter of her heeled boots descended the staircase. Rachel left through the dining room.

"I'll go and find Thomas."

"Addie, you look nice." Jonas blushed.

"Jonas, I can't remember the last time I put on my dancing skirt. I'm looking forward to the evening in the village." Addie had childish glee from ear to ear. She took his arm and they went to the veranda to wait.

The night was clear, with the sky full of stars and a gentle breeze across the vineyard. The foursome took their time down the tractor lane toward the blazing bonfire.

Addie talked to almost everyone, old friends and new. She knew most of them by sight, as every new employee hired on the estate had dinner in the main house with Addie and Zach, welcoming them into the Ducharme family. While Addie and Jonas were mixing, Thomas and Rachel spotted some older couples sitting on hay bales.

"Hello, I'm Thomas, and this is my wife, Rachel, Addie's niece. Addie was raving to us about the old days."

"Indeed, no one misses Saturday night. After dinner there will be music like you've never heard, a ukulele, harmonica, banjo, saw banding, fiddle and an accordion. We're the Colemans, Lil and Luke. Have a seat, there's room."

"Thanks, have you been on the estate for long?" Rachel asked.

Lil spoke up again. "Oh, how long, Luke? A good twenty-five years, if my memory serves me. Luke loves working with his hands in the earth and the vines."

"So, would you have known Zach's parents?"

"Indeed, the manor house was bursting with people. Zach had taken over by the time we came. Most of Zach's brothers and sisters stayed until they married and had children. Then, lore tells that Francois and Margaret-Louise gave them a chunk of land bordering the east side of the vineyard. Several of them still live over that way."

Rachel said, "Do you have children?"

"Oh yes. Four boys and two girls. Two of the boys work on vineyards further down the valley. You know, they wanted to spread their wings. One of our daughters married David Wilkes's son; one of our sons married a Hanson girl; and our two youngest sons work here."

Thomas sat up straight, leaning in to hear every word.

"Who are the Wilkes and the Hansons?" Thomas asked.

"They're both second generation families."

Rachel said, "That's wonderful! Do you have grandchildren too?"

"On the Wilkes side, we have a grandson—he's fifteen and still in school; on the Hanson side, we have another grandson who's eighteen and works over on the Delacroix estate."

Thomas smiled politely at the news.

I'll remember they have a grandson at the Delacroixs.

"It sounds like a close knit family. Do your kids come here on occasion for the barbeques?"

"They used to, but they've gotten busy with their lives."

"I'd love to hear more about the old days, Lil." Rachel said.

Thomas and Luke had drawn closer to the bonfire, where some of the men were shooting marbles and whittling.

The evening drew on past midnight, with the laughter and music growing into the night.

Addie collapsed, exhausted, onto a bale of hay. She stared up into the starry night.

Zach is there watching over me. Our hearts are one in this moment.

"Are you alright, Addie?"

"Jonas, do you mind returning me to the main house. I've truly had a wonderful time, but I'm a few years older than before. These old dancing boots have had enough of a workout for one night."

She reached for his hand to pull her up.

"We're all older. In spite of the years, laughter is still our best medicine."

Addie stopped halfway down the lane and turned to Jonas. "Have you ever been to the Delacroix farm?"

"Why, certainly not, Addie. Why do you ask?"

"I knew you hadn't, but I wanted to hear it from you."

Still, Jonas's integrity had been slightly bruised.

Thomas and Rachel followed a half hour later.

"Rachel, don't turn on the light. I don't want it known that we are home."

Stepping lightly toward the window, he looked into the telescope.

"Fire! Fire in the west field!"

"No, Thomas, it's the bonfire from the barbeque."

"Rachel, the barbeque is east. The fire is in the west."

Thomas stretched three steps at a time to the main level, yelling as he went. Outside, he pulled the emergency bell and siren. Rachel was behind and called the Fire Department. She pounded on Addie's door with the news, and ran down the steps.

Outside, shouting voices pierced the air in the distance.

Workers were running from the compound; Jonas and the foremen took the positions they'd been trained for in practice drills.

With a megaphone, Jonas shouted, "Fire! West field! Man the water vehicles. The tanks at the station huts are full! Everyone, men and women. Grab rakes, shovels and sacks."

Jonas had the first truck ready, already filling with workers taking night lanterns and battery torches.

Rachel turned back from outside to look at the kitchen door. There was Addie, her long wavy hair blowing in the wind. She looked like an angel guarding the house. She grabbed a throw and ran down the slope of the lawn.

"You know I have to go too." She looked at Thomas. "Where's Matthew?"

"Addie, I'm going to drive down in your car. You come with me. The men know what to do, we don't want to be a worry to them. You should get dressed, I'll wait right here."

Matthew's nowhere in sight.

FOURTEEN

Court was to be in session at 1:00 a.m., and Addie insisted they allow plenty of time. The District Courthouse in Vallejo was a short half hour scenic drive. Thomas stopped at a charming tea house outside town.

"We still have plenty of time," Rachel said, "and this will ease your nerves. A nice cup of English tea, Addie."

Thomas added, "Zach has been gone for six weeks. We're here to see justice is served for him."

Rachel said, "Aunt Addie, we're going to hear some graphic detail. Take my iPad and plug the ear phones in when it gets rough."

"I'm good, Rachel. I spent time this morning asking God why. Then I talked his ear off. I'm not alone, I have faith and family."

Rachel squeezed her hand.

Judge Carter was introduced promptly at 10:00 a.m. and rules of the courtroom and instructions to the jury were read by the bailiff. The charges were first degree murder.

Opening statements by the prosecution described Zachary Ducharme's upstanding character and contribution to the community bringing prosperity for hundreds of families, as well as tourism and industry to the valley.

Thomas watched as the defendant flinched in his seat and put his head down. The jurors looked at Lane without empathy.

Gregoire Delacroix had two sons living on the estate. Lane was tall and dark like his father, but a fiery temperament and spirit of a lone stallion. He was resentful and bent on overshadowing his elder brother, Seebe.

From the looks of the jury, he's going to have a rough go. Lane, you coward, you have no remorse. You've already shown your stripes.

When Lane stood and answered "Not Guilty", he looked only at his lawyer and then the judge.

The prosecution attorney's statement portrayed Lane Delacroix as a greedy man; a man without remorse who incorporated those around him to join his deed.

Lane Delacroix's fingerprint on the detonating device raised the level of tension, along with the promise of eye witness testimony. Lane volunteered Rocky as an accomplice to divert suspicion. However, Rocky had been missing since shortly after the incident.

I suspect he knows exactly where Rocky is, and it's a cold place.

Addie, Thomas and Rachel sat behind the prosecution. Matthew arrived late and took a seat behind. Gregoire Delacroix and his younger son Seebe sat in the rear.

Thomas turned to survey the courtroom.

He whispered to Addie, "Jonas and the other foremen are sitting in the back row with Maria and her sisters, and several women from the compound."

Addie smiled with pride for her extended family.

For two hours, the prosecution presented convincing evidence of motive, starting with the Offer to Purchase. He portrayed the devastation to the Ducharme family, how his wife and daughter were left with the burden of the vineyards.

Zach was presented as a vintner and connoisseur of wines. The prosecution suggested the jealousy of the Delacroix family led to the murder. The court was told of their intense envy for his lush crops and the jealousy over Zach's annual awards for his wines.

Such an extreme cost for a wine label.

"Is it true, Mr. Delacroix, that you made several offers to buy the Ducharme vineyards? Did you act alone?" the prosecution asked.

Lane sheepishly glanced at his father sitting behind.

"About a year ago, the Delacroix vineyards did make a generous offer. The principals were my brother, my father and myself."

"Was that the only offer?"

"No, Sir. I made an offer with an acquaintance a few hours before Mr. Ducharme was killed."

"Remember you are under oath. Name your acquaintance."

"Dexter Kincaid."

"Your Honor, I intend to call Dexter Kincaid at a later time."

The court adjourned for lunch. A prosecution lawyer met with Jonas to help prepare him, as he'd be next when they resumed.

"Jonas, a half fingerprint belongs to you. The defense will tear your credibility apart and present you as an angry employee, being unjustly treated. They'll even propose that you should be suspect of murder."

"That's rubbish! Zach and I were close friends. Any of the estate workers will vouch for me. We are a loyal family—the defense lawyer can't break that. I'm not worried about the questioning."

"You need to look at the defense as a lion ready to shred you. Only answer his questions with a 'Yes' or 'No'. Too much explaining opens the door to interrogate you under cross examination."

"Do I have time for a quick coffee?" Jonas's arms were crossed projecting an invisible barrier.

"Of course, Jonas. Please study what I have said. We are trying to protect Zach and Addie."

Turning, Jonas left the courtroom. A gathering of friendly faces waited for him.

"Jonas, we are defiant. The defense cannot break up a family," Thomas said.

Throughout the afternoon, Jonas held his own. Each of the four foremen were called and vouched for his character. It appeared to the jury that the suggestion of any involvement was preposterous.

FIFTEEN

After the first day in court, Thomas was conflicted.
Why would Lane's lawyer even bring up Rocky's name? It wouldn't be good for them. We've got to be prepared.

Thomas and Rachel took the tractor out to the west quarter fence. Matthew was not invited but saw them leave.

Dusk had fallen. They shone flashlights along the trail to the repaired fence, walking through charred remains of the fire that destroyed so many vintage vines.

"That fence is not much of a deterrent," Rachel said. "As a last resort, electric fences and security cameras should be installed in this section. That would send a message."

Thomas directed the beam along the fence. "Look at all the footprints in the mud. So many people have been back here, nothing would be considered proof."

"Thomas, you have something specific on your mind. Spill the beans."

"Rocky, the scapegoat, must be somewhere back here. He disappeared within a few days of Zach's murder. Look for a mound or anything that might look like a grave. It was important to Lane to conceal evidence."

"Wow! I didn't expect that."

"Stop!" Thomas put a finger to his lips. "Listen for a minute."

Rachel turned off her headlamp and crouched to the ground. She couldn't hear anything and thought about how the silence of expectation can be deafening. Then she heard the distant purr of a truck engine.

The truck puttered to the property line, then went silent on the other side of the fence.

Thomas signaled to Rachel to back away from the area and stay quiet. Still crouching, she stepped back onto fragments of a decaying wooden wagon. Surrounded by rocks, it seemed out of place. She motioned to Thomas, and he joined her behind the wagon.

Three men from the truck mounted the fence, and Thomas and Rachel moved twenty feet further to some heavy shrubs.

"Do you remember where it is, Dexter?"

"I know exactly where it is, I planted it myself."

"Are you sure no one will see us?"

They're talking about Rocky. His body must be buried here.

"Hanson, over here." Dexter was standing by the wagon. "Under the rocks".

Rachel had figured out the Hanson-Delacroix connection.

I wonder who gave the orders for this nocturnal excursion.

Rachel inched closer to Thomas, watching in silence as Hanson and the other man heaved rocks into a new pile.

Seebe Delacroix was giving the orders. He was in his late twenties with fair hair and blue eyes. Although he was shorter than Lane, he made it up in brawn.

"Come on boys, we can't waste time. The detectives are staying in the room with the telescope. There's a rare chance they could see us, however they are too dumb to figure this out."

Thomas was tempted to stand up and reveal himself. He felt in the back of his belt for his revolver.

Delacroix's men came to a halt. "Here it is."

What do we do with him?" Hanson asked.

"There's a floor rug in the back of the truck. The neighbor kid got from the detectives' room. Wrap Rocky in it."

"We're not moving him?"

"No, we're setting a trap."

Rachel poked Thomas in his ribs.

Thomas made an eight a.m. call to the DA, offering new evidence about Seebe's nocturnal visit to the vineyards.

As court resumed, defense was to take over questioning, but before the first witness was called, the prosecution asked to approach the bench. A long sidebar followed. The judge announced a recess stating that new evidence would be allowed.

The first witness called by the defense was Thomas York. He had expected that, and he carried an envelope in his jacket to the witness stand.

"Mr. York, is it true that you are staying at the Ducharme estate to assist in the murder investigation?"

"Yes."

"Did you know Rocky Morse?"

"No, I've never met him."

"Are you staying in the bedroom, the one with the panoramic view of the vineyards where a high powered telescope sits?"

"Yes. I suppose, but I haven't seen the other bedrooms to know the difference."

"Therefore, you can view a large expanse of the vineyards from your room."

"Yes."

"Rocky Morse was interrogated by Officer Murdock, the day after the murder. He was uncooperative. Was that for your benefit?"

"I know nothing about that."

"As you heard in testimony yesterday, the eye witness identified Rocky Morse as being around the Ducharme's truck, minutes before the ignition was turned. Did that make you angry?"

"It meant nothing to me."

"Come on, Mr. York, why do you deny knowing Rocky Morse? A field worker, on the Delacroix estate, has recently come forward to tell of an argument between you and Mr. Morse."

"That's a preposterous set-up." Thomas exclaimed.

"Set-up or the truth?"

"May I have the court's permission to relay my knowledge of Rocky Morse?"

The defense agreed, stating he would still cross-examine.

I'll make mincemeat out of the defense. He set himself up for target practice.

"I wasn't even in California when Zachary Ducharme was killed. I arrived with my wife the day before the funeral. That say day, Officer Murdock came to the house and brought us up to date on the investigation. He told us Rocky had disappeared, and that Lane Delacroix had been arrested."

The defense lawyer attempted to object.

"Overruled. Please continue Mr. York."

"My next encounter with Rocky Morse was last evening." There were murmurs in the audience, and the judge ordered silence.

"My wife and I were tracking footprints in the back west quarter that is the scene of a recent arson fire and trespassing. It was public knowledge that Gregoire Delacroix was jealous of Mr. Ducharme's recent Bordeaux award success with his grapes from the west quarter.

"Objection! Conjecture."

"Overruled. I'd like to hear this; please continue Mr. York." The

wanted Thomas's full account.

"One of the Ducharme's foreman, that I recognize to be Cole, retrieved a sack on the property, with the Delacroix name imprinted on it. The sack contained Ducharme vine slips and I have it here. It can be verified by other witnesses."

Thomas pulled the sack from a pockets using a tissue.

"This may have suspicious fingerprints on it," he said.

"Objection!"

"Overruled."

"Last evening, I was in the back west quarter when a truck arrived at the location of the trespass fence."

Lane's head flung around to look at his father.

"My wife and I concealed ourselves and watched Dexter Kincaid, Seebe Delacroix and a younger man called by the name of 'Hanson'. They went to the sight of an old decaying wagon that was on Ducharme land. Under the wagon and a pile of rocks, was the body of Rocky Morse."

"Objection! Objection!"

The judge leaned toward Thomas. "Please continue."

Gregoire Delacroix's face was beet red.

"It is further complicated, by the fact that the floor rug stolen from my bedroom was used to wrap Rocky. It was a grotesque scene. The intention was to plant evidence to implicate me.

"I have here, a glove that was left behind last night, and several cigarette butts that will have DNA of those at the sight. With my cellphone, I have photos of the scene and a video of the activity and conversation." A court employee took his phone to the judge.

The prosecution lawyer was smiling, and the defense had his head close to Lane in a discussion. Gregoire was gripping his hands tight, containing his rage toward his sons.

The prosecution lawyer rose.

"Your Honor, in view of Mr. York's statement, I request a delay to allow for time to subpoena the accomplices in this case."

"Mr. Delacroix, do you wish to change your plea?"

Lane's face was flushed, while the prosecutor and defense lawyers discussed a deal with the judge.

Following another recess, Lane rose reluctantly to face the court. "I would like to change my plea to 'Guilty' in regard to Zachary Ducharme. However, the murder of Rocky Morse was not my doing."

"Bailiff, remove Mr. Lane Delacroix until sentencing later this week. And take Seebe Delacroix into custody, for the alleged conspiracy to murder. It is further recommended to the prosecution that charges be laid against Dexter Kincaid."

"Addie, do you have an address for Charles Ducharme?"

"Funny that you should ask. At Christmas, my card was returned as address unknown."

"Can you give me that address as a starting point? I'm unsettled why Zach's own brother didn't attend his funeral. Certainly Matthew would have wanted him there."

"Yes. You're right Thomas, I did feel brushed aside."

Addie opened her address book to Ducharme.

Hmmm, Vallejo.

"Does Matthew talk about his adoptive parents much?" Thomas asked.

"I haven't heard a word, Thomas."

"Rachel and I are going to take a drive this morning, and we'll be back until after lunch."

Enroute to Vallejo, Thomas and Rachel stopped at a couple of wineries. Posing as tourists, they delved into local conversation whenever they had the chance. Town folk had heard about the current court case involving the Delacroix boys.

At their last stop, Rachel found some pleasant older women chatting and sharing a little gossip. It was the rumors that Rachel wanted to hear. She asked if they had known Zachary. One woman was very glad to tell all she knew.

"Oh yes, I knew him. Zach was a nice man, and a master with wines. He was kind enough to hold a workshop last summer and allowed other vineyards to join him. Zach wasn't a selfish man, but was always eager to help a friend or neighbor. The Ducharmes were always proud of their Bordeaux heritage and he gave us valuable tips about our grapes.

"One year, our crops suffered a blight and he happened by with a couple of burlap root sacks. He said they were from the old stock from France, and that they would multiply quickly. Such a generous thing to do, we couldn't thank him enough. We might have a chance at competitions this year."

"Do you know Gregoire Delacroix, or his sons?" Rachel asked.

"I can say that he's not a nice man. He was disqualified last year when Zachary received top recognition. A witness saw him tampering with some wines, and he's barred from this year's competition. As far as his sons—there are two, Lane and Seebe. There had been a young one that was killed in a tractor accident as a wee lad. Can you imagine losing a child right before your eyes?"

Rachel said, "Yes, the pain of losing a child would be unimaginable."

"Indeed, it is."

"I wish you success with your wines," Rachel added. "Thank you for the chat. Do you know much about the Hanson family or of a connection between them and the Delacroixs?

"My goodness, no! I can't believe that Nathan and Caliste would cross the fence, so to speak. They have a lovely little cottage in Charron and enjoy retirement. You can find them on Washington Boulevard, a couple of streets behind Main. You'd see their wonderful red and yellow window boxes. I would be surprised if there were a family connection."

Mr. Stewart, the estate lawyer in Charron, was direct. "For the documentation, Matthew, I need to verify your heritage. What is your birth father's name?"

"Can't I give you my adoptive parents' names?"

"No, the rules are rigid."

Matthew squirmed. "Can I request the information be sealed from the public?"

"I can make that request if you like? What would your reason be?"

"An error on my original certificate."

"What kind of error, Matthew?"

"My birth mother is Caliste Delacroix. That is true enough. I didn't find that out until my late teens. She hasn't even tried to see me. My letter, letting her know where I was didn't come back, so I presume she received it."

"And your father?

"My handwritten birth certificate states that my father is Charles Ducharme."

"He's your adoptive father! You said you are the legitimate son of Zachary Ducharme. Isn't that what this is all about?"

"I am. Charles Ducharme took me in to avoid the humiliation of an unwed mother."

"Do you have proof of that?"

"I have answered your questions as best as I can. Please just show my father as Zachary Ducharme."

"You know, Matthew, I am also the attorney for Addie. This will be considered privileged information, and a possible conflict of interest."

"Absolutely, you cannot reveal any of this. You said you would seal the records. Do you want money? I'll give you $5,000 cash to do it."

"I'll make the request. Nonetheless, the true record will be preserved, birth records are never expunged. You should be aware that this may put your inheritance into question. Also, you have bribed an attorney pledged to the courts of California."

"No. You can't allow that."

He reached across the desk, and glowered, then grabbed the lawyer's shirt. "Did you hear me? I can't allow that."

"I don't want your money," Stewart said firmly.

Matthew stormed for the door.

The cache and the winery will be mine; whatever the cost.

SIXTEEN

Matthew disappeared into the wine caves with the key marked '1967' in his pocket. On each previous attempt, he returned frustrated and empty-handed.

The multiple storage rooms and wine stacks presented many challenges to search. Strategically, he divided the rooms into quarters and chose the last section. The rooms were dimly lit but his vision adapted quickly to focus on the wine bottles and crevices.

A five foot wide wrought iron gate stood at the end of a large cavern. It was higher than a man, and securely locked with a rusty padlock.

Surely the cache is in one or more of the wine bottles or in a crack in the walls. I don't even know what I'm looking for—cash, jewels, or gold?

He became so absorbed that he tuned out another noise. With his flashlight he focused on a crack along the walls.

He was startled when Addie called him from the stairway.

"Matthew? Matthew?"

He turned to find her ten feet behind him. He spun in her direction, and in his bewilderment, he knocked a case of Beaujolais from the shelf, a nouveau waiting for a storage assignment.

"Oh dear!" Addie jumped back at his knee-jerk reaction.

"I'll get it cleaned up, Addie; no need to fuss."

Addie was smarter than he presumed.

Sensing agitation in his voice, she was determined to know why he was in the caves.

"No one knew you were down here, Matthew. Why didn't you notify a foreman or log the inventory book. We all do that for security."

"Come on, Addie, I don't need permission on my own property. Have you forgotten we're partners?"

Matthew tried to keep his cool; he dearly wanted to shove her out of his way—to get her out of his life. In his anger, he bumped her shoulder, deliberately knocking her off balance.

Addie faltered three steps to the wall, hitting her head on a ceiling rafter. Without Matthew noticing, she reached for the intercom switch.

"I don't understand your change in attitude, we've been getting along so well since your father died."

Matthew sneered and shook his head.

What is he saying? Where are the memories of Zach? Thomas and Rachel should be back soon and I hope they hear this in the house.

"Addie, my dear step-mother, I am taking over as head-of-the household. As a full partner, I have that right."

"What has happened to you?"

"I'm tired of being looked down upon. I've been treated like the fifth wheel, excluded from all those tête-à-têtes you have with your niece. A step-son surely outranks a niece. Now, we have your detective friends checking up on me.

"Also I overheard Jonas being a snitch. I've been waiting for a reason to dismiss him. I could let him stay on as a laborer, to put him in his place and give him a dose of humiliation."

"I won't allow that," Addie snapped.

"You don't have a choice."

"We'll see about that."

Addie turned to leave, then turned back.

"By the way, you won't find what you are looking for."

Thomas and Rachel stopped at a country style restaurant at the edge of Vallejo. His mind was on a full breakfast and Rachel settled on a Swiss omelet and toasted bagel.

"Today we will find Charles Ducharme," Thomas said. "We'll put our heads together. What are our best options?"

"We could start at the post office," Rachel suggested, "and then the check the tax rolls."

"But first, let's try the address Addie gave us. Also, Matthew seems to be mechanical, the way he babies the Harleys. Perhaps his Dad was a mechanic. They have to renew a license every year to post at their place of business. That might be easy to check."

Charles Ducharme's house was easy to locate with Addie's address, and the GPS. He lived in the south sector where many streets were lined with ranch bungalows and palm trees. Landscapes were meticulous, lush and green, except for his house.

It was apparent the house was unoccupied, with the windows covered in sheets. The lawn hadn't been mowed and a pile of newspapers and flyers were faded by the sun at the front step.

The next door neighbor came out, glad to see any kind of attention to the house.

"Are you folks the new owners? If so, I hope you'll get this lawn in order. It's shameful for the whole street. My wife

Agnes is ready to call the city office to complain and have the weeds removed."

"Hello, I'm Rachel Redmond."

"I'm Wilson Bennett. I didn't mean to blurt all that out without even a greeting."

"Mr. Bennett, I'm sorry. We are not new owners. Was the property for sale recently?"

"There was a sign in the New Year, but it fell down and I put the sign at the side of the house."

"When did you last see Mr. or Mrs. Ducharme?"

"Haven't seen them in a long time. It was only the boy that came around."

"Do you know his name?"

"Oh sure, it was Matthew."

Thomas rifled into his pocket for American bills.

"Mr. Bennett, here's a fifty dollar bill. If you can mow the lawn for the Ducharmes, everyone will be much happier."

"I'll do that right away. Mighty nice of you."

Before Thomas and Rachel left, they walked to the back of the house for the realtor's number and called her voicemail. He presented himself as a potential customer, hoping for a fast callback.

"Maybe, she'll call back while we're in town."

He looked at his watch. "Okay then, so now to the post office," Rachel said.

The postal supervisor pulled out recent change of address applications. "Well, their three month COA expired and wasn't renewed. The mail was to be redirected to a postal box in Charron. The name was Matthew Delacroix."

"Thank you, this really helps."

Thomas jotted down the box and phone numbers and Rachel pulled some mechanics' addresses.

His cell rang and he winked at Rachel. He expected the realtor, but it was Addie. Her breathing was heavy and he detected alarm even before she spoke.

"Please, Thomas, I need you back at the house. It's Matthew. I'll explain when you get here. I don't feel safe."

"Addie, we're on our way. Take the tractor to the second station hut; Jonas should be working around there. We'll be half an hour."

Addie said, "I have to go. Hurry!" It clicked.

He held the phone from his ear and Rachel watched his eyes. He pointed at the car. "We have to run. It sounds like trouble."

"It's Matthew, isn't it?" Rachel's brow tightened.

Thomas nodded. "I know you have strong suspicions."

"I don't want to make assumptions, but I am concerned."

"The problem is that we don't have authority to intervene. Their partnership is equal."

"All this going on under Zach and Addie's roof must be distressing to her," Rachel said.

"There is safety in numbers. It's time to invite Melissa and the children back for a farm visit. Furthermore, there will be a new rumbling in the fields. I'll get Jonas involved."

"Are you talking about a revolt?"

"More like cleaning house," Thomas said. "That's where it is headed. "We'll soon find out as Matthew is supporting the sale of the estate."

Rachel put one finger in the air and laughed. "And he doesn't know about the strength of the Cumberland women."

Thomas sped back and drove directly to Jonas's hut. He skidded to a stop and ran to the door, but no-one was there.

Rachel called him. "Thomas, listen. Voices over there." She led the way into the rows of vines, with grapes in full bloom. The high foliage obstructed a view, but soon the voices were clear. Thomas relaxed. It was Addie and Jonas picking grapes.

"Hey, Addie," Thomas said in a low voice.

"Are you hiding out back here?" Rachel piped in with a chuckle.

"Thank goodness, you're back," Addie said. "Come on, Jonas, we're going up to the main house for lunch."

Jonas nodded at Thomas, then walked with Addie back to the tractor. It had been moved to the back of the hut, out of sight.

"Addie, you can tell us back at the house. Remember Cumberland women are strong and in charge."

Addie laughed at the reminder.

"Zach used to tell me that, whenever I had to go through struggles of a sort. Addie, my dear, Cumberland women are invincible. You are in charge." Addie mimicked Zach's low voice.

Matthew was in the kitchen going over some business papers, when the troops arrived. He put his coffee down.

"Are you feeling better, Addie, from that bump on your head?" He sneered with sarcasm. "You should have seen her, Thomas, tumbling down the stairs."

The words sickened Thomas. "Rubbish, Matthew. You and I know the truth."

"Ah, the truth! You have no idea what that is."

Thomas kicked his chair back and charged at Matthew, grabbing him by the collar.

"You never hit a woman! You don't deserve the Ducharme name! Don't ever again show such disrespect!"

Thomas was inches from Matthew's face. He tightened his grip on Matt's shirt and glared into his eyes. With another yank on the collar, Matthew's face went red and he struggled to speak. Thomas threw him to a chair and returned to the other side of the table as if nothing happened.

But Addie wasn't ready to let things go.

"Matthew, you can't march into this family under false pretenses. This house has years of secrets and I know a good many more of them than you do. Are you really Zachary's son as that's in question here? It's time you watched yourself. It would be easy for me to take you to court and have this relationship absolved."

Matthew stood again. His voice boomed with over-confidence as he shouted down at Addie.

"I have papers to prove it. I am the son of Zachary Ducharme and there's no way you can challenge that. I'll put you in your place, little woman."

"No, Matthew! You're not . . ." Rachel stopped herself short of denying his birthright.

Thomas's eyes went to Rachel then quickly back. "Take your coffee outside, Matthew," he said.

Matthew didn't move. Inches from Matthew's face, Thomas yelled, "Whatever you've got going, we'll tear you to shreds. Don't ever let me hear you being disrespectful in this house."

"Big fella, you can't take care of all your women at the same time. Take a step back."

Rachel gripped Thomas's arm to hold him back.

The four of them stood looking at Matthew. He toyed with rebellion, but kept his strategy under wraps. The kitchen door slammed with all the force he could give it.

Maria had been silent in the laundry room and came out with a basket of folded sheets and towels. Her face was red, guilty for unintentionally overhearing the tiff with Matthew.

Rachel said, "Maria, the four of us will be having lunch in the sunroom. Let me know if I can help."

"Thank you, but no. I have lasagna and salad already made for you. It will be out of the oven in five minutes."

"Okay, Addie," Jonas said, "tell us from the beginning what happened." He reached for both her hands and held them together. Addie blushed but let her hands linger.

Trembling to find the right words, she recounted the story.

"I went looking for Matthew to talk about our accounts. After several hours, I decided to check the caves. Deep inside, I heard shifting and scratching, and at the bottom step, Matthew saw me. He was angry and pushed me back against the wall. I hit my head on the rafter and lost my balance.

"Zach would never stand for a man to treat me that way."

The moment flooded back to her and she dabbed a small pool from her eyes. Rachel found a box of tissues on the sideboard.

Thomas clenched his fist. "He'll pay, don't you worry."

Gathering composure, Addie went on. "I appreciate it that you want to protect me."

She turned to Jonas, "Matthew was going to demote you. I overruled that decision, you can be assured."

Jonas showed a different determination than Thomas had seen before. "Don't worry, Addie, Zachary always encouraged me to stand up to oppression in whatever form. I won't listen to Matthew. He won't have the satisfaction of seeing insult on my face."

"Be careful, Jonas. Remember that the clear facts are not good," Thomas said. "Matthew has control of the financial accounts. With equal authority, he can't be overruled technically."

Rachel said, "Addie, this may sound ludicrous but it's time to invite Melissa and the children. There's plenty of room." She looked at Jonas then Addie.

"Jonas, for safety concerns you should move into the guest suite in the addition," Thomas cautioned. "You can keep tabs on Matthew from there. Is that okay, Addie? The more numbers in the house, the safer we are. He will be less intimidating."

Addie had been staring into her lap, pondering the situation. She looked up, facing the three of them and nodded.

"You see me, as I want you to see me. I know what Matthew wants." After a moment's pause, she said, "Thomas, I should have been more forthcoming with you when you searched into Zach's affairs. I knew about the newspaper clippings. The way things were exposed, one at a time, I realize that your intention has been to protect me. I am committed to protecting my husband's good name.

"Zach and I had a long talk, about a year ago. He didn't write Matthew's Will a few months ago, nor did he rob a bank in Brazil. We knew that someone was trying to set him up. He was a bit of a sleuth himself; and set some traps of his own."

Jonas took another stern tone. "Addie, dear, it's time to lay it all on the table."

"Yes, Jonas, I know. I know about the traps . . . and about the cache."

SEVENTEEN

Addie had the foresight to dismiss Maria for the evening, detecting flirting with Matthew, and wanted to be sure the walls didn't talk.

"Let's start back at the beginning. Help yourself to another cup of coffee and Maria's warm butter tarts, as this will take some time. But first, does anyone know where Matthew is?"

"He often heads to a bar down near Ascot," Jonas said.

Addie looked at him astounded.

"You don't mean the Rusty Nail, do you?"

"Yes, that's the place."

Addie stopped briefly. "Jonas, we have to talk about that, when I've relayed my involvement in this chaos."

Jonas was embarrassed. "One of the Wilkes boys works there. He is a fine lad and enjoys chatting, especially with women. I go there to pick up beer as they offer the best price around."

"On our first anniversary in '73, Zach and I did our Wills with the family lawyer. It was the same firm as Mr. Stewart, but that lawyer since passed away, and our papers went somewhere else in the firm. The entire estate goes to the surviving spouse, less a portion to the workers.

"Thomas, you found the original taped to Zach's desk drawer?"

"Found it. May I comment?"

"Not, yet, but don't lose it"

"My copy of my own Will is taped to the back of my dresser mirror. That's rather irrelevant right now.

"Unfortunately, the following year, our first child died within a few days of his birth. We had named him Matthew. Life continued as life does, and two years later, Melissa was born. She was the apple of her Daddy's eye.

"Jacob, Jr. was the perfect son, and patriotic. He was born after Melissa—the baby in the family. He gave his life in Afghanistan ten years ago; never married and no children. His fiancé grieved for months, and then moved away and married.

"One romantic evening in San Francisco, over a few bottles of wine, Zach revealed the Brazilian caper to me. He was tortured his entire life by it. Although he didn't take part in the robbery or know what happened to the others, he felt guilt for surviving. When he left Brazil, his shoes and apparel were stuffed with jewels. His leather jacket was lined with money. The cash amount of the booty came to over 80,000 Brazilian Cruzeiros in notes.

"We continued to live on the estate using the bedroom that the two of you are sharing. Zach spent hours with that telescope and knew every inch of the vineyard."

Addie paused to regroup, and the other three sat in silence.

"I should have told you this before. Thomas and Rachel, there's a secret passage at the back of your closet, entering from a false door on the landing into the servants' quarters. It eventually goes to the closet in the laundry room. This old house is full of secrets.

"Zachary made me promise to never change the wallpaper in that room. It has stayed the same for forty plus years and always gave me an eerie feeling. When his father Francois passed, we moved into the master bedroom. It was larger with a corner window and an ensuite, but Zach would still come back to use the telescope.

"Zach had nightmares about the Brazilian coming to find him. He transferred a large cash sum from the company investment account into one in my name as security. In private, he would tease me, calling me Marie Antoinette.

"For more than forty years, the jewelry cache remained hidden. The key for the box was left in a tiny envelope in his desk drawer. Matthew has taken that. Zach gave me the box to hide, insisting I never tell him where it was. That is what Matthew was looking for this afternoon down in the wine caves.

Addie rose and stood at the screen door, her hands on her hips.

"A wrought iron grate is at the end of the final cavern. I know where the key for the padlock is, however I'm sure any master key would work. It's been like that for so many years, I never had an interest to check.

"When the Ducharme estate started winning wine competitions, our world became cursed. Gregoire Delacroix never hid his envy of our grape crops, especially the French Bordeaux stock. We received embarrassing offers from him, and gave him a solid rejection each time.

"He claimed that his land was higher, and that the drainage sent his most fertile soil into our fields. Our soil is fertile due to the lava, and he must have also benefit on his own property."

Addie sighed and took a deep breath.

"I need a drink of water. Let's take a five minute break."

Addie remained with her hands covering her face. Her shoulders shook gently. Jonas gave her a gentle rub on her back, a silent understanding.

With a fresh tea, Addie continued.

"My supposed step-son made his first appearance on the estate two years ago. Matthew doesn't think I remember. His straggly red hair and unruly beard didn't thwart me. He had a ridiculous straw hat with a red feather pulled halfway down his face.

"He came to tell us he was in a partnership with Dexter Kincaid, who was still serving time in prison for the bank robbery. There was a letter. I'll get the original later, but the gist of it was that we were to give him the cache.

"Zachary asked him what the password was. Stunned as a man hit by a swinging door, Matthew lost his composure. His truck spun out of here pretty darn fast."

Addie's shoulders jiggled when she laughed.

"Is something the matter, Addie?" Rachel asked.

"No. There wasn't a password, Zach was joshing with him. Then about six months ago, there was a break-in one night when Zach and I were in Vallejo for dinner. It was hot, and the drive in the night air with the windows down was wonderful.

"As we approached the house, a red Silverado tore out of our lane. Zach said he didn't recognize the truck. But at the house, the kitchen door from the veranda was smashed inward and things were taken apart, to appear like a robbery.

"We called the police, and they looked for fingerprints on the door and around the main floor. It didn't look like anyone had gone upstairs. The list of missing items was short—a petty cash box from Zach's desk, a collection of silver medallions from his father, and a set of my sterling silver knives. The only real value would have been the medallions.

"The next day though, Zach thought someone had been through his papers. He noticed the new Will and the letter, but he let it be. Baby Matthew's birth certificate was taken—that broke our hearts. The pain was like yesterday. I would have given him anything he wanted, if he had only left that alone."

"Zach told me the letter left in the drawer was bogus. I told him straight, that I had a box of love letters upstairs in a shoe box. There was no resemblance in the writing or the manner of speech."

"Why did you continue to play the rouse?"

"I can see you all have questions, but I am feeling exhausted. Can we continue this later?" Addie left the table and went upstairs.

As Jonas stood to leave, Rachel gave him a gentle hug. "Thanks for your support, Jonas. She is my mother's sister, my aunt, and I'm grateful."

"I can't help but worry about her," he said. "It's like I'm her soldier, she's my Queen and the King has fallen. I would guard her at all costs. You won't need to worry when you go back home, I'll be here."

EIGHTEEN

The red Silverado was parked at the Delacroix winery. Lane was working alone in the barrel room, on bail and awaiting sentencing.

The door flew open and slammed against a barrel. Dexter Kincaid stood in the doorway, looking rough.

"Hey, Lane!"

Gregoire was in the garage below the bunkhouse. The floor grate was open and he listened in disgust.

"Lane, when I get the booty, I promise to put a cache away for you like we agreed."

Lane's face was pale and haggard. "It's not looking good for me. My attorney tells me to be prepared for life in prison."

"Once you get used to it, prison isn't so bad. You make friends and hear stories. Lane, I'm not even the real Dexter Kincaid. He blabbed the whole story until we were sick of it. Got himself murdered in prison."

Lane stiffened and reached behind for a tool in case he would need it.

"Who the heck are you, then?"

"I'm not a bad imposter. Same build and I keep a scruffy look to confuse them."

"What's your name?"

"Keep on calling me Dex. If I hear you've blabbed, I know how to get you back."

The Silverado sprayed stones. Gregoire stepped outside to watch him leave, then went into the testing gallery. He heard Lane call his name.

"I'm busy right now, Lane. Go up to the winery and have a glass. I'll be up in about ten minutes."

Putting down the acidity tester, he returned the lid to the barrel.

What did I get us into? Dexter has been nothing but a curse. If only Zach had cooperated, this wouldn't have happened. The con man is now into us for shares.

This has all come to a pinnacle. Lane's going to rot in prison, Rocky's dead, Seebe is trying to be exactly like Lane, and my wife is gone. The only good that could come would be if the Ducharmes would sell. I never wished harm to anybody, but it's out of my hands now.

Gregoire took long strides up to the winery. He wasn't tolerant of Lane's friends, and now had reason for concern for the safety of his son in prison.

It was early afternoon and some of the lunch crowd still lingered. Lane had settled into a table by the front window, drumming his fingers.

"Well, Lane, what good news do you have for me today? I was getting some tools from the garage and overheard your conversation with Dexter."

Lane's face was red.

"That was your decision to listen. My inside man says he'll have the goods tonight. Join me at the Rusty Nail. It's at

Ascot, and nobody there will recognize us. Mind you, I've had a few chats with the barkeep."

"And what have you chatted about?" Gregoire asked. "Don't you know to keep your blasted mouth shut? That's what it means when you are told to stay low!"

"No worries, Pop. I didn't say anything about you."

Gregoire whispered in a loud rasp into Lane's ear. "Keep your voice down!"

"Okay! I've got it."

"Is there any sign that Matthew and Addie will agree to sell?"

"Why don't you come with me, and meet the Matt kid. Dexter connected with him once when he was on the prowl in the vineyards."

"I'm heavily implicated already. I don't need to connect with another villain. I've heard he claims to be Zachary's first born. How did he manage to convince them?"

"I really haven't had cozy conversations with him. Sometimes the less you know about the person, the better. Right?"

Gregoire sat back and took a sip of chardonnay. "I agree."

"I detect cynicism."

"Lane, get going, but it seems Dex drove off with your red truck. When you use the bunk house, leave the truck out of sight behind the garage? It don't like it visible in the driveway.

Melissa and her children arrived by car. She was tall and good looking like Addie, with freckles across her pale complexion and the same blue-green eyes. Her nature was quiet and withdrawn, but the moment she stepped through the door of her childhood home, her face lit up.

Hazel was Melissa's oldest at seven and Isaac, the mischievous one was five; the youngest was adventurous

Marcy. Together, they ran squealing into their Grandmother's arms.

Addie brought out a basket of wrapped gifts and they shrieked as each small token was opened. Their favorites were the personalized vineyard work shirts, with their names embroidered on the back in red, blue and yellow.

The children were assigned tasks to spend mornings in the fields with Jonas and Thomas to teach them about the grapes, and afternoons in the kitchen with Addie and Melissa.

Carmen, the house boy, carried the luggage up to the bedroom that overlooked the front gardens. It was fitted with a queen size bed, a set of bunks, and a pull-out sofa. Hazel and Isaac claimed the bunks, and put Marcy into tears.

"Don't cry, Marcy'" Hazel said. "You get the big bed with Mommy."

Addie left the room in a hurry when they'd gone. She found Thomas in the yard.

"I forgot to mention something. Yesterday during my confrontation with Matthew, I turned the intercom on. My hope was that you would hear I was in distress. As it turns out, the only person in the kitchen was Maria but she didn't come to help."

Thomas reassured her. "Don't worry about it." But he knew Rachel would be interested.

Maria was in the vegetable garden at the side, pulling carrots and beets, green beans, red peppers and cucumber.

Rachel searched the house, and saw her from the bedroom window.

"Maria. Wait there!" Rachel waved as she climbed the rise to the garden. Maria was startled, and finished putting green onions and tomatoes in the basket.

She didn't look at Rachel right away, and Rachel thought Maria was stalling. She removed her garden gloves and wiped the perspiration from her brow with her apron.

"Hello, Rachel. What brings you out here?"

Maria moved over and sat down on the lush, cold grass for a rest. Rachel followed and settled beside her.

"I wanted to talk to you for a few minutes."

"Of course."

"How long have you known Matthew Ducharme?"

Maria's face became red and stern.

"Are you asking me for a specific date?"

"If you have one, it would be great; or even a description of the circumstances."

"Am I in trouble, Rachel?"

"Oh no, Maria, you're a godsend to Addie. You're family."

Maria gave a sigh of relief and relaxed, throwing off her shoes to blend her bare feet into the garden soil.

"I met Mr. Matthew when he came to the house around the time of Mr. Ducharme's funeral. He looked familiar but I can't recall meeting him before."

"Has he paid special attention to you?"

"I apologize. Mr. Matthew finds me in the kitchen when everyone else is gone, and he puts his arms around me and whispers nice things in my ear. I didn't think it any harm to tell the part-owner about what I knew."

"Certainly you were in a delicate situation. Were you in the kitchen when Matthew and Addie had a confrontation in the caves? Did you hear through the intercom?"

Maria put her head down. Rachel leaned over placing her hand on Maria's arm.

"Maria, I would similarly be curious if suddenly voices were coming from somewhere through the intercom. Instinct would encourage me to try to figure out what was going on. Did you ever wonder if Addie could have been in danger?"

"I was about to go down to see, when I heard the yelling."

"Thanks, Maria. Do you need help with the garden?"

"My basket is almost full, Rachel, but thanks."

Rachel started back down over the rise in the lawn, then turned back.

"One more question, Maria. Have you ever met Zachary Ducharme's older brother, Charles?"

"Oh, my goodness." Maria gasped. "He is not a nice man, Rachel." She stopped. "That is where I saw Matthew before. About six months ago, I was sitting on the veranda in the moonlight. It was quiet and no-one would know I was there. I'd finished my work and was taking a rest before walking home.

"Matthew came out from the shadows behind the garage, and skulked toward the veranda door. I was too scared to move. Zach and Addie were out for the evening and I knew I was alone with no way to get help.

"When he went into the house, I stayed back behind the row of lilacs over there and made my way in the dark toward the vineyard. I heard a truck coming from the compound and thought I would be rescued. But no, it was Charles Ducharme. I saw his face in the truck, but I don't think he saw me. The people in the house don't talk about him.

"The father was old Francois, rest his soul. He banished Charles from the estate years ago, and I could tell you some stories I heard, but I wasn't here then. I wasn't even born.

"There was bad blood between Charles and Zachary. That night, I heard Mr. Charles tell Matthew to burn the whole thing down. Matthew had been in the house for at least twenty minutes. When he came out he notched the railing along the porch.

"Although Addie says she remembers him as a boy, she is being kind."

"Do you remember what the issue was that caused Jacob Sr. and Francois to send Charles away?"

"He caused trouble with one of the girls in the compound. I heard she had been with child. She had a pretty name, Cally. That's all I know."

Thomas was working deep in the vineyard with Jonas and his three little workers, when his cell phone rang. He stepped away out of range and left Hazel and Isaac in training with the water pail.

"Hello, I'm looking for Thomas York. My name is Miranda Robinson from the realty office in Vallejo."

"Oh, thanks for returning my call. I was interested a property you had listed. I believe the owner is Mr. Charles Ducharme. It's in the south sector."

"Yes, you mentioned it in your message and I looked into it. When the listing expired, there wasn't a renewal. However, when the listing expired, Mr. Ducharme called and asked me to forward his accumulation of mail to an apartment in Charron."

"I'm not at liberty to give you any personal information. I'd suggest though, that you pick-up some of Ricky's Pizza on Barber Road. That's all I can say."

Matthew had been on a mission to find Jonas, and found their site while Thomas was on the phone.

Hazel, Isaac and Marcy were pulling weeds. Then they saw the boots, the alligator cowboy boots with the pointed steel toe.

Matthew strode up to Jonas with intention. His face leaned close. "Jonas, my man. I have taken over full responsibility for the vineyards. You are hereby demoted to field laborer. I have reason to doubt your loyalty."

Jonas kept his back turned the other way, but was ready. He had prepared for the moment. He dropped his pitchfork, striking Matthew gently on the toe of his boot. The children saw it and laughed, making Matthew angrier.

Hazel and Isaac had rehearsed the scene, to move the water bucket behind him, and Matthew had no choice but to step backward. They needed to be quiet, no giggling, but they burst into laughter when Matthew put his foot in the pail.

He lost his balance and sprawled on the ground, with the bucket drenching his jeans, drawing more hearty laughter.

"Matthew, I'm sorry I didn't see you there," Jonas said. "How did that pail get there? The children are training to be good vintners. It's in their blood, being Ducharmes and all. They're getting a feel for the soil's soft, rich texture. Someday, all this will be theirs."

"You ingrate," Matthew muttered, struggling to his feet.

Jonas continued, "Oh, by the way, Matthew, Addie asked me to move to the extra spare room near yours. She needed to be kept up-to-date on daily issues. Apparently she felt left a bit out-of-touch.

"Unfortunately, management has gotten loose. I know Addie has been distracted, but she's ready to take back the reins. I'll be happy to help you learn. I know you've tried, but running these vineyards takes years of experience."

Matthew was thrown off his game. He was about to raise his arm, when he looked down at the three little faces. Instead, he returned to the main house.

"Excellent job with the pail, Hazel and Isaac," Jonas whispered. "You too Marcy." They did high fives all around.

NINETEEN

Remote Island off the Normandy coast, present day

The weathered rowboat neared the sheltered shoreline. It wasn't visible in the fog, but its oarlocks groaned in the rolling sea. A man in a long religious robe stood on the dock waiting for relief to arrive.

He turned his head to listen for a voice, and finally heard the call from the boat.

"Ah, Brother, I brought a Florence Nightingale to lend her mercies."

The man on the dock leaned out for the bow rope and extended his hand to the nurse. She wore a grey dress and white apron, and her hair was tied by a plain gray scarf.

"Bonsoir, Mademoiselle. Welcome."

Her eyes were dark brown and her skin creamy beige. Looking directly into his eyes, she introduced herself.

"Call me Sister Katrina."

He turned to the other man who had come down to unload the boat. "Do we have new instructions regarding the patient?"

"We should pull back on the drugs, if we want truthful answers. How is he today?"

"He is sitting up, but only stares out the window in a trance. I'm not sure if he even knows who he is."

"The dear Sister will try to help restore his health. She received her own instructions from America."

Napa Valley, California, present day

Melissa lounged on a hammock under a giant oak by the veranda, reading a book. The children had eaten lunch, and Marcy was tucked in for a nap. Melissa was insistent that Hazel and Isaac have one too, but Addie won the tug of war.

"Melissa, I have plans with the kids for the afternoon. We are going to dig for buried treasure. I already enticed them with lemonade and chocolate chip cookies. They can sleep all they want when they get back home. Grandmas' houses are supposed to be places to create memories. Right?"

"Ma, you're a grown up kid. Go ahead, have your fun. I'm going to hang out with a good mystery book."

"Huh. Good mystery? Keep your eyes open, Melissa, and you'll find that there's one right under your nose."

"Ma, is there something you need to tell me?"

"Later, Mel; over a cup of tea. Right now, my pirate ship is about to depart." Hazel and Isaac were tugging on her skirt, anxious to find Jonas.

Armed with honey pails and trowels, Hazel and Isaac marched alongside Addie deep into the vineyard.

Addie carried towels, a cooler, and a folding camp stool to spare her back. Jonas had wooden crates ready for them.

"Ahoy, mates, into the crates."

Jonas, the pirate, tied ropes to the crates and dragged his captives over some bumps and through the vines. "Heave ho! Land ho! Off here to bury ye treasure."

Addie called from behind. "Quick! Get away from the pirate, so he doesn't take the jewels."

"Yargh!" Jonas, with a patch over his eye, swung his arms and his deep, raspy voice sent the children scattering in squeals of laughter.

Addie removed a burlap package from the cooler. "Ah ha, the treasure! We must bury it where no one will find it. Remember pirates never tell where their treasure is, it would be terrible luck. Have you heard about Captain Jack?"

The children were wide-eye, nodding in agreement, but their eyes were only on the burlap as Addie unwrapped it. She laid out a brilliant necklace with a cluster of rubies, and another with golden strands of sparkling emeralds.

"Oh, Grandma, can I keep mine instead of burying it?"

"No sweetheart, not this time."

Hazel ran toward the service hut in the shelter of a clump of trees.

"Grandma, I see a squirrel's home way up in the tree. Could you hide the rubies up there?"

"Sure, Hazel, we'll find a stump for me to stand on so I don't fall."

Isaac was enamored with his gems and reluctant to part with them. "If you are to be a true pirate, Isaac, you must bury your treasure. Maybe someday when you are tall like Grandpa was, you can come back here and find it."

"Okay, Grandma, mine wants to go in the hornet's nest up there."

"I'm afraid not, you can never disturb a hornet's nest. If you awaken them, a thousand hornets will gather together and put all their stingers into you. Can you see another place?"

Isaac pointed to crumbling foundation. "What about that deep hole under the stone, the broken one?"

"Excellent."

"Now that our treasure is buried, let's find some lawn for our snacks. Over there, see the big oak tree? That will give us some shade.

The trio ate, sang and danced, letting their bellies jiggle with every 'Yo, Ho, Ho'. Skipping back, home, they sang over and over, lowering their chins to their deepest pirate voices.

For I am a Pirate King!
And it is, it is a glorious thing
To be a Pirate King!
For I am a Pirate King!

"Now you know we have a pirate's oath never to reveal buried treasure," Addie whispered. "You have to spit on it."

Isaac looked at the spit all the way to the veranda.

"Grandma, this was even better than the toad Jonas caught for me. Do I have to keep the spit forever?"

"As long as you can, but even when it is gone, you must obey your oath of secrecy."

"I will. Yargh!"

At the national registry in Charron, Thomas investigated the legal relationship between Matthew and Addie. The only relevant birth record for Matthew Ducharme, was the baby who died within a few days of birth, born to Adelaide Cumberland and Zachary Ducharme.

He dug again for evidence of Caliste Hanson or Caliste Delacroix as the mother on a birth certificate. There were several legitimate births while Caliste was married to Nathan Hanson, but none fit the scenario.

Another thought struck Thomas, and a search for Caliste Delacroix and Charles Ducharme brought back a hit. He paid for a copy of the birth certificate and folded it in his jacket pocket. It was within a year of Addie's child.

Before Thomas left Charron, he drove to the law firm. He didn't have an appointment and it was late in the afternoon. The lawyer was about to leave his office when Thomas came up the outside step.

"Sir, could I have a few minutes of your time? You can bill the estate."

"Highly inappropriate. What are you looking for?"

"Who gave you the Will for Zachary Ducharme?" Thomas asked.

"Why, it was Matthew."

"That is odd. Addie had little contact with Matthew until the day of Zach's death. There wasn't any contact between them until Addie found a mysterious letter introducing him. At the registry, there's no record of his birth to Zachary Ducharme.

"What I did find interesting was a birth certificate registered to Caliste Hanson and Charles Ducharme for a son by the name of Roderick Matteo Ducharme. Do you have any knowledge of that? Has it occurred to you that you are working for an imposter?"

"Mr. York, I am not under questioning. Please make an appointment with my secretary for the morning."

His voice trembled as he continued down the steps. At the bottom, he fumbled for his keys, his hands shaking.

Matthew was angry that Jonas had moved into the guest room in the extension. He also detected a new distance from Maria, as she was pulling back from his advances.

I have to teach Addie a lesson. The vineyards are mine. I'll be glad to sell it and kick that family out of the house.

Agitated, Matthew stepped out to the back veranda for a smoke. The late afternoon sun was casting long shadows and he went to the railing to admire the lawns. Behind him, he heard gentle rocking.

It must be Addie.

Without turning around, Matthew began.

"You've been waiting for me, haven't you?"

"Yes, Matt, I have. I thought we should talk in private."

"Don't get me started. You have dinner guests."

"No, we are all family; my daughter, my grandchildren, my niece and her husband, and my dear trusted friend. I have been thinking hard about passages. They can be very enlightening if you really search. How do you know that ugly man Dex? Is he the one responsible for the scare tactics, or was that you?"

Matt bristled. "That's none of your business. You're being cantankerous. What's your point?"

"With all the complications and outside involvement, it's best if you move back in with your parents. I'm giving you a twenty-four hour notice, before I request a restraining order."

"Not at chance!"

Matthew dropped the cigarette onto the porch boards and ground the ashes. Addie continued to rock persistently and whistled 'Just slip out the back, Jack'.

Matthew stamped off the veranda, without showing enough respect to look at her.

Before dinner, he took one of the pickups out for an errand. After the pickup left, Thomas started up one of the Harleys. He kept a safe distance behind and watched Matthew pull into the Delacriox laneway.

He's going for reinforcements. But Gregoire is too smart to get involved in Matt's dirty laundry. I wonder what their connection is.

Slamming the driver's door, Matthew took a deep breath and stormed to the front door of the big Georgian house. He rang the buzzer twice and pounded his fist on the door. With his ear to the door he heard shuffling.

He shouted. "Mr. Delacroix, it's important!"

The cook answered. "Who should I say is calling?"

"Caliste Hanson's son."

There was a long pause as Matthew waited on the steps. Thomas parked the motorcycle by the ditch and crept up along the side of the house to within hearing range. The door opened and Thomas regretted not packing a transmitter in his pocket.

Gregoire stood at the door with his arms crossed in defiance. "So you are Caliste Hanson's son. What's that mean to me?"

"Let's not play cat and mouse, Mr. Delacroix."

"Are you related to Nathan Hanson?"

"No, I'm related to Caliste Delacroix. She's my mother and your half-sister."

Matthew watched Gregoire's face as he couldn't make the connection at first, but then felt the heavy burden of the relationship. Matthew enjoyed seeing the anguish.

"For heaven's sake, lad! What you say is impossible."

"Putting two and two together, I presume I was born illegitimately."

"My stepfamily ignored me, and then my adoptive family disappeared. So I now present myself as the heir to the Ducharme fortune. A man's got to look out for his future."

"You are the son, the one at the funeral! That is blatantly rude, but granted it's brilliant. Is Addie on to you?"

"I was welcomed with open arms. The books on the vineyard are under my control as well as the field supervisors. Having a half interest gives me a great amount of power. Power to negotiate a sale, and then the cache would be ours too."

"Let's talk in my office, I want to hear more about the cache. Come back to the tasting rooms."

Thomas stayed out of sight, and returned to the bike.

TWENTY

Addie rang the dinner bell as she heard Matthew's steps coming across the veranda.

Matthew went straight to the head of the table, to Zach's empty chair. He didn't look, but hoped the insult would tarnish Addie's cheeriness.

Thomas sat at the other end, with Addie to his right, Jonas across from her, and the children in between. Rachel and Melissa were sitting on either side of Matthew's chair when he arrived. Everything about the seating was strategic.

Serving bowls were abundant with the vegetables that Maria had gathered in the afternoon, and a honey-glazed ham was ready for carving.

"Ahem." Addie rose and stood behind her chair.

"One moment before you delve into dinner. I would like to say grace."

"Bless us, O Lord, and these your gifts, which we are about to receive from your bounty. We pray for those among us, for health and safety, truth and love. We ask that you watch over each member of the family at this table. Through Christ our Lord. Amen."

Matthew glowered at her, then forced a gracious smile for the sake of the children.

"Well, Isaac what did you learn today?" he asked.

Melissa's eyes went to Addie waiting for her to intercept but Isaac was bold.

"I learned to keep a promise, and I learned to help people get their own."

There were a few chuckles at Isaac's innocence, and he fell quiet with embarrassment.

Jonas put a gentle hand on the lad's shoulder. "Tomorrow, I have another adventure for you and your sister."

"What's that?"

"Well, if I told you in front of everyone, it wouldn't be a secret. I hope you will come back for many more summers."

"What do you mean, Jonas?"

Isaac searched for understanding but Matthew hung onto every pointed word.

"No matter where you go on this vast estate, there are eyes and ears. The house holds many mysteries too. I understand from your Grandma that tomorrow you get to ride in the dumb waiter."

"That's not a nice thing to say about Carmen. Only bullies use the word dumb."

"I'm sorry Isaac. We'll explain that better tomorrow. We weren't referring to Carmen."

Rachel assisted Hazel as the bowls passed. "Grandma, are these the beans we snapped this afternoon?"

Matthew stood up.

"Enough of these pointed conversations using children. I know what is taking place. I'm going out to find some adult company."

He threw his napkin on the table and slammed the kitchen door. Addie relaxed at the roar of the truck in the distance.

Melissa took the children to their baths to clean the mud from between their toes. Addie encouraged bare feet on the lawns and the vineyards, thinking that it toughens them up and builds character.

"Now I want to continue our conversation of the other day," Addie said to the others.

"Without going further than where you left off, I have some new clues to contribute," Thomas said. "Do you mind, Addie?"

"No, it's a good time for that."

Thomas said. "Rachel, you should go first with your conversation in the garden with Maria."

Rachel whispered of the visitation of Matthew and Charles Ducharme, verbatim as Maria told it.

"This would tie into the time of the break-in. Maria wasn't sure if she had seen Matthew before, but with his red straggly hair and beard, she knew the silhouette and the tone of his voice."

Jonas said, "Addie, shortly before Zach's passing, I saw Matthew at the Rusty Nail. I was picking up beer for the barbeques. Zach was speaking quietly to the Kincaid fellow, and after Zach left, the kid came over and took up the conversation with Dexter."

"Thanks, Jonas," Addie said. "From the moment Zach saw the bogus Will in his desk, he became sharp to 'the rustling in the weeds; and the words of the whippoorwill came to his ears'. It's a funny expression, but believe me, for weeks his days were spent keeping an eye on anything that moved in the fields.

"He knew there was an ambush in the planning. The bogus Will was part of it. Then the red-haired man, the poaching, the burglary, the busted lock in the garage, Rocky's behavior, and the red Silverado. Then the invitations to the Saturday night barbeque stopped." She hesitated. "There were the guilty faces on the workers who'd betrayed us, and all these offers to get us out.

"Zach took precautions. He planted a silent trigger in the back west field that went off when poachers trespassed, and the intercom in the caves. The loyalty of all the foremen was vital and he set a provision for them. Jonas, can you describe it?"

Jonas picked up. "A few months ago, Zach held a meeting at the bunkhouse, explaining his concerns.

We all had suspected that the Delacroix farm was stealing Bordeaux vines through the west fence. Some workers had accepted bribes, and Zach asked us to be vigilant. He also suspected that someone was forging documents.

"Each of the foremen would receive a cash sum from the estate for their loyalty. I meet with each of the foremen daily for an accounting of anything suspicious without Matthew knowing. I know we can trust our foremen."

Addie wiped a tear. "This land belongs in a way to fathers, grandfathers, great-grandfathers, and great-great-grandfathers. Countless people were born here and spent their lives in the vineyards. That cannot change."

Addie leaned in to speak, and their heads followed. "The west field had the ancient Bordeaux vines. We have endured trespassing, murder, and recently fire.

"Two years ago, Zach, Jonas and I moved the Bordeaux grapes to the east quarter over a few weekends on a Sunday. Once transplanted, they received specialized care, without anyone's suspicion. In the second season, they flourished and received awards." She laughed. "And all this time, the Delacroix people have been going after the west quarter vines. Zach planted weak vines back there that won't produce quality wine for a few more years. No one would know."

When Addie finished, she sat back to enjoy the laughter at the success of their mischief. Jonas took a bottle of cabernet from the cupboard and Rachel put some glasses out.

"Wait. There's more!" Addie said. "After the fake Will was found, Zach took fingerprints around his desk and photographs of them. He applied them onto a vinyl surface with packing tape. The photos are digitally noted with the date and time, and saved in a steel case and online.

"It would have drawn too much attention to have them analyzed in San Francisco. However, now would be an appropriate time and I have them on the premises. It's enough evidence to convict him of break and enter."

Rachel said, "I'll retrieve Matthew's glass at breakfast for a fingerprint sample."

"Zach removed the business papers from his desk that had his own signature," Addie said. "The ones remaining were in my own hand, forging his John Henry. I left a lipstick smudge on the backside of each one I handled. Also, the last Offer to Purchase wasn't in the desk the morning of the accident."

Jonas began, then paused, swallowing on his guilt.

"Addie, I hadn't been able to contact Matthew when Zach passed; he arrived at the kitchen door all the same. It leaves a question about how close he was to the estate in the days surrounding the accident."

He thought for a moment and said, "He'll get his own."

Those words echoed. "Did you hear the kids say that?" he asked. "They picked it up in the pirate field. We may have overlooked the children. Rachel could you get Melissa's permission to talk with the kids; they might have noticed Matthew do something of interest."

Rachel nodded, "Good thought. Children love secrets. And Addie, with Matthew being asked to leave, can I arrange for a locksmith?"

"You've got guts! He'll be riled for sure. Do it."

At 9:00 a.m. Thomas arrived at the lawyer's. He didn't particularly like Mr. Stewart, as the man seemed weak and tentative to him.

Stewart's secretary announced Thomas promptly. He thumbed through a ragged magazine and threw it on the table. Finally he was ushered to the legal room.

"It's a pleasure to see you again, Mr. York. I gather from our rather informal meeting on the outer stairs, that you have questions regarding Matthew Ducharme as beneficiary."

Stewart peered over his glasses, and Thomas came straight to the point.

"I believe the man who has presented himself as Matthew Ducharme, is not the birth child of Zachary and his first wife. That child was deceased at birth. There's also no record of Zachary being married before Addie. Not a single match in the entire county."

"Doesn't surprise me."

"Did Matthew present a birth certificate to you? Federal records are open to the public, so there is no confidentiality issue here."

"Yes, you're right. He was anxious for me to validate the Will and I didn't receive any objection. His driver's license and passport were satisfactory."

"I have done some leg work for you," Thomas said. The only marriage is that of Addie's. There is a child by the name of Matthew coinciding with the age in the woeful letter left in his desk. Comparing examples of Zach's true handwriting authorized by his own wife, there's no resemblance to handwriting in either the letter or the Will. The unwitting culprit was obviously unaware of Addie's intervention."

Stewart listened and wrote some lines on a legal pad.

"Did you ask him for a birth certificate?" Thomas asked.

"Matthew came a week ago and asked me to conceal a record showing his birth mother as Caliste Delacroix and his father as Charles Ducharme. He attempted to bribe me to make the alteration."

Thomas jumped to his feet. "You could be disbarred for that!" He slammed the door as he left.

He made two more stops in Charron, the first on Barber Street. Ricky's Pizza was an old establishment, however already full of patrons by 11:00 a.m. Thomas pushed down the aisle between the metal booths and sat down to wait. A bald man seemed to be in charge, with a pot belly and a greasy apron.

That must be Ricky.

A young lad worked at the oven and two girls prepared toppings. The lad resembled Ricky, with signs of premature balding.

Several office buildings were within a few blocks, and the lunch crowd was lined up at the counter. Thomas stood to order a slice.

With hot pizza in his hands, he took a lone seat at the counter. By 1:00 p.m., the staff turned to clean-up.

Thomas called out.

"Hello, are you Ricky, the owner?"

"I am."

He wiped his hands on the apron and placed them on his hips. Do you have a complaint?"

"My name is Thomas York. I'm visiting at the Ducharme estate down the road. I was told that one of my uncles, Charles Ducharme, was staying in one of your apartments. Do you know where I could find him?"

"Well, it's mighty nice to see some kin. Charles's wife left him before Christmas, and he threw himself into the drink. Didn't keep himself or the apartment in good shape. By the way, I have a raft of mail, including last month's pension checks. Would you take that off my hands?"

"Sure, I'll take it back to the estate for Matthew. He's staying there. When did you last see Charles?"

"He left sometime in January, but the kid popped in since then."

"What did the kid look like?"

The description suited Matthew to a tee.

"He hasn't been here since that awful incident that killed poor Ducharme."

"Do you have an address, or phone number for any of them?"

"No. They have all disappeared."

"Did Charles have a job that you know it?"

"I don't think so, he paid his rent with a government pension check."

"Thank you, Ricky, for your help. I had the deluxe pizza and I'd have it again."

TWENTY-ONE

Running late, Thomas drove over the speed limit to Motor Vehicles. The risk had a price, a $150 speeding ticket.

At the registry, luck was on his side, with only one person waiting in front of him for the clerk. As a government office, he still was required to pull a number from the dispenser.

"Hello, I was run off the road by a pickup recently. I would like you to check this partial plate for a red Silverado."

"A partial is all you've got?"

The clerk looked out into the office, hoping there would be a line up and she could dismiss Thomas. She grimaced and reached for the tattered note.

"Did he cause any damage to your car? It's not too late to make a report. Drivers with those big pickups presume they own the road."

The clerk chatted while her eyes were fixed on the monitor. She was now onboard with the mission.

"Appears only one recent model red Silverado is registered in town. I have a full license number for you. It is owned by Gregoire Delacroix."

"Thanks. Can you tell me where I can go to check up on locals with speeding violations in town?"

"Sure, at the police station. Follow Main Street to Richmond, turn right and go two blocks."

Rachel kept a ham sandwich for Thomas, with a skim of Dijon, tomato, lettuce and mayo; exactly as he liked it in Paris.

She placed two cups of coffee on the table, then wrapped her arms around him from behind as he ate.

"Thomas, let me know what's going on."

"Sit with me Rachel. A lot is happening at a rapid pace. It's time for Addie to challenge the Will and expose Matthew."

He paused for a large bite of the sandwich and a gulp.

"I tried to track down Charles, but he's a needle in a haystack. Can you search for any tidbit?"

"Sure. I'll do that when we've finished."

"I went to Motor Vehicles and they confirmed that the Silverado belongs to Gregoire Delacroix. Although, he's the owner, both Dexter and Matthew have been driving it. Shows a clear relationship between them. What's new around here?"

"Matthew is still here. He lit into Addie this morning. He's been drawing the business account down and there's not much left. Then he ranted about being defrauded and accused Addie of embezzlement."

"Is Addie alright?"

"Oh sure. She enjoyed it. Matthew was right, she has been redirecting funds, but to protect herself."

"While in town, I had a speeding ticket. I was annoyed at first, then I wondered who has had tickets in the section?

Perhaps Matthew, Dex, Charles or maybe Lane. Rachel, I hit the jackpot. I don't know where to begin."

"At the beginning please." Rachel came around the table and kissed him.

"Matthew and his father both had speeding tickets in December. Matthew was in his Toyota and his father in an older pickup. It was on the same stretch of road heading south of town, within a half hour of each other on the same day. The location could be the farm in Ascot. It's possible they were renters on that property. Before they left Barber Road, they paid rent with their pension check.

"The speeding tickets might indicate that Matthew was chasing Charles."

"We'll have to talk later, Jonas is coming down the stairs."

Jonas walked into the kitchen as Thomas and Rachel cleared the table.

"Is Addie around?" he said. "I need to talk to her."

Rachel noticed that since Jonas moved into the house, he'd been more assertive, even overruling Matthew in the fields. But in the house, the two avoided conversation.

"I believe she's hanging her whites out on the line."

Addie walked in with a basket full. Jonas took it to the laundry room for Maria.

"Can you sit for a few minutes, Addie?"

"What is it?

Rachel walked over to the hallway extension to be sure Matthew wasn't in hearing range. She nodded back to Thomas.

Jonas started. "Addie, can you tell us about the cache? We all wonder but are afraid of appearing greedy. Since we have an open forum to save the vineyards, we need to know."

"And how would Matthew have known it existed?" Thomas added.

"I don't know about Matthew, but Dexter Kincaid knew for sure. He spent a lot of years in prison, where secrets get spilled. Matthew and Dexter both came here knowing about a sack of jewels and bundles of cash from Rio.

"I'd like Matthew to conclude that the box I hid at Zach's request is still somewhere in the wine caves. It would keep him occupied. But no one will ever find the gems, until the next generation."

"The box you hid . . . is it the box for the key?" Thomas asked.

"Yes," Addie said. "The key that Matthew has. And he asked me the other day about the gems, in a nasty tone.

"I have my suspicions about the bank notes too. Thomas, can you see what 80,000 Brazilian Cruzeiros from 1967 are worth today?"

TWENTY-TWO

Spirited and flirtatious, Caliste Delacroix stood out amongst the village girls, with flaming red hair and freckles across her nose. She enhanced her reputation with the boys, always in flirtatious clothes, and bright red lipstick.

She found employment in 1972 as a housekeeper and nanny in the village, but she maintained full range of the compound and often ventured into the vineyards to fraternize with the men.

There was harmony between the two neighbors in those days. But in 1973, Francois Ducharme discovered his son Charles with Caliste in compromising circumstances in the bunkhouse. He was outraged.

Both Charles and Nathan Hanson had vied for her attentions. Guilty of the tryst with Charles Ducharme, she produced a child. Caliste cried foul to her parents and insisted she had nothing further to do with her disreputable man, Charles.

A confidential financial settlement was provided by the Ducharmes, and Charles was evicted from the property and forever banned. His birthright was snatched from him.

Nathan had remained sweet on Caliste and married her, not knowing who the father of the child was. They both agreed they couldn't live with the shame of the newborn, and within a few days, the child was removed until arrangements were sorted out.

Charles was sent to work in a vineyard near Vallejo where he met and married the daughter of a local businessman. Evelyn was slightly older than Charles and soon found she was unable to bear a child. Hearing the situation, she offered to take the infant in. Charles and Evelyn raised Matthew.

Nathan Hanson worked for Francois in the vineyards and they were always treated like one big family. Nathan and Caliste raised four boys and two girls, who never knew the existence of a half-brother. The daughters and sons all married and moved away.

Matthew was never mentioned, and whenever he brushed shoulders with his step-brothers in the community, they had nothing friendly to say to each other.

After Grandfather Jacob retired, Zachary prepared to take over by studying the art of villa management in France, and to learn to create award winning wines. He became a member of 'The Vintners of Beaujolais' in Lyon and 'Bordeaux Master' and studied with the monks to produce prized chardonnays.

Under Zach's management, there was a sudden boost in the demand for Ducharme wines in the Napa Valley. Five star establishments lined up for as many cases as they could get.

Meanwhile, Charles and Evelyn, were never invited to family celebrations. Charles maintained no family connections, feeling like the biblical parallel of Esau, stripped of his birthright.

As Zachary thrived in the business, Charles hoarded resentment for being bypassed. He felt he should have been entitled to a portion of the vineyards, in spite of the incident.

Charles's other brothers Pierre and Robert built wineries in the Sonoma Valley, but still returned for holidays at the farm. Antoinette and Marie-Louise married local men; one went to Los Angeles, the other to San Francisco. Celia fell in love with Jeremy Davis, a foreman on the estate. When they married, they moved back to Arizona.

As a teenager, Matthew found papers showing his birth information, and in a typical first reaction, he was angry. He ran away from home trying to find his way, but returned with a thousand questions. He insisted on locating his birth mother, but Evelyn constantly deterred him.

"Matthew, we can't change who you were born to be." Charles said. "We have given you the best we could. Your mother didn't want to raise you, but Evelyn lovingly brought you into our home. Be thankful."

"Why didn't you tell me?"

"What good would that have done?" Charles challenged.

Evelyn begged, "Matthew, you should know that I always loved you like my own son. Please don't do this."

Matthew turned to Charles, his neck veins bulging. "You deceived your own son and deprived me of my natural mother. Where is she? This is your fault—your fault."

"Matthew! Suck it up!" Charles blurted.

In his late teens, Matthew stormed into the workers' village on the Ducharme property, in search of Caliste Hanson. She was making tortillas by the open bread oven.

Caliste stared for a moment, then looked away. She knew Nathan wouldn't return until late afternoon.

"Caliste Hanson?"

"Who are you?"

"Look again. They say a mother never forgets her child. Is that true?"

"It's my understanding from this little piece of paper here, that you and I have Delacroix blood." He handed her the folded birth certificate. She slowly and carefully smoothed out the paper, and her eyes began to well.

Sitting down on a tree stump, she sobbed.

"Don't you have something to say to your own son?" Matthew was pleading with genuine wanting for her to beg forgiveness and embrace him.

"Please sit down, Matthew, I want to explain."

He pulled over a bale of hay to sit on. His own mother wouldn't look at him, keeping her head down.

"I was raped by Charles Ducharme. Your father is a monster. I was unmarried and couldn't bear the shame. Your father was happy to have you in his own family."

Matthew was stunned.

"My father is a monster! At least he cared enough to bring me up in his home, and never raised a hand to me."

"It was the Delacroixs that took me in while I was pregnant. Then I married a wonderful man, Nathan Hanson. I have no place for you in my life. I can't bear the reminders. Every time to see your face, I see Charles."

"You're my mother! You might as well spit in my face, the way you deny me."

"So be it." Caliste rose and walked away.

Matthew kicked dust in her face and stomped back toward the driveway.

TWENTY-THREE

At three a.m. Thomas opened his eyes suddenly but didn't move. In the darkness, he turned his head toward the scratching in the closet, then listened to the floor creak under a footstep in the room.

What would Matthew want in here at this hour? There must be an entrance from the extension.

Rachel changed position, settling into a gentle sigh then a purr. He was glad she was asleep. The dark shadow tip-toed to his dresser and removed an item, then quietly retreated toward the closet.

Thomas silently reached for his gun from the nightstand drawer, then bolted upright with his revolver aimed at the intruder. Turning the lamp on, he was surprised to see Carmen, one of the house boys.

"What the devil are you doing, Carmen?"

"So sorry, Mr. Tom. I didn't want to do this, but Mr. Matt gave me a pure silver medallion if I would take your wallet. He said you have a document belonging to him."

The commotion woke Rachel, who sat up. Then Addie heard the shouting from down the hall and listened. She knocked, and to confront the loud voices, she eased the door open to Thomas's bedroom.

Addie was abrupt. "Carmen. There is nothing you can say. Pack your bags immediately. I'll see you get a ride to town."

"Miss Addie, I didn't mean any harm." He passed her the medallion.

"Where did you get this, Carmen?"

"As I said to Mr. Tom, I was asked to come up the back way through the old staircase from the servants' quarters. Mr. Matthew wanted me to take the wallet. The medallion was a terrible temptation. It is pure silver."

"Addie, I'll give him a ride into town," Thomas said.

She nodded and held a raised index finger.

"Carmen, what can you tell me about the old staircase? Where does it go, besides the bedroom?"

"It is lengthy and in bad repair. You could break your ankle if you didn't pay careful attention to your feet. I was curious one Sunday and went to a door that was barricaded, but the wine caves were on the other side. There are halls behind all the bedrooms. I've heard old talk about slaves been hidden here, that's why the route is so extensive."

"Can you draw me a map?"

"I'll show you what I know."

Thomas and Carmen didn't speak for most of the drive. Finally Thomas spoke.

"Where am I taking you, Carmen?"

"My grandmother lives in an apartment on this side of Charron. I know where she keeps the key. Turn right at the next side road.

"I'm sorry about what happened tonight, Mr. Thomas. Miss Addie has been good to me, I can't apologize enough. Tell her how sorry I am. I would do anything to make it up to her. "

At seven o'clock, Addie and the grandchildren were in the kitchen, helping Maria make breakfast. The aroma of fresh baked buns and cinnamon rolls would wake up the rest.

"We're going to have a grand breakfast. Hazel, you will be scrambling eggs. Isaac, are you big enough to set the table?"

"I am big enough, but Mommy says I can't touch knives."

"Isaac, just spoons and forks then. Marcy, you can push the chairs in around the table."

Melissa came downstairs in a flower print dress.

"Morning, Mom. I thought I might take a jaunt into town. I'm overdue for some shopping. Can I tempt you to come with me? Maybe lunch in that tea shop, we used to go to?"

"I'm afraid, I'll be going into Charron to tend to some legal matters. I have no doubt you will shop very well without me."

"That's a shame. Another day, promise me?"

"Promise."

Addie turned back to ensure the bacon didn't get too crisp. Maria's waffles and home fried potatoes were ready and she brought out a jar of her home made salsa and strawberry jam.

Melissa put her handbag down. "Mmm, smells good. Perhaps I'll stay, and go after breakfast." "Ma, we need to have a talk. Can you squeeze me into your schedule?"

"Tomorrow morning I'm yours, dear. Let's have tea in the sunroom. I have some old family pictures for you."

Matthew walked into the kitchen and took the head chair as usual. There was little conversation until Jonas arrived.

"I'm starved, Maria," Jonas said. "I could smell the bacon from the hallway. Good morning, Hazel and Isaac. Where's Marcy?"

"Here I am." Out popped Marcy from under the table, her arms open wide, waiting for a spring lift into Jonas's arms.

"Addie, did you have a good sleep?"

"Well, Jonas, we did have a night visitor. I retrieved one of the silver medallions." Addie's eyes were on Matthew as she spoke.

Thomas wasn't so polite. "Matthew, what did you want out of my wallet? Are you running short on cash? Shameful, setting up an innocent houseboy, to do your dirty work. Carmen is gone, fired on the spot. He won't be able to sleep at night for a long time. Some people don't stop to realize how they affect the lives of others."

"Maria, I'll have my breakfast in the dining room." Matthew took his coffee through the adjoining hall without answering.

"Mr. Stewart is expecting us. Thomas York and Addie Ducharme." They stood and waited, and the lawyer was prompt this time to greet them.

"I've had a long talk with my nephew, by marriage. You have some legal matters to straighten out in that regard."

"Please take a seat. Can I offer you coffee, tea or water?" Mr. Stewart was more anxious to please this time.

"I'll have Earl Grey with lemon."

"Black coffee, please," Thomas said.

Mr. Stewart paused and sighed.

"The first matter is the proof of birth for Matthew Ducharme. Can we start there?"

"Go ahead," Addie said.

"Mr. York met with me yesterday and produced a certified birth certificate for Matthew showing his birth mother to be

Caliste Delacroix and that Charles Ducharme is his natural father."

Addie said, "You know, in thinking back past the cobwebs, shortly after Zach and I were married, there was a lot of attention directed at Charles. After that, we never saw Matthew until Evelyn sent me his graduation photo. He is Zach's brother's son, my nephew by marriage.

"Without a doubt, it was Matthew in disguise in the fields about six months ago. He wore a straw hat with a red feather and dyed his hair red and left it straggly.

"Before Zach died, there were skeptical circumstances." Addie leaned toward Stewart. "I'm smarter than you calculate, Mr. Stewart. I knew Matthew's fabricated letter and Will could be reversed within ninety days. Also, my mortality is a condition. I like to be thorough when I clean house. If there are rumblings in the fields, we must rectify the problem."

Stewart was silent and Thomas added, "Mr. Stewart, did Matthew address the ninety day provision?"

"Yes, he did. At the first meeting."

Addie put her elbow on the desk, taking charge. "Let's fix this up then. What was his question regarding the provision. Did the words 'if Addie doesn't survive ninety days' come up?"

"I'm sorry, Addie." The lawyer bowed apologetically. "Where do you want to begin?"

"Revoke his authority over all affairs on the vineyard. Advise the bank of an illegal imposter and remove him from authority over the estate. Re-introduce this original Will for probate."

She pulled a legal size envelope from her purse. This is Zach's legal Will that was filed years ago with this firm. See, it is witnessed by one of your lawyers. This validated copy was taped under his desk."

"A hearing is necessary to legally change Matthew's status."

"Start that process."

"A restraining order needs to be served to restrict him access from the house. Again, that goes before the court."

"Do that immediately. Today. I'll sign an affidavit now to allow you to represent me in court. Further, deny Matthew information regarding the estate from this point onward."

Mr. Stewart buzzed for his secretary to take notes.

Addie continued. "You should also know, I'll be laying assault charges against Matthew. I know there is nothing you can do about that. Any cooperation you provide will be to a felon, and that won't look good to your partners. I'm sure you anticipate a partnership in your firm in the future."

TWENTY-FOUR

Island underground chamber, Normandy, France

Sister Katrina gentle hand's felt her patient's forehead and raised his head to take a sip of tea.

"Welcome back to the real world."

"Where am I? How long?"

"First, I have some questions for you. What is *your* name?"

Daniel struggled to find an answer.

"We found your passport in your pocket . . . are you Thomas York?"

Napa Valley, California

Dexter Kincaid had served forty years of his sentence in the notorious Bangu Penitentiary in one of the most populated districts of Rio de Janeiro, where hard labor kept him fit.

The band of eight from the robbery had each faced their own demise. Kane and five others in the shootout at the scene. Roberto tried to get back out through the collapsed tunnel, but his body was never recovered.

Sharing bunks with a man known as Spider, Dexter embellished the heist, making the story more glamorous and the fireworks longer. But the details of the boy in California remained the same. Dexter had memorized his address.

In turn, Spider shared the story with his own daughter. Julia obtained a work visa and moved to the San Diego area in the '90s as a nanny. It was here that she met Rocky Morse; they married and went to work on the Delacroix farms.

Two years shy of being a free man, Dexter became arrogant and loose tongued, boasting of his impending release and wealth. It was unfortunate that he got his head stuck in the window bars of his cell.

Rocky Morse contracted with an ex-con who resembled Dexter in appearance. Similar in build, he needed a beard and to speak with a raspy voice. Rocky found his man in California and cut a scheme. After listening to the story for forty years, Spider wanted a cut of the cache.

His greed became an obsession and he saw an easy target. In his mind, Dexter Kincaid's fantasy life could go on after all. Nobody would go back to Rio to check the prison records. No-one would care that the real Dexter perished after forty years in prison.

One day in the vineyards, Rocky approached Lane with the preposterous story of treasure on the Ducharme estate. Dexter Kincaid, the California version, was eager for Rocky to spill the beans.

"Lane, I have it from a reliable source Zach has an old Brazilian buried treasure. I'll share it with you, if you support me in infiltrating their winery. They're always hiring field workers."

Lane looked at Rocky in amazement, but the wheels of greed spun in his head.

"I'm interested. Tell me more."

"When Zach was sixteen, he went to the Carnival in Rio. An innocent kid wanting to see the world.

"The story is fascinating, as he was forced into collusion with a crew of bandits. Zachary's role was to be inside the bank, then escaped with a sack of jewels and bank notes, with instructions from my accomplice.

"He was to go back to California. The convict, who left the sack, had an agreement to meet up at the Ducharme estate. When he first came to California, we devised a plan."

"This is ludicrous." Lane rubbed his chin then burst into laughter. "This is a lot to absorb in a few minutes. We'll talk again tomorrow. In the meantime, hustle yourself over to the Ducharme vineyards and worm your way into a position in the west quarter."

Rocky said, "I need to have an agreement with you. What do you want? Is it the cache or the grapes?"

"Why can't we have both, Rocky?" Lane patted him on the shoulder as if they were old friends.

Rocky accepted the pat but wasn't convinced that Lane could be trusted.

"Later, pal," he said.

Napa Valley, California (Previous Harvest)

As harvest approached, the Ducharmes were short of workers. One of the Wilkes boys, who worked in the west quarter, had been mugged in a bar near Ascot a few nights before. Witnesses claimed the assault was instigated by a burly stranger with some beard growth, a mean looking fellow.

Zachary was standing at the north service hut close to the main house, when a lad approached him. His claim to have had experience at the Delacroix vineyard raised red flags.

"Tell you what young fellow. "I'll give you a thirty day trial. As it happens, one of my guys got his arm broke last night. What's your name?"

"Rocky Morse. Thanks, you won't be disappointed. I can pitch in right now."

"Mr. Morse, why did you leave the Delacroix farms?"

"I was ready for a change and through the workers, I've heard good things about the management here." Rocky's flattery hooked Zach.

"First you need to meet the main foreman and he'll assign you to an area." Zach stood on his toes looking over the vines for Jonas's hat.

"Jonas, over here."

"Coming, Zach."

"I've taken on a new fellow. I thought we could replace the Wilkes boy on a temporary basis in the west fields."

Turning to Rocky, Zach said, "Jonas will be your foreman."

"Do you have a bunkhouse for single men? I'll be needing a place to sleep and hang my hat."

"There's one in the worker's village and another over the garage. Jonas will show you around."

Rocky knocked at the Delacroix kitchen door. Lane peered out. After a moment, he kicked the door open.

"Rocky, our relationship is under wraps; I don't want anyone else getting curious. My father isn't to know about it and you have to be invisible. You can't talk to my father; only myself and my brother, Seebe."

"Sorry, Lane."

"Come on, we'll have a walk down to the well."

"I did as you said. I got a job at Ducharmes. Had to break a fellow's arm at the Rusty Nail to clear it. Then I get this rulebook foreman, called Jonas."

"What's your plan, Rocky?"

"The fence in the back corner. We can dig up the Bordeaux grapes. It's not the season yet for taking slips from them. Many rows of the grapes were destroyed last week in the fire." Rocky laughed.

Rocky shifted his feet, waiting for a reaction. "Are you chickening out, Lane?

"What do you need? I said we'd do it!"

"Transportation and equipment to your side of the fence corner. Assuming you are going to help me, we need one extra man."

"I'll bring Seebe and the Hanson kid."

"We'll start tomorrow night."

Rocky's night trespassing and tampering continued for the next two weeks, but halted when Zachary and the head foreman caught on to their night tracks. Zach had been watching from the telescope, pacing his timing to be ready to expose the Delacroix crew red-handed.

Seeing the flashlight approaching, Rocky and the other Delacroix workers made a quick exit through the broken fence.

In their haste, a sack of cuttings was dropped, creating the confrontation between Zach and Gregoire.

Rocky was on edge. He and Lane were on the brink of chaos, and if they didn't deter Zach now, the ship was about to sink. Zach's cache was the other big prize and they couldn't risk losing it.

Kincaid had the lay of the land even before his encounter with Zach. Rocky and Lane schemed to remove Zach's cache. The Delacroix vineyards would flourish on a grander scale with the Bordeaux grapes.

Rocky called a meeting at the pub with Dexter and Lane to go through the scheme. "The kid with the red hair, I met up with him in the fields. He's got his own plan, but he'll co-operate.

"The kid bragged about breaking into the house and altering Zach's Will. He's not interested in continuing to operate the winery; but needs to vindicate his father."

"How do I know you're telling the truth? Lane asked.

"He told me to call him Matt. He intends to stay under the radar until there is a good opening."

"What do you mean by a good opening? The kid's scheme sounds too grandiose."

Rocky said, "Matt told me to get rid of old Zach, and he would challenge the widow as Zach's son.

"Once we take control of the place, the cache will be ours. The Ducharme coot doesn't deserve his good fortune. When we get the rights, we'll comb those wine caves and tear the house apart."

"Exactly, Rocky, who is the 'we' you are talking about?" Lane glared while he quietly judged the man.

"And Dexter, the way I see it, you're looking for a fabled old cache of currency and gems."

Dexter leaned and showed his teeth as spoke. "Lane Delacroix! What would happen if I told your father of these schemes? The police will be interested to know that I was here six months ago casing the place and crossed paths with Matt."

Lane gritted back. "You'll be going to the police over my dead body. Nobody's going to believe an ex-con."

"I'll take care of it, Lane," Rocky said. "Get a detonating mechanism for me. You can claim you're blowing out stumps."

"I'll take care of that, but I'm steering clear of the murder. Make sure nothing comes back to me."

Napa Valley, California (present day)

Officer Murdock and his deputy skidded into the driveway as dinner was being laid.

"Hello, Addie."

"Well, come on in and join us," she said.

"I'm here on official business. Where is Matthew Ducharme?"

"He's in his suite in the extension. He's refused to leave. Jonas will show you them where."

"Come this way, Officer."

An adjoining hall lead to an extension including two suites, and an office.

"Is he in?"

"I'm not sure, but it's the second door on the left."

"Jonas, I have a search warrant. Remain where you are?"

Officer Murdock knocked on the door to Matthew's suite. There was no answer, but a second knock brought a shout. "What now?"

"Matthew Ducharme, I am Officer Murdock of the Charron Police Department. I have a search warrant. Open the door slowly."

There was silence, then the sound of shifting furniture. The door opened an inch and Matthew peered out.

"What are you looking for? You could ask!"

"Stand aside, Matthew, we have a warrant."

Murdock pushed passed him followed by his partner. He looked in drawers, closets and the bathroom. Suitcases were opened on the bed, and the zippers examined. Matthew paced at the window.

I must be close if he's so nervous. Look for the smallest detail.

The cases were all empty, except for one with a shaving kit. Checking each zipper, he found a bulge in the lining. He cut it open and a handful of silver medallions fell onto the futon. He turned to Matthew.

"Matthew Ducharme, you are under arrest for theft over five thousand dollars, for violation of a restraining order and assault. We're taking you in."

Matthew scowled at Jonas, as Murdock marched him by. Melissa had taken the kids into the living room until the arrest was over. Thomas, Rachel and Addie watched Matthew leave.

There was a hush in the room. Then a tiny voice called out. "Grandma was that a bad man?"

Gregoire Delacroix picked up Matthew's call from the Charron jail. His tires screeched as he floored it on the road to town. Bail was posted and Matthew was ushered out in his custody.

"You fool. Why on earth would you rob your own Sugar Daddy? If I wasn't so confused about your claim to his name, I'd leave you in jail to rot. You had a perfect set-up. Stay in the bunk house with Dexter for a few days until I come up with a plan."

"Mr. Delacroix, you can't turn your back on kin."

"Shut up."

The rest of the ride was silent. Gregoire didn't speak. He didn't realize, he had just put two evil men together.

TWENTY-FIVE

An hour later, the intercom buzzed at the bunkhouse. "Dexter, meet me beside the garage." Gregoire bellowed. "Now."

"Yes, Sir."

Dexter was down the stairs in seconds.

"I want you off my property immediately. I don't understand why Lane let you stay and mooch off of us. If you have a good reason, then spill the beans."

Dexter was coy with a snicker. "Perhaps you should've asked your son first."

"I'm asking you."

"I had a deal with Lane. The truth might be hard to bear, but I murdered Rocky Morse. We wouldn't want him going around saying things that might implicate you or Lane. The prize, of course, is the Ducharme land."

Gregoire's face turned white.

"Are you telling me that Lane was party to this conniving scheme? To murder?"

"Yes, Sir."

"Tell me, did Lane have anything to do with Zach's murder. And Rocky's now?"

"Yes, the Delacroix's are in up to their necks." Dexter jeered.

"I had a feeling he was up to no good. I'll alert the authorities. I thought the evidence was circumstantial, but you're telling me it was true. There's no reason for Lane to appeal."

Dexter's tone changed. "No, you won't do that, Gregoire." "There are several reasons. I'm a shareholder of Delacroix farms, and your signature is on an Offer to Purchase dated the same day as Zach's murder."

"I've no knowledge of that."

"You should pay more attention to your children and your grandchildren. I took ten shares; one from each of your grandchildren who were happy to part with them for a few silver medallions. Another twenty-five shares assigned to me by Lane; then fifteen from your errant daughter, Sylvia. By the way she is living in Arizona now and sends her love."

Gregoire's eyes were wide with anger. "If I had my gun, I'd shoot you right now."

"I'm not going anywhere until I get my stake. For forty years, a man rotted in his prison cell with his dream of finding the cache. No way that I'd walk away from that."

Thomas and Rachel took a drive into town to deliver papers to the court house. Matthew was out on bail and rumored to be back mooching off the Delacroixs. The scheme he had envisioned was now unraveling, one day at a time.

It was two months since Zach's funeral and Addie grieved in her own way. She dreaded the day of Thomas and Rachel's departure and the black cloud that would be waiting.

Addie paced the lawn dragging the picnic tables and outside lights in preparation for an old fashioned dinner. Melissa and the kids would be leaving on the weekend, and Addie wanted it to be an occasion they could never forget.

She knew there were only three more days for treasure hunts with the children, and she still had pirate songs for them. Melissa was amused in the beginning, but the persistent pirate singing got on her nerves.

"No more singing in the house—only outside." Melissa said.

"But Mama, we're pirates!"

"Pirates aren't allowed in Grandma's house."

The trio sauntered out the kitchen door and could be heard singing on the lawn.

Craving time alone, Thomas and Rachel drove to a breakfast house in town. A quiet table by the window was what they needed, away from the perils of the estate.

Rachel ordered, "The Quiche Lorraine, please, with mixed salad and balsamic."

The cook pointed at the chalkboard at the door. "Did you see the special, sir? A hot Reuben with warm chips drizzled with blue cheese and a tomato bisque?" Thomas took the easy route and nodded.

"Thomas, when should we be going home?"

"I've been troubled about that too. Zach's murder is solved, but Addie isn't safe yet. There's still the cache to be discovered."

Rachel was biting her lip, holding back. "I know, but I long for our privacy. I miss your spontaneous arms around me, romantic candlelight dinners and snuggling on the couch." She reached for his hand.

His brown eyes burrowed into her heart and they were both speechless as they savored the moment.

A gunshot rattled the window where they sat, crashing the plate glass to the ground. They both dove to the floor, and other customers, out of range in the corner, ran to the kitchen.

"Rachel, are you alright?"

"Yes, and you?"

"Stay here! I need to see who shot at us."

The tail light of a motorcycle was the only glimpse of the culprit, as it sped up the rise.

I know who that was.

Shards and splinters of glass covered the table and the floor. Sirens were on, crowding the street in front.

"Who was it, Thomas?" Rachel asked.

"It was a vintage Harley."

Rachel was unnerved. "Matthew . . . He's running wild and dangerous."

Thomas was on his knees searching in the broken glass for the bullet. Finally he found it lodged in the wooden frame of his chair. He turned to the shaking hostess.

"Have the police analyze this bullet. They're coming in now. I have a suspicion of whose gun did this!"

Rachel was still on the floor and he leaned to help her stand up. "Rachel, you're bleeding."

"Only a scratch, Thomas, must be a piece of flying glass." Within inches of her, he saw a shard embedded in her forehead.

"I'm taking you to the hospital." An ambulance with paramedics were already in the restaurant and they took over instantly. Following the stretcher, an officer continued to ask him for information.

"Not now," he said. "Meet me at the hospital."

At midnight, Rachel was released, bandaged and repaired. It was one more moment realizing the life and death risks of their profession.

Gregoire stood at the bunkhouse lower level, knocking first, then pounding.

"Matthew, let me in! I demand it."

The other men who used the bunkhouse were at their shifts. Gregoire's master key opened the door and he checked the back room. Taking two steps at a time to the top of the stairs and called again.

"Matthew? Dexter?" He flung open the closets and bathroom door. The alligator boots were toppled on the floor.

I've never seen Dexter without his boots. I guess he didn't take my eviction order seriously. Why would he come back here?

The hair on his neck stood up and the lights went out for Gregoire.

Not knowing how long he'd been unconscious, he stumbled to his feet with his hand on the back of his neck. There was blood in his palm.

Staggering to the kitchen, he picked up the First Aid kit. He dabbed the blood from the back of his head and examined the gash in the bathroom mirror. The blood kept coming.

I need stitches.

The red Silverado was gone.

Gregoire ran to his truck, a cloth pressed to his head. He had to get to the clinic fast.

Grape harvest had started and Napa Valley was filling with tourists. Every vineyard bustled, with tractors, trucks and wagons running until dark. Guest tours were limited but still operated with high demand.

Matthew and Dexter climbed through a fence opening. Unnoticed, they made their way to a stone doorway near the winery, leading down into the volcanic caves.

Addie and Maria had taken the tractor to the north field, and Thomas and Rachel were with Jonas in the east field.

"They just up and walked away, Dexter," Matthew said. "They left the till open." They both laughed. "Follow me."

Slipping into the lava caves, their urgency was to find the cache. Matthew carried a box of tools from the Delacroix garage.

Dexter shone his flashlight into the back. "I've checked the front tasting rooms but it looks like there's a large vintage aging room back here. If I were to hide a box, that's where it would be. Do you know what's beyond the grate, Matthew?"

"I think it is fallen rock back there. It's put there for safety. No one has passed those gates for a long time."

Well, then, let's start there," Dexter said.

Leading the way to the aging room, Matthew deliberately kicked over a case of wine by the archway, creating a pattern of red boot tracks.

"You take that side, Dex, and I'll take the south wall."

As they chipped and chiseled, they tested every few feet in the rock. Matthew pulled out bricks and checked cracks and crevices.

"I've got something!" he shouted.

Reaching his hand into Zach's crevice, Matthew's heart raced with excitement. He stretched as far as he could, and touched a something metal. It was heavy and he wiggled it out, an old oversize cash box. His hand was wet.

"It's full, Dex."

He felt in his shirt pocket for the key, but common sense told him he would have to deal with Dexter Kincaid first.

Before opening the box, Matthew picked up a hammer from the tool box. Greed and vengeance took over him. The muscles in his arms tightened when he saw movement behind and made a full swing about face, smashing Dexter on the top of his head.

"Did you really expect I would share all this with a criminal?" Matthew sneered.

He looked down only for a moment at the fallen man, and returned to the tin box. He slipped in the key and pulled back the lid. Addie had filled it with rocks and monopoly bills.

"Well played, Mrs. Ducharme." In a rage, Matthew kicked over the milk stool and some large stones rolled, breaking a row of wine bottles. Fraught with frustration, he kicked over the next rack of bottles.

Thomas and Jonas were walking from the field on the stone pathway past by the cave entrance. At the sound of the crash, they stopped abruptly.

"Someone's down there. I hear a voice ranting."

With the dim lighting from the aging room, they inched toward the archway at the bottom of a steps.

"Who's there?" Thomas called.

"Well, Tommy boy, would you like a bottle of wine?" Matthew called with sarcasm. "How about some of the best Ducharme Bordeaux. A real prize-winner! Oops, looks like the whole rack fell over."

Dexter was on the floor but alive. He mumbled, unable to rise to his feet but looked at the cashbox contents dumped on the floor and spurt out a weak laugh.

"Addie outwitted you again! That's your cache!"

Jonas went to assist Dexter who was bleeding.

Thomas held a gun on Matthew and flicked on the bug in his pocket. Addie and Rachel picked up the transmission from the kitchen. In minutes, police sirens pulled into the lot.

"Matthew, did you have a part in Zach's murder?" Thomas prodded.

"It was Lane and Rocky. I learned of the plan, that's why I was standing by to console the grieving widow. It was all easy, no one suspected me."

"That's where you're wrong, Matthew. Zach had foreseen his murder and took precautions. Addie was part of the scheme—it was her in control, not you!"

Paramedics and four policemen barged into the room.

"Everyone, stay where you are and drop your guns!"

Dexter had faded to unconsciousness. The medics placed him on a stretcher.

"Who is responsible for this mayhem?" The officer looked at Matthew with the hammer at his feet.

"This man was a greedy convict trying to intervene, it was self-defense." Matthew spit.

"What is his name?"

Thomas said, "Dexter Kincaid. He served time in Rio for bank robbery. Old prison rumors led him to believe buried treasure is on this estate. You know how inmates tell fantastic stories. "

"Matthew, let it go. You're not going to take over the winery, but you will likely go to prison for murder"

"So, you figured that out, did you? Charles was on to me. He was my partner in crime, when we took the medallions. Evelyn found out and wanted us to confess. I was tidying up loose ends."

Thomas let him talk. "What about Zach's murder?"

"It was Lane and Rocky. I was aware of the plan, that's why I was standing by to console the grieving widow. It was all easy, no one suspected me."

Matthew was cheeky and over-confident.

No prison is going to hold me!

One detective wrote as another collected IDs.

Thomas said. "I suspect he's involved in the arson fire in the west fields we had about a week ago. He is mixed up Lane Delacroix."

"I'll need the whole story." He pointed at Thomas and Jonas. "The two of you need to follow me to the station to make statements."

"We have his recorded confession to the murder of Rocky Morse. Good luck keeping him under wraps in the prison. He'll be determined to find his way back here."

TWENTY-SIX

Thomas stood alone beside the bed in Dexter's hospital room. "How is Addie taking all this, Rachel?" His cell phone was wedged between his ear and his shoulder.

"Listen as much as you can. My instincts tell me there is more to the mystery of the cache,"

"Has anyone else been to visit Dexter?"

"Yes, the police detectives. They came about ten this morning and again at four this afternoon. The routine here is simple, but I don't want to leave him unguarded. Are you on your way here now?"

"Yes, I'm on my way with a new Robin Cook mystery book to keep me on my toes."

As soon as Rachel arrived, Thomas headed back to the winery to inspect the scene again. An hour later, Rachel called him.

"Thomas. We lost Dexter. He passed away without regaining consciousness. He never spoke a word and his witness testimony died with him."

At the atrium dining room, Thomas picked up The Herald at the door. He ordered coffee and a menu—Rachel took first crack at the paper.

"Thomas! Listen to this article!

"Two bodies were discovered in a burnt out shell of an abandoned farm near Ascot. Their remains are decomposed and investigators suggest they may have been there for several months. The woman was wearing a charm necklace with a locket engraved EW+CD. It is considered a possible homicide." Rachel gasped.

Thomas said, "We don't know Evelyn's maiden name, but the rest fits, and ties to Matthew's words. We'll stop by the police station.

"He's already up against grand theft, assault, and violating a restraining order. And he has to face charges of being an imposter, fraud and embezzlement. Now murder could be added."

Rachel said, "Lane withdrew his appeal for the explosion, admitting he obtained the fatal device. So Matthew's might be clear of that.

"At the house, I became afraid of him. He has years of built up rage towards his adoptive parents and his mother. He was resentful that Gregoire wouldn't accept him and saw Zach and Addie as his answer."

"It's not up to us to analyze him." He checked his watch. "Are you ready to go to the station?"

"Alright, Thomas, but I do feel a bit shaky." She touched the bandage on her forehead.

"Let's go home instead."

"No, I'm fine."

They pulled up at the police station, a block off Main Street. The duty clerk looked up as they entered.

"Hello, can we help you?"

Thomas explained the purpose of their visit, and they were ushered into an interrogation room.

"I'm Officer Turnbull. We'll need an official statement. Can you start from your first knowledge of the alleged victims?"

"Have you ever been to the farm at Ascot?" The officer searched both their faces.

"No, the first we knew about it was the newspaper article." Thomas said.

"Do you know where we can find Matthew?"

"He's out on bail, living on the Delacroix estate."

"Can you provide a picture of him?"

Thomas found one in his phone and sent it to the Officer by text. He said, "The injuries that you see to my wife are the result of Matthew attempting to murder us. He must have followed us from the estate hoping to isolate us. The bullet wasn't random. You can add that to the long list. We saw him leave on the Harley."

On Saturday morning, Thomas read the Charron News over his second cup of coffee. There was an update regarding Charles and Evelyn.

CHARRON, Calif.: Police have identified the bodies found at abandoned Ascot farm, as Charles Ducharme and his wife, Evelyn Wye. Their bodies had been in the burnt shell of the house for several months. Both were inside the front door that had been nailed shut. If anyone saw a suspicious person on or around the farm in early January, please notify the police. It is believed to be arson and homicide.

"In the pit of my stomach, I know what happened to them. I can't fathom how such an evil deed can come out of a Ducharme. Charles hadn't accepted responsibility in life, but there was no evil in the man. It is God that decides our time, not family, and not strangers," Addie said.

Rachel said, "At the police station, the officer told us that there was evidence nearby the bodies. Arson started the fire trapping Charles and Evelyn in the house, and they died of asphyxiation. Both had blunt force trauma to the back of the head. Whoever is responsible will be brought to justice."

"I'm surprised Matthew hasn't made a run for it," Thomas said. "I saw the red Silverado in the Delacroix parking lot yesterday. He's likely armed and has a clever hideout planned."

Rachel said, "He won't leave without his undiscovered treasure! But why does Gregoire Delacroix continue to post bail?"

Addie hired interior decorators to repaint Matthew's room. She needed a fresh start. A life without Zach, and now without Matthew.

When will this all come to an end?

Jonas was passing through the kitchen, and Addie stepped up quickly from her chair to stop him.

"Jonas, before you go to the fields, can we talk?"

"What is it you're worrying your pretty head about?"

Addie blushed and continued.

"With all the upset around here, how are we doing with the Bordeaux wines. Are we still in award contention?"

"We're right on track with processing procedures. Why don't you come to the barrel room tonight? You can do some tasting. Let's schedule regular grape inspections, field walks, and that way you and I supervise tasting and bottling. We also have the Beaujolais and Chardonnays coming along well.

"I agree. I'm ready to roll up my sleeves."

After dinner, in the tasting room, Addie and Jonas stopped at the sound of a slight crack in the ceiling. The tasting room was built ten years before, located behind the winery and atrium. Zach and his helpers built it with teak and stucco, with the teepee roof crafted out of pine beams. Sunlight filtered through the skylights.

The eerie silence was recognizable as events of the 2008 earthquake flashed in Addie's memory. Trembling, windows breaking, ditches breaking apart, and enormous crop damage. The West Napa Valley Fault had been active many times in their years at the vineyard and she knew could happen at any time.

Groaning arose from the floor and roof opened.

"Jonas, it's an earthquake!"

"Bolt all the lids, Addie."

Addie locked the wheels and spigots, and restraint bars were tightened to the barrels leaving the pressure release ready.

"I'm opening the release; it's better to let them roll than break apart."

A second louder crack shifted the building. Addie's face was pale. Jonas held her tight; they crouched together under the concrete reinforced archway, the safest place for them.

The splintering got louder and the barrels began to roll off their cradles. A crack was now visible in the ceiling and the lights failed. Glass reigned down.

Jonas called through the darkness to see if anyone else was in the tasting room. No answer.

The wine tasting room had been built with heavy French pine and steel girders approved to withstand a quake of 6.0.

Jonas had completed his safety inspections last week and hadn't found any gaps or faults in the walls.

Ceiling fractures gave and slabs of roofing fell between the beams. "This is a big one," Jonas said.

They could see the black sky and hear the frantic barking of the German shepherds outside.

"Addie, we're going to be alright. I promise." Jonas bent over her, shielding her against the wall with his body.

"Jonas, I'm scared."

The barrels rolled as the floor heaved and shifted. Rolling from side to side, a wayward barrel landed on Jonas's leg, pinning him and Addie to the wall. Two more barrels crashed into them and one burst open, flooding their crouched area with red puddles.

Jonas tried his cell phone but he got a 'No Service' message. He stretched to reach the intercom with his fingers, and called for help, aware it was unlikely to be heard. Addie heard him mumble a prayer to keep her safe. She knew they'd be protected under the arch, and considered a run herself for help if she could get out from under the barrels, but she'd face the falling debris, still coming from the collapsed roof.

The earthquake lasted two minutes, and Thomas and some of the men came to their rescue with hardhats.

Addie's eyes fluttered open. She instantly realized Jonas was still embracing her, but not moving.

"I'm alright, but please help Jonas." Addie cried looking stunned and frightened. Terrified by the siren, it was like losing Zach all over again.

The beam was removed and Jonas laid on the floor with an emergency foil blanket over him. Addie was at his side.

"Jonas, I need you. Don't go. Please!" He didn't speak, but his hand inched over to find hers.

The paramedics were shown into the room by Maria.

"What's your name fella?" The medic asked while he took vital readings.

"Jonas Barstow."

"Where does it hurt? Can you move your fingers and toes?"

"I feel pretty bruised, but no bones are broken, except maybe a rib."

"Thank goodness for that," Addie sighed.

"It appears you took a knock on the head. We'll take you to the hospital for x-rays."

Jonas wanted to stand on his own, and leaned a few inches, but his ribs instantly seared with pain. Sinking back to the ground, he gave in to the medics. His breathing was difficult and he gasped for air.

"Mr. Barstow, we're going to give you some oxygen to help you breathe. You'll be back home within a few hours."

Addie was bruised and scratched, but climbed onto the tractor with Cole to examine the earthquake damage in the fields. They went first to see the large fissure over the wine caves, but the area was taped off for safety until examinations were complete.

Cole said, "Addie, we should go to the major crack in the west field. Some cement blocks there pinned one of the boys. He was taken by ambulance with a concussion and that area is off limits, but I brought hard hats for us."

The vineyard tour took three hours, and they turned back to the house when the light rain turned to rumblings of thunder from the direction of Yountville.

The rest of the buildings on the property were solid, except for a tree branch that damaged the garage roof. Windows were broken in the main house and a chandelier had fallen in the dining room. The stone block building had withstood many an earthquake before and was strong enough for more.

TWENTY-SEVEN

Island underground chamber, Normandy, France

One of the cloaked men along with Sister Katrina helped Daniel to his feet. Through the small window he could see a glimpse of the blue sky and shimmering seas. Faltering on the stairs, Daniel let the railing support his weight. As he reached the ground floor, his eyes were on the door leading outside.

Another cloaked man raised the handle, and as he pulled the door inward, a blaze of sunlight poured on Daniel's face. Confined to the underground chamber for weeks, the only people he'd seen were the two men in robes and Sister Katrina.

Feeling the heat of the sun, he turned his face to the rays to soak in the energy and life that he'd missed.

"Where am I?"

"As you can see, we are on an island. Above you on that mountain is a secret monastery. We do our best to shield our location from satellite images and radar. No one knows you are here, Mr. York."

Daniel absorbed the scene quickly, feeling initial defeat that an escape would be difficult. The shoreline was wooded with breaks of sandy beaches and rocky cliffs. High on the hill was an ancient castle encircled by a road leading to the dock.

"Mr. York, we have some questions for you. If you are truthful, you'll continue to have outdoor benefits. But if you lie, you know the consequences."

Daniel contemplated the name they used.

Mr. York? What's going on? Be calm, play it cool.

He answered quickly. "Do you think my choice would be to stay in a musty dungeon? I'm confused about what happened and I can't tell you my name, because I don't know. Weren't there other people with me when you found me? They would know who I am."

Napa Valley, California

Rachel organized a team to help clean up in the wine caves, as a significant shipment of Bordeaux had been lost. At five o'clock, Thomas, Cole, Chavez and Maria met her at the entrance. She had taken an inventory of the spilled cases.

Jonas was returning to the winery nursing his bandaged broken ribs, and in minutes he gathered three more helpers. His voice echoed as got close to the entrance. "It's quite a mess down there, so be careful where you walk and how you handle the broken glass."

Maria piped up. "We brought mops, brooms and heavy gardening gloves."

"I'll get some bins from the garage for the glass and a couple of shovels," Jonas said.

Rachel intercepted him. "No way, Jonas! That's too much weight on your ribs. We'll get it. You supervise, if you insist you're fit enough."

Starting outside the stone passageway, the group moved through the various rooms to understand the scope.

Thomas motioned for Rachel to come over. "Here is where Matthew was standing when we came in. The wine is diluted and there's a dribble of water coming from a crevice here."

"Thomas, you remember the piece of paper we found that read 'Cave6' followed by a north and an east direction. I think we've found it."

Rachel reached her hand into the crevice where the cash box had been hidden. The rock inside was porous and damp. The fissure from the hole to the ground had opened and water seeped through.

Peering into the opening with a flashlight, Rachel was aghast. "Thomas, this opens into another tunnel with a small stream." She moved the beam around. "The lava cones are magnificent."

The others gathered behind and Rachel backed up to allow them to take turns with the flashlight.

"It's magnificent." Jonas said. "I'll bring Addie down." He quickened his pace through to the daylight.

"Cole, where there's a jack hammer?" Thomas asked.

"In the garage, but it hasn't been used in a long time. And a working auger that Matthew had fixed."

"Can you lug them down here?"

As Addie and Jonas joined the group, the others stepped back. She took longer with the light and shone it on every section.

"Ah, it's beautiful. This must be Cave6, however 4 North and 3 East don't meet the coordinates you've found. It would seem more like it's beyond the grated gate."

Addie was slowly putting pieces together in her head. She examined her compass.

Jonas said, "I'll call up a couple more men from the vineyards to help with the jack hammering. We have some small explosives in the service hut. Harmless to people, but strong enough to clear rubble. Addie, we'll clear a walkway at the fissure and then we'll go behind the gate."

"Yes, Jonas," Addie admired his take charge attitude. "I'm still not clear why Zach left me those directions. It was something he felt worth keeping a secret."

Jonas supervised the sculpting and digging, as the men quickly cleared the entrance through the fissure.

Rachel watched for Jonas's nod, then made a nervous invitation. "I guess the four of us should go and take a peek."

"Do you want to lead us, Rachel?" Jonas asked.

They gingerly stepped through to the lava tunnel, and stopped to observe the contrast of the smooth ceiling on one side, to the sponge-like cascading lava cones on the other. A larger stream from the past had left a stone bed walkway. The water in the pool was crystal clear and less than a foot deep.

Jonas said, "The stream is headed south. If we keep walking this way, there might be a sign of an opening where the grate was. Have you noticed these lava cones are similar to the crumbling material in Addie's caves?"

Before he could say another word Addie shot both arms in the air. "Does everyone feel that? The ground is starting to shift.

"We're fools to stay in here," she said. "An aftershock could seal us in."

Jonas didn't delay. "Okay group, let's get out fast. Cole can you see that the access is boarded for now."

The crew stuck close together, feeling along the walls bumping into one another, in panic, until they were outside. Falling rock and the echo of stumbling feet followed them.

Jonas gathered them again outside. "We'll come back and search the lava tunnels in a few weeks when the aftershocks have ceased. But nobody will be allowed beyond those boards without the permission of Addie or me. And what I'm about to say is very serious. Absolutely no mention of this to anyone!" He looked at each face.

In the morning, Thomas and Addie sat in the lawyers' reception area. The chairs were chrome and imitation leather, a world away from the luxurious trappings Thomas remembered at the big firms in New York. Addie interrupted his recollections.

"Thomas, there shouldn't be a problem sorting out the Will." She looked at the receptionist and whispered. "I hate tending to legal business and that Stewart man. It's time to remove the ninety-day provision. The foremen have a loyal support group. It was Zach's wish for fifteen percent of the estate to be distributed amongst foremen with him for more than two years at the time of his death."

"Zach was a generous man."

"Indeed he was. We were two of a kind in this decision. He was determined to give an additional $5,000 to each of the loyal workers that are not foremen. That would be thirty to forty people. Remind me to talk to Jonas about that."

Thomas nodded. "Jonas is a reliable man and has your best interests at heart."

Addie didn't answer, but looked into space until they were disrupted by the attorney.

"Mrs. Ducharme. It's nice to see you again."

"Mr. Stewart, I'm not much for formalities. Let's get to the matter of the Will."

Stewart straightened a pile of papers.

"We've had some progress. Matthew's will has been dissolved, and the false birth certificate naming Zach as his birth father has been revoked."

"That's good."

"Instructions have been sent to your banker. However, the specifications of Zach's will haven't yet been completed."

"What specifications?" Thomas asked."

"The fifteen percent."

Addie stood. "Mr. Stewart, Jonas and I will distribute the fifteen percent to the foremen from my account. Also, the waiting period for the provisions needs to be removed. I'll send a list of the payouts so you can complete your file."

Thomas rose beside Addie. She turned back as they walked. "I'll expect it to be done immediately."

Matthew was uncooperative with the police in the Rocky Kincaid homicide.

In private with his lawyer, he slurred with sarcasm. "Kincaid's nothing more than a common criminal. I saved the county prison costs."

"You are not judge and jury, Matthew," his lawyer said. "Be careful how you answer things and are perceived. It can influence the outcome."

The defense knew upfront that the evidence would be overwhelming to a jury. Tire tracks matched Matthew's Toyota and a jerry can of gas was in the wheel well with his fingerprints. A matchbook from the Rusty Nail was in the car. A speeding ticket and an eye witness account put Matthew at the Ascot farm at the time of Charles and Evelyn's death and a recovered cigarette butt proved a DNA match.

For the townsfolk of Ascot, this put them in headlines. Coffee shops flourished with media and tourists, and weekly sales of 'The Truth about Ascot" boomed.

At Matthew's first court appearance, bail was set at $200,000 for the murder of Charles and Evelyn Ducharme.

His lawyer appealed. "The evidence is circumstantial and my client has surrendered his passport. He is not a flight risk."

The judge listened to that position. "I find this case to be a heinous crime and my first instinct was to deny bail. However, there are parameters in the law to allow the bail offered. If the client cannot pay, he will be remanded until the court is ready to proceed. The first hearing will take place in two weeks if the prosecution agrees."

The prosecution stood. "Thank you, Your Honor. We agree."

Matthew looked to the back of the court, hoping for support.

Uncle Gregoire will have his bail refunded now that Lane's case has been decided. He owes it to me now to come to my aid.

Matthew was returned to his cell and his lawyer joined him minutes later.

"Do you have a bail solution, Matthew?"

"I need one call."

Gregoire Delacroix was in his kitchen when he saw the incoming call on his phone. Call display said 'Vallejo Prison' and he let it ring. He opened the door and stared out into the fields. His face twitched and his hands were white knuckled on door frame.

Turning to the pantry, he poured a glass of Jamieson's Irish Whisky, then sat in the old rocker and rocked for a long time.

Without showing remorse for his parents, Matthew was oblivious to the reality surrounding him, and remained focused on the cache.

In prison, he was able to control his anger but still initiated a few scraps with inmates when it was in his interest. One day, he used such a fight to his advantage, with a plan to end up in sick bay for sutures. He knew the room before, and needed to examine it again as a possible escape route.

With the stitches in place above his eye, Matthew faked a fainting spell, and the nurse helped him to a cot. His eyes scanned the ceiling to memorize the detail.

A broken air duct, with several of the tiles down. I'll need access, opportunity and rope with a grapple. If I can get into the ventilation system, there'll be an exit. Don't count me out, Addie Ducharme!

His plan was in play, but had to be between night guard checks.

I'll barely have twenty minutes.

Rachel woke at 6 a.m. and took a warm cup of cocoa to the TV. She scanned the cable news channels for world news, then the local network station.

"Thomas! Thomas!"

She called up the stairs from the kitchen.

"What is it?"

Rachel held her hand over her mouth and pointed at the screen.

"He's gotten out. Last night."

Thomas pulled at his hair and paced.

"Call Addie and Jonas on the intercom," he said. "Say it's urgent that we meet in the kitchen."

Addie's slippers shuffled quickly down the stairs and Jonas, in a robe, came from the back suites.

"Do you kids know what time it is?" Jonas teased but stopped as he saw their faces.

"What's happened? I have a bad feeling, Thomas," Addie said.

Thomas flipped to another news channel and found the headline—Murder Suspect Escapes Vallejo Prison. He turned up the volume and they sat in silence.

A picture flashed onto the screen and the announcer's voice boomed the story.

A daring prison escape through the ventilation system went unnoticed last evening, until a role call found that Matthew Ducharme was missing. A forensic team has confirmed the ceiling air vent was the access point. He must have been in the tunnels for hours before punching out the grate on a south wall.

Anyone seeing him should not approach as he is considered dangerous and likely to be armed. He is six feet tall, reddish-brown hair, muscular shoulders with a tattoo of a silver medallion on his right bicep. Please call police with any tips.

"A silver medallion! When did he know about those? He must know about the treasure chest," Addie blurted.

"Addie, what are you talking about?" Jonas asked.

"Yes, Addie," Thomas stood and watched her face. "We've been here for two months. When were you going to tell us there's a treasure chest? You led us to believe the cache was the bank loot."

Sinking back into her chair, Addie put her face into her hands and cowered over the table.

"When Zach asked me to hide the cache and not tell him, I should've said 'no' and left the cost of his involvement in Brazil as his own cross to bear. But see where this has gotten us?"

"Addie, I need to ask this and want a 'yes' or 'no' answer."

"I know, Jonas."

"Do you know where Zach's cache is hidden, at this moment?"

"Yes, I know."

"Is it your better judgment not to tell? Will it cause more destruction to say where it is?"

"In time, it will find its way into deserving hands. For now, I don't see that anyone *needs* to know. Everyone has overlooked the true cache. Matthew must have heard childhood rumors from Charles to make any connection to the silver medallions."

"The police recovered a handful from Matthew's room. Were there more?"

"Oh, yes, much more. Somewhere in the attic rafters there are old documents. I have never seen them, but the grate at the end of the wine caves has something to do with it."

Thomas and Rachel looked at each other, comprehending Addie's implications.

"Where would Matthew go to hide out?" Rachel asked. "You don't think that was him on the motorcycle last night?"

"He would either try to get as far away as possible or be secure in not being discovered in a familiar place. We'll be on guard," Thomas said.

Jonas said, "I'll double-check all accesses to the house." We might need to be armed at all times.

"Is there a secret tunnel or old forgotten entrance into the house or the caves, Addie?"

"This is all too much to recall. The house is old and suffered through earthquakes and renovations in the last one hundred years. Zach told me about the trunks in the attic but I never ventured that far." She froze before continuing. "You don't think Matthew could be somewhere in this house?"

Rachel said, "Since I've been here, Thomas, I've had a weird feeling about our bedroom. Now knowing of the secret halls, I feel I've been watched."

"Thomas, you and Rachel should go to the attic. Inside the small trunk, you'll find maps to the wine caves. You'll remember from the incident with Carmen that the back wall of your closet moves into a labyrinth of footholds and ladders. From outside the house, there are dormers up on the third floor that were never finished. This house is as old as the freedom route for slaves."

TWENTY-EIGHT

Overwhelmed with so many memories of the house as a child, Rachel poured out her favorite stories to Thomas and Addie.

"Amy and I became princesses in the Heirloom room and our kingdom was the panorama of the vineyards. We vowed to Uncle Zach we wouldn't call it that to anyone else. That's the only time he was ever firm with us.

"We adored him, his swing rides, propellers." She closed her eyes. "When he tossed us up on his shoulders."

Thomas said, "Keep opening these gems, Rachel. The solution is more than forty years ago, but until we know the difference between folk lore and reality, the estate will be hounded by treasure seekers."

Rachel had dressed in faded jeans, a sweatshirt and runners, ready for the dusty rails behind the walls.

Addie said, "Before the attic, Rachel, let's finish the clues to the wallpaper and see what treasure is so important to Matthew.

"When you and Amy were on your summer vacations. I know Uncle Zach admonished you for picking at the wallpaper. You came and told me."

"Yes, I remember. That was the only time he was ever stern with us."

"I'm sorry, dear, that he was strict that time. He adored you both."

"Oh, I know that, Aunt Addie. We loved him too." Rachel squeezed her hand.

"It must have been a terrible experience for Zachary as a teen, being a hostage for two months and threatened with his life. It breaks my heart. Over all the years, he only talked to me about it once. He was ashamed for his part.

"He hid this box behind the closet door and thought about it every day when he passed your room—The Heirloom room. It's time for you and Thomas to unravel its secrets."

"What do you mean?"

"It's the wallpaper, dear. But Rachel, Matthew will return for the currency and he knows it's in your bedroom."

"We understand the danger," Rachel said. "We'll be ready for him."

Addie hesitated. "About the Heirloom room . . . I've often thought about it, lying awake on the big poster bed while we looked out at the stars.

"When Zach and I first got married, Papa Francois gave us that room. I thought it was wonderful. As you know, the wallpaper is old and the tapestry pattern out of date; I wanted many times to redo it. Zach would get upset and say he didn't want anybody to touch it."

"Is it time, Aunt Addie, to tear a few strips off the wall?"

"I was hoping you would suggest that. It's been a burden to me."

"Where do you want to start?" Rachel quipped.

"By the window. There are already a few tiny shreds."

Addie took the first strip and gasped, then two. Then three more.

"Rachel, look it is money! There are hundreds of Brazilian bank notes pasted under the wallpaper. Let's get this out of my house!"

"We can rent a steamer in the morning."

"No, now! I'll get some pails of warm water. That'll do the trick."

Addie started to the kitchen, calling to Jonas as she went.

Rachel continued to peel. There were different colors and sizes of bank notes. As she sorted the bills into piles by color, a panic thought hit her.

Has it devalued since 1967?

A quick google told her she was right. Brazilian currency had changed to the Real, suggesting the 80,000 cruzeiros could be worth less than one hundred US dollars. Small quantities of Chilean, Argentine, Columbian and Bolivian notes were with the haul.

The famous cache has been severely devalued, if I'm right. What a mad caper for treasure, and this is it!

"Addie, Look at this. I can't read the Portuguese, but it has itemized serial numbers and the words 'Para destruicao'."

She picked up some bills. "These have all been through a perforated punch."

"What are you worried about, Rachel?"

"These were all marked for destruction by the Centrale Banco. They're worthless."

TWENTY-NINE

Julia Morse started her waitress job at the Rusty Nail the same day Rocky was hired at the Delacroix vineyards.

In her early twenties, she had cropped blonde hair and two tattoos on her right arm, a spider web and the words 'Rocky Forever'.

After Rocky's death, nobody acknowledged her as a widow and she became withdrawn without him. Surviving on minimum wage and tips, she lived in a bachelor apartment in Charron. Saving her tips, Julia made a deposit on a ten-year old Ford pickup.

Although on occasion she had hitched a ride with both Matthew Ducharme and Dexter Kincaid, neither was aware of her connection to Rocky. But vengeance stirred inside her.

Although Rocky had been a rough and courageous man, Julia adored him and he had promised her the world. It was only the Brazil cache that she wanted now.

Spider, a former inmate of Dexter Kincaid, had given Julia a phone number for emergencies like this. Rocky had often told her too that the underground security was there when you needed it, that prison connections were woven into a network of ex-cons, available for a fee.

A few hours after calling the number, she connected with Matthew. She had read about his escape and he seemed to be her best resource to search for Dexter's booty. Dangling the threat of her powerful prison connection, she contacted him.

Matthew answered on his new disposable phone. "How did you reach me?" he asked. "And how do I know that this is real and not a trap?"

"This is the real thing, Matthew! I'm recruiting you. Otherwise how would I get your new number? These guys aren't good for petty theft; they go after the big stuff."

Keeping her ears open, she was on the inside of good information at the Ducharme winery from naïve workers who came on Saturday's for beer orders for the barbeque.

Julia stopped at Ducharme's, then eased her pickup around the circular driveway to the parking lot. She turned it off behind a row of palm trees. The winery was busy considering the parked vehicles.

She smoothed out her tee shirt and went to the entrance of the atrium restaurant in front of the main house.

"Table for one, please."

The server looked her over, deciding whether or not to invoke a dress code.

"I've heard the lunch here is fantastic." Julia looked him in the eye and gave the waiter a flirty smile. "What is the special today?"

"This way, there's a table by the window. You're lucky, we've been busy today."

Listening to voices floating above the patrons, she heard enthusiasm about Saturday's barbeque.

I need an invitation. If old Zachary had only given up the cache, Rocky wouldn't have got messed up in the murder.

She motioned for the server. "I see you're busy here. Are you hiring? I've got experience from the Rusty Nail."

"You'll have to talk to the Manager. I'll let him know you're interested." Julia's eyes followed her to the man behind the bar.

Returning with cheeseburger and fries, the server placed a form on the table. "Fill this out and give it to me before you leave. He'll have a look at it and call you later today."

Julia smiled and picked up the pen to create a convincing resume. Pleased with her effort, she drove back to her shift at the Rusty Nail, but her mind stayed back at the vineyard.

A rebound offer came from the Ducharme's restaurant for short shifts while on probation.

The barkeep called her with disgust.

"Julia, you're off in dreamland. I have two more drink orders. Do them pronto!"

When her shift ended, she left immediately and drove back to the vineyard. She stayed off the main driveway and parked near the road on the east lane.

I wonder if there's a women's bunkhouse. That would set me up fine.

Julia knotted a scarf over her head and strolled down the lane to the worker's village, self-conscious in her dirty jeans. In bold print, her tee shirt said "What's Yours is Mine, What's Mine is Mine" over a caricature of orangutans sharing bananas.

She passed Enrique, chopping corn cobs from the stalks and tossing them into an open trailer. He stepped out from beside the tractor and called to Julia.

"This is a private area, Miss. Where are you going?"

"Hello, I'm a new hire; I work in the restaurant. I'm walking down to see the workers' village. Do you know if there are accommodations for women?"

"Go to the end of the lane and ask for Mrs. Wilkes; she'll know if there's a place." Enrique brushed the sweat from his forehead and returned to the corn husking.

Julia was satisfied she'd passed the checkpoint. She walked by rows of cottages and a common area with brick bake ovens. One side had a chicken coop and pig sty beside a cement hut. A circle of stumps surrounded a fire pit, and the barbeque spit was already in place.

Matthew forged through the woods to a lumber road. His thinking was irrational, but he was desperate, knowing that the dogs would be on him as soon as he went missing. At an abandoned shack, he pulled some dusty clothes from a shelf and changed into a red flannel shirt and dirty dungarees.

Must be a hunter's cabin. If I can get to the main road, I'll hitchhike to the estate and make myself invisible. Julia should have gotten into the worker's compound. I'll blend in there unnoticed.

In the distance, Matthew heard the orchestra of barking bloodhounds on his trail. Stumbling through fallen branches and brush to a stream, he stepped into the fast current with his arms high in the air for balance.

A thought occurred that the dogs might be thrown off the scent in the water, or even confused to give him a slight edge. Thrusting into the waist deep water, he pushed ahead against the direction of the current.

He soon felt defeated by the strength of the water, and after twenty feet he swam to the opposite bank. A rusty briar fence was at the top of the hill, and climbing over, he tore off a chunk of his shirt, leaving blood from his gouged arm.

At a secondary road, he stood out on the pavement edge to flag down a ride. A truck and a van passed before a cable van pulled to the side.

"You going to Charron?" he asked.

"I can drop you near enough. Hop in."

At close to midnight, Matthew got out of the van near the estate. The sky was clear and a slight warm breeze whispered over his head.

He knew how to get access to the garage and the bikes.

Most of the workers had returned to their homes. Julia heard the putter of a motorcycle in the distance. She turned in her bed, hoping Mrs. Wilkes hadn't heard.

Creeping out of her room, the creak of the screen door stopped her for a moment; Julia stepped out to the small porch. She held a flashlight and watched the silhouette of his motorcycle closing in. She waved the light.

He'd better cut the engine, or I'll get evicted.

Through the darkness, Julia ran to the back of the black Honda. She secured the sleek point-back helmet and hugged her arms around his leather jacket.

"Where'd you get the ride and clothes?"

"If it ain't locked, it's meant for borrowing."

He twisted the handle to gun it, and at the burst of speed, the front wheel rose and she grabbed Matthew tighter.

The pair of overstuffed armchairs were next to the telescope in front of the bedroom window. Rachel took one as Addie stood at the telescope, watching for Jonas and Thomas. Toward the workers' village, Addie saw a light move.

"There's a motorcycle near the end of the lane." Addie adjusted the zoom. "Two people; it's moving now.

"It's that new waitress from lunch the other day. What is she doing back there? And who's the man? With the helmets, I can't make out their faces."

She sent a text to Jonas.

Cole had some workers with him in the cornfield when the bike sped past. In the next field, the African Pygmy goats were roaming at their duties of grass and weed control. In their role in land management, they feasted on noxious weeds, thistles, and invasive plants that would otherwise overwhelm the vines.

The chorus of goat cries stopped Cole, and he went to the lane.

"Julia, you can't bring a motorcycle back here! You'd better check with the boss before you return."

The bike faded in the distance and Cole's words were lost in the exhaust. The goats continued to snort and spit. Cole sliced two of them an apple from his pocket, but had to share with two more who nuzzled up.

"Thomas! It's gone. Someone was in our room." He raced up the steps to Rachel.

"Right over our heads while we were in the kitchen," Thomas said.

Jonas and Addie rushed upstairs.

"I'll call the police,"

"Let's be cautious." Addie said. "If the police come they'll find out about Zach's Brazil involvement and we don't have solid evidence to blame Matthew. He won't be far. The other night I saw the new waitress with a guy on a bike coming up from the compound.

"My instinct says that Matthew is the guy. He could be nearer than you think, Thomas. You should start scouting the hidden walls."

At 7:00 a.m., Thomas brought two coffees on a tray to the bedroom. "Rachel, are you ready to go hunting?"

The autumn days were getting shorter and an orange sunrise over the vineyard. The morning sun had long shadows through the window.

In the kitchen, Thomas felt the edges of the secret door, built flush with the wall. Only the hinges and the keyhole gave it away. Fumbling, his fingers found the key on the dusty ridge of the wainscoting above.

"I wonder how Matthew knew about this key."

"Maybe from Maria, or one of the other servants who knew of the root cellar?"

As the door creaked open, they covered their mouths and noses from the pungent odor from dozens of empty unclean apple barrels and exploded preserve jars.

From the bottom wooden step, they could see the worn dirt path leading to the next room. They stayed to the middle, past shelves blanketed by cobwebs, and containers and broken chairs on the floor.

A narrow route led to the left, clear of the cobwebs. "This way," Thomas said. "It's been well used lately."

On the other side of the room, they went back up a staircase. Following a narrow passage behind the dining room and parlor, they reached the steps to the upper level. A wide fireplace surround on each floor was covered in plank.

They stopped behind the secret door leading to their own closet. Rachel shone her flashlight on a box between the trestle beams and opened the cardboard flaps. Kneeling, she lifted out a bundle of love letters tied with a velvet ribbon. Beside it on the ground were rolls of left over wallpaper and a satchel of yellowed newspapers.

"We can get those later through the closet," Thomas said.

Continuing to a door behind Addie's room, they stepped over a small travel trunk with steamship labels from France. A Family Bible was on top.

Rachel picked out some things. "Here's a pair of lace up leather shoes and a pine box with infant christening gowns. And some birth, marriage and death certificates. But they're not all Ducharme."

"We'll let Addie see this."

"Thomas, I see slits of light ahead, like another door. Let's try it, my calculation brings us to a landing or library."

Rachel was right. The wall opened into the upper landing, near the bedroom that Melissa and the children used.

"It's odd that we didn't notice the crack in the wainscoting. Are we losing our acute skills, Thomas?"

"Wouldn't Melissa and Jacob Jr. have found these suspicious doors when they played as children?" Thomas said pausing to survey their next move.

"We haven't checked the third floor dormers yet. There's likely an access through Addie's closet."

"Okay, to the left we can connect again with the ladder." Rachel began the climb.

She looked over the top. "Oh my gosh!

The third floor over the master suite had rows of rusted metal cots, one with a polyester sleeping bag and a pile of clothing at the foot. Small trunks were in the corner, with dusty blueprints sitting on one. A panel of the fireplace casing was ajar.

"Rachel, there's a crude dumb waiter pulley here." Thomas peered in.

"It goes to the main floor."

"Ah, there's Matthew's ruse!"

THIRTY

The Yorks joined Addie at the dining table to lay out the boxes. Rachel laid out the papers, but Thomas got up abruptly and went to the fireplace in the main parlor. The rest followed.

He tapped into hollow space, then with a pen knife, he ran it down the seam.

"There should be years of paint covering this panel but someone has chipped that away: I can barely make out small hinges."

Thomas pressed the panel and heard a pop and he felt the leverage in the door. He pried it open.

"A crude make-shift pulley, similar to a dumb waiter, but large enough for one person to squeeze inside." Thomas said. "Addie, have you ever seen this?"

Her face was pale and she shook her head.

"No, Thomas. I'm imagining how we have been violated over the years. This is incredible. Are you thinking Matthew used this?"

"Could Maria possibly have known, if Matthew did?" Rachel asked.

"She's in the laundry room, I'll talk to her right now," Jonas said.

Rachel dug into the box. "Here's a deed from 1880, another one from 1950, and a stack of tax rolls. This is good—a layout on the vineyard and sections showing grape varieties. And sketchy notes of recipes and procedures."

Jonas reached in.

"This is a hand drawn map of the wine caves. It looks like those tunnels have more tributaries than we thought. Before we go down there, I'll check if the seismic activity has returned to normal. We'll take the last blueprint of the property, I brought it from Zach's office.

"There's a marking on the map, suggesting something of significance in a cavern to the west. If it's safe, we can go down after lunch."

Jonas said, "I'll pick up gear and helmets at the service huts, to excavate where the creek wanders."

Thomas laid out the blueprint of the skeleton of the house and marked its hiding places.

"We'll establish a twenty-four hour watch until Matthew is apprehended. How about rotating eight hour shifts for three people. Jonas, do you have a third man we can trust for relief?"

"Cole will be our guy," Jonas said.

"We can't rule out that Matthew might hide out at the Delacroixs or maybe even the Ascot farm. We don't know what he is capable of doing."

Rachel said, "During the night shift, someone should sleep in the living room where the inside access begins."

"That can be me to start," Thomas said. "We'll take this blueprint and check that the old accesses are sealed. I'll plant a sound transmitter in the attic and another in the root cellar, to pick up any movement."

"Chavez can provide surveillance for the cave entrances. My instinct tells me that's where the medallions are."

"Addie, this box marked "Heirloom' was near the closet door to our bedroom," Rachel said. "It's tied with hemp rope."

Addie lifted and held it on her lap. "I knew it was there—it's been there a long time. I'm afraid to dig any further into Zach's past. So far it has been a curious ride. But go through the other boxes and tally up a list of questions."

She quietly left the dining room with the box and returned it a few minutes later with a cup of tea.

"Aunt Addie, are you alright?"

"Of course, I am. I'll be fifty-six this year, too young to be a widow. I was counting up my blessings."

Rachel noticed the box was untied.

Thomas laid out the original map to the caves. It was brittle and cracked at the corners as he unfolded it. Addie was surprised but happy it had been found. They all leaned close to see it.

"Look at this, Addie, there's an 'X' on the map. What would that be?" Thomas asked.

"I saw this years ago, and Zach told me it was nothing to worry about, that I shouldn't give it another thought."

"Wouldn't you like an answer?" Jonas added.

"I've had enough surprises in the last few weeks. Why don't you both let me know what you find?"

"Where's your spirit of adventure, Addie?" Jonas teased.

Her head shook. "This fiasco with Matthew has drained me, I'm afraid."

Rachel said, "Aunt Addie, if Zach were here, wouldn't he tell you to perk up and be one of those strong Cumberland women."

Addie didn't answer. Her eyes were moist and she went to the kitchen window. Staring into space, she closed her eyes and mumbled quiet words.

"Aunt Addie, are you alright? I'm sorry pushed you." Rachel put a comforting arm around her shoulders.

"I'll come, but without enthusiasm. We'll go right after our morning meeting in the worker's compound." She stood up, ready to go. "Jonas, you and I should go down now before the workers start their chores. Maria can prepare a canteen for us in case we find Captain Morgan's pirate treasure. Pirates, huh, they are the death of me."

The air was still and the birds were singing. Walking down the lane to the east village, the cornfields stood higher than their heads.

"I'm glad of the walk, Jonas. I have opted for the truck or tractor too often. It's wonderful to case out our own land. Look there, Jonas, the raccoons have been at the corn. Do we need more scarecrows?"

Jonas said nothing but her words lingered.

Was it a slip of the tongue? Did she say 'our own land'? I'm sure it didn't mean anything. I'm too sensitive.

"Did you hear me, Jonas?"

"What do you mean, Addie?"

She reached for his arm for support.

"You heard me. I said 'our land'. I want to give you shares. I can't thank you enough for all you've done."

"Addie, that isn't right. I'm paid more than adequately for my job. There is no price for my loyalty and friendship."

Her face showed disappointment and the rejection in her heart. Jonas was quick to see it.

"Addie, I don't mean to hurt your feelings."

Tears rolled down her cheeks.

"Addie. Let's stop." He took her by the hand. A stump was at the side of the path and she sat and looked up at him.

"We need to talk," Jonas said. "You've got something heavy on your mind. My shoulder is always here for you."

"It's difficult, Jonas. 'Always' is a tentative word, and so quickly forgotten. Zach told me he would be with me forever. He's been gone almost three months, but in some ways it seems like an eternity.

"You were at the scene to hear his dying words, and you stayed at the hospital to comfort me. Since then I have relied on you for all my thoughts. Jonas, you have come to mean more than I can say. My offer of land was my way of telling you how much I need you. To be truthful, I thought it would bind you to the land so you would never leave."

Jonas felt a heavy lump in his throat. He tried to speak, but couldn't. Kneeling beside her, Jonas took her hands in his and looked into her pooling eyes.

"Addie, you can count on me forever. I promise. There is much to be said, but for now, let's go to the village. On our way home, we'll take time." Jonas trembled with his emotions as he leaned down and kissed her soft lips. She lingered and didn't pull back.

At the village, Jonas rang the bell. A few heads poked out, and seeing Jonas and Addie, they called for the others. The meeting started quickly, rallied around the circle of stumps.

Jonas stood in the center to speak on Addie's behalf.

"We are bringing good news on this beautiful Sunday morning. This is a day I will never forget." He winked at Addie.

"As many of you know, Zachary Ducharme was a generous man beyond his death. There have been delays in finalizing the estate, however, it was his wish that $15,000 would be given to each of the foreman who have worked in the vineyards for more than the last two years."

The silence of the workers turned into mumbling, laughing, and gratitude. The eagerness of the foremen was overwrought by the sullen faces of the workers.

"The generosity of the Ducharme family is also extended to the wonderful field workers, who will each receive a payment in the amount of $5,000. Your checks can be picked up today in the office. Remember that we are family. Whenever you are suffering or in need, the same generous spirit of Zach will continue to be respected."

Cole stepped forward and shook Jonas's hand, then Addie's. "On behalf of the whole team, we thank you like our sister and our brother. Most gracious."

Trevor raised his hand.

"Miss Addie, come back into the fields to see us more often, we'd like to see you."

"I appreciate that, Trevor."

Jonas saw that she was fading and addressed them again. "Don't forget Saturday night. We'll be hosting a barbeque at the main house. You're all welcome."

An accordion started the impromptu celebration, then a guitar, then singing and dancing, on a Sunday morning to be remembered.

Safety helmets and steel-toed boots were at the back door beside Maria's picnic basket and a hot coffee thermos. Maria had filled a fishing tackle box with flashlights, batteries, matches and a first aid kit. The shovels and tools were still in the wine caves from the last excursion.

Rachel ran up to the bedroom for her camera, and stopped at the window. Addie and Jonas were on the east path heading toward the house. He was holding her hand and they were both laughing. "I hope Aunt Addie's dreams come true."

She made it back to the porch as they arrived. "Did you want to wait awhile, Aunt Addie?"

"No, no. I gave my word and we'll stick to our plans."

Addie put down the hardhat, and insisted on her straw garden hat. Golden strands of loose hair hung to her shoulders and her sparkling green eyes were on the brink of adventure. A visual flashed to Rachel, imagining Addie like this on the cover of *Harrowsmith*.

Rachel brought heavy work socks for all of them from the laundry room. Thomas carried the basket and carafe while Jonas led the way.

Taking the outside stone staircase down into the caves, an awesome feeling prevailed. Damp smells of the underground were indescribable and the venture soul-searching.

Rachel pulled her sweater up under her chin and tightened her belt. A water flask, cinched to the leather strap, bounced as she quickened her step to catch up to Thomas's arm.

Jonas stopped the group at the entrance to Zach's crevice to confer over the map. They opened it on the flat ground. The crevice and gate were both marked and Thomas pointed to a date in pencil on the bottom right corner. It was faint, but visible—1946.

Jonas tapped the boards away from the opening and stepped into the darkness. Oil lanterns were hanging inside.

"One lantern to each couple." Jonas lit each with a match.

Thomas set a lamp on the walkway, to allow his eyes to accustom. On the other side of the creek, erosion and water marks showed a water level that had been at least two feet higher. On a rock above that was an old rusted lantern.

"What would cause the drop in water level?" Rachel asked. From the map's date, the schematic was written more than sixty years ago."

"The creek flows east," Jonas said. He shone the light on his compass. "But the grate is on the west side."

Rachel reached for the compass. "I hear water dripping from the west, but I can't see the ceilings or the caverns either way."

Thomas skipped a rock east, then another west, listening each time and counting until the rock dropped.

"They're my caves, and I say we go west." Addie put the end to the discussion with a laugh. "The grate has a reason, and I want to know what it is."

Jonas held his lantern ahead to shed a path for his feet.

"Come on, Addie, take my hand. Walk slowly; watch for the lava cones in this area, you could easily bump your head without warning."

At ten paces west, they came to another stop.

Thomas raised his hand "Look on the other side." Their voices all echoed. "The cavern widens and there's another crevice that appears to be jammed. Could it be another tunnel? There's only a trickle of water from that direction."

"The grate shouldn't be far from here," Addie said. Are we moving southwest? There should be a glimmer of light from our caves."

Jonas said, "The walkway widens soon and the ceiling is higher, like a midpoint in a large cavern. Possibly the tributaries all converge here."

"Jonas, look ahead. It's a dim light. Do you see it?"

"Oops!" Rachel cried out. "And there's something around my feet, Thomas."

He picked up an old canteen with a tangled leather strap. "You're safe," he laughed and lifted it to the lantern. "What vintage do you think this would be, Addie?"

"It's the era of World War Two."

"If it's military, there should be a government stamp on the bottom. Let's take it back with us and we'll check that out," Rachel said.

"Does anyone know how far below ground level we are at the moment?" Addie asked. "The sound of trickling water seems to be from a crevice higher than the creek bed."

The creek water was pristine, without barnacles or weed growth. Rachel suggested that from her experience, without vegetation, there'd be no rats, as animal life can't survive or stay in these conditions.

Thomas smiled at the memory of Giverny. He said, "Also, likely few humans have been this way, or bits of soil and seed from boots would be here."

Fifteen feet later, they came to the wrought iron grate.

"I knew it, Jonas." Addie was excited, and reached for his arm. Swaying the lantern, she leaned to pick up a weathered leather boot near the wall. "This looks to be the same vintage as the canteen—1940's. A small size for a man's boot."

THIRTY-ONE

A crude stone step took them the final few feet to the grate.

"On the few occasions when my grandchildren toured our wine caves, they were most fascinated about the grate. They named it 'the forbidden door' conjuring up images of pirates and ghosts."

"Children have such imaginations," Rachel said, "and adults too." Addie laughed at the inference.

"I've got the coffee canteen," Thomas said. "Where's the picnic basket?

"I really feel like I am in a pirate's cave," Addie giggled.

"Argh! The next time our grandkids come for a visit, this will really freak them out," Jonas said.

Addie blushed and turned her head away. She did notice what Jonas had said.

"Thomas, give me the lantern," Rachel said. "I'm going to walk on the other side of the creek. I see a dark shadow and I'm curious."

With her arms stretched, she balanced from stone to stone through the creek bed to a sandy cove on the far side.

"Over here!" Her shout echoed through the tunnel. "It's a treasure chest! A steamer truck!"

The other three splashed across the creek.

"This is really ancient," Thomas said. "These are French passenger labels for Atlantic crossing. They have to be very old, they're so brittle."

Addie said, "Before we get too wound up, remember old Jacob's warning, that something bad happened down here years ago."

Jonas pried the lid open and the four stood breathless and wide eyed.

"It's a treasure," he said. "Addie, those silver medallions you had in the house—this is where they came from."

The trunk was filled with hundreds of medallions on the upper tray, along with a rolled parchment script tied by a strip of leather. Thomas slowly unfurled the scroll.

"Being in this vacuum has preserved the parchment from disintegrating. But the wax seal has already been broken."

Jonas held it up to translate.

"It's in French, but I'll do my best." He mouthed the translation to himself, then tried it out loud.

"It says that King Louis Philippe I of France authorized Francois Delavere Courchelles to invest in California land development. That he would farm his allotted land and return twenty-percent annually to the Treasury of the King of France.

"Also, he is authorized to retrieve smuggled silver and gold from poachers infringing or pillaging from the Boranalli, a sunken pirate ship on the Coast of California."

Jonas stopped, hoping for a reaction, but no-one spoke.

"It is signed and dated August 24, 1844."

"What about the other pages?" Thomas asked.

They waited in silence as Jonas read the next part.

"It doesn't exactly say it, but from my understanding, France needed to defend its territories around the time of the American Revolution, so incentives were given by Louis Philippe I, who was the King before Napoleon. They wanted French soldiers to settle in America and defend their farmlands from Spaniards looting ships along the California coast.

"The settlers could salvage any silver or gold treasure from sunken pirate ships in the shallow waters off the coast. A portion would be returned to France and the balance considered a reward."

He looked at the next scrolls and placed them down.

"Much more is here in French, but what I read explains the medallions. Have you ever heard of Francois Delavere Courchelles, Addie?"

"In Grandfather's day, a family named Simpson came for a picnic and a tour of the vineyard. Distant relatives somehow, and I didn't pay much attention."

"We should get those old records from the attic. The Courchelles name did appear in the old documents," Rachel said.

Addie continued. "When we gathered for family celebrations, Jacob, Sr. always stood at the head of the table and said grace. Each person's name was mentioned, and a reminder of those who passed before us. There was sadness and hesitation when young Jeremiah's name was mentioned. Once when I asked, Mother Ducharme scowled at me and told me to hush, that the mention of his name was painful enough, the memories were too much to bear.

"The family viewed the tunnels as a curse and that greed had taken poor Jeremiah. I didn't understand what they were talking about."

"What should we do with the trunk?" Jonas asked.

"Leave it where it is for now, but bring a few medallions so we can compare with the others in the house," Addie said.

Plodding further west, they reached a convergence in the creek, and kept to the right tributary.

Thomas laid the blueprints and surveys out again.

"We're a fair distance from the house and I suggest we head back. If we keep going to the west, we'll be under Delacroix land."

The aroma of Maria's pot roast filled the kitchen, flavors of Yorkshire pudding, braised Brussels sprouts, snap green peas from the garden, and sour cream whipped potatoes.

Rachel stopped at the door. "My goodness, Maria. Thomas will have an adjustment when we go home. You've spoiled him. Could I could take a few of your recipes?"

"Of course, Rachel."

Jonas appeared. "They're all my favorites," he said.

"Have either of you seen Addie?"

"A half an hour ago, she was in the sunroom."

Addie looked up when Jonas entered. "Melissa, her husband and kids, will be coming on the weekend for the barbeque."

"Sounds like a fine idea."

Thomas and Rachel sat on a mat in the attic, sorting the names of husbands, wives, children and their spouses.

"Here it is," Thomas said. "Francois Delavere Courchelles! He emigrated from France to California in 1800 and bought land near San Francisco. He had eight children including a daughter, Annette, who married a Ducharme. It was this Jefferson Ducharme that purchased land in the Napa Valley.

"Annette received a dowry from her grandfather in the form of silver medallions. The discovery of the caves and tunnels offered a secure hiding place for the Courchelles's dowry. I presume that over the years, family members have checked on it and no doubt pilfered some medallions.

"We can search the geological records since 1800 to give us time periods coinciding with earthquakes and tremors that could have sealed the tunnels. It is likely the fault line buckled within the last two hundred years.

Rachel said, "Zach's fissure was man-made, but there is also a natural entrance into the tunnels. And the date of the installation of the gate could match to death records from a supposed accident probably Jeremiah."

"Don't take on more than you can handle," Thomas said. "Do we really need to know all these answers, or should some mystery remain for a future generation?"

"Are you trying to douse my fire, Thomas?"

"No, but I feel you should consider the depth of your research, whether it makes any difference to what we need to know." He grimaced until she laughed.

"Tomorrow, I'll spend two hours at the Vallejo library and not a minute more. I promise not to be obsessive." A twinkle was in her eye. "Let me have some fun."

Thomas stood and took Rachel in his arms and caressed her.

"To each his own, my love!"

He led her to the porch and pointed to the sky. "C'mon, babe, it's a perfect night to walk under the stars."

Rachel sidled closer beside him with her arms around his waist. Her eyes sparkled and told him yes.

"I'd love to. I'll let the security patrol officer know we're out there, so he doesn't suspect we're poachers."

Addie watched them from the screen door, drawing on her own memories.

She called to them. "Have a nice walk. The sky is clear and the stars are out, the best time for star searching. The Big Dipper is my favorite."

Looking back at the main house, Rachel noticed Addie and Jonas had moved out to the veranda with their tea.

"We're being watched, Thomas." Rachel held his hand and nudged him to look back. "They're such a match, and they don't realize how much they depend on each another. It would be nice for Addie . . . but a widow needs time."

He poked her ribs. "Don't even say it."

From the east, the lights shone from the workers compound, and the fields were even brighter with the half moon.

Absorbed in conversation, Thomas and Rachel didn't hear the purring engine near them. They continued toward the east, and a breeze caused Rachel to shiver. She stopped in her tracks. Three mangy coyotes watched her from the path, the glint of hallow grey eyes piercing the moonlight.

"Don't move, Rachel. They will move on."

The coyotes were on their own mission and returned seconds later with wild rabbits dangling from their mouths, then ran back into the dark.

"That was unappetizing, yuck!" Rachel recoiled.

"The circle of life. The fit of the fittest."

"I don't have to like it."

"Did you want to go back?" Thomas asked.

"No, but let's stay on the main path."

"Look, Rachel there's a new light over in the west field. Are you up to checking it out?"

"I suppose, but give me your jacket for this chill."

They walked fast, stepping through vine rows and stopped twenty feet back from the corner fence. The light was on the Delacroix side.

Rachel spoke softly. "Who would be working there at this hour of the night?"

Thomas advanced to the fence line, peering past the hanging light into the darkness of the Delacroix farm.

He called out to two moving shadows. "Ahoy, neighbor!" Both shadows froze, and one replied.

"Who's there?"

"Thomas York. Who's that?"

"It's me, Thomas, Gregoire. A pack of feral coyotes has been tearing my vines apart. Also a pair of red foxes."

"We were out for a moonlight walk and came across some ourselves. Is this unusual in the Napa Valley?"

Gregoire said, "It sure is for me. We find a few small animal carcasses here and there. When they're on a chase and the vines are in the way, they plunge ahead anyway and create this damage."

"I'll ask our security night patrol to tractor down this way at night. It might deter them."

Returning on the tractor path to the main house, Rachel's eyes faced into the night sky.

"I see Orion's Belt." Her head leaned to his shoulder.

"Let's get down on the grass and look up into the galaxy. I haven't done that since my brother Randy and I were kids."

"Me too."

Thomas raised his hand and whispered. "Over there. Something is moving toward the main house." He pulled the pistol from his leg holster.

Rachel gripped his hand tighter.

"Looks like our security man has gone for a smoke. I don't see him anywhere."

They crouched, inching along the path. The shadow stepped out from the cornfield and strode toward the main house.

Rachel breathed the words. "Is it Matthew?"

"That's my guess. If we had backup we could take him."

"Don't underestimate your wife, Thomas York."

Thomas chuckled and squeezed her hand.

"Addie and Jonas went in, so it's the two of us, honey."

"Don't honey me, I've been trained by a military expert in karate chops." Rachel flexed her hands but her eyes stayed glued to Matthew.

"Alright, what if you scamper up to the back porch, visible to him. You could even hum a tune or whistle. Matthew will either back up or take you from behind as a hostage. You need to expect either move. I'll be close behind."

Standing straight, Rachel took a deep breath and moved away from Thomas. She started muttering 'This Old House' as she skipped up the lane to the back lawn, exposed by the bright moonbeams.

Matthew stopped at the sound, then skulked into the shadow of the house. Satisfied she hadn't seen him, he continued toward the fireplace and disappeared into the walls.

Rachel stepped into the kitchen. Addie was cleaning some tea cups and Jonas was rubbing beeswax on a corner chip of the table.

Rachel thought it out again.

Thomas, we didn't discuss a plan if he made it into the house.

Jonas was the first to notice her demeanor, as she stood with the door open. Locking on his eyes, she put her finger to her lips and quietly mouthed, "Matthew". He moved closer and she whispered, "Fireplace".

"Thomas isn't far behind me, he's armed. Take Addie where she is safe. I'll be okay, but Matthew is in the house."

"No, Rachel. There's safety in numbers."

THIRTY-TWO

Island underground chamber in Normandy, France

Yannick leaned his face close.

"Mr. York, you must understand that someone has gone to elaborate lengths to be sure you stay alive and remain in confinement. We're confident that you'll remember your real name."

Daniel's memory was fuzzy but the voice seemed familiar.

"Who are you working for and why do you want me?" Daniel asked.

"Mr. York, you are merely a pawn in a trade. Don't think you have the privilege of negotiating."

"It seems to me that you've started negotiations by asking me who I am. You insist I'm Thomas York because of a passport you found. Perhaps I am simply a courier, or worse, a master of disguise. Let me know when you are ready to barter."

Daniel felt confident in his verbal attack. Yannick and Sister Katrina exchanged fast glances. The cloaked man in sandals took out a phone and made a hushed call, then turned to Daniel.

"No need for that, Mr. York. Our Master will be arriving in a few days to convince you to co-operate. For now, you will return to your chambers where you can re-think it."

Daniel took a last glance at his location, burning details into his memory.

They walked him up the dirt hill from the beach to the monastery that rose tall above the island. The path twisted and turned past boulders and trees. A cloaked man stood in the courtyard above, watching his every move.

Out of the bunker, Yannick made a call to New York. "Sir, he is not co-operating. Is it possible that his memory has been compromised by head injuries? Is your guy for sure?"

Napa Valley, California

The three sat frozen in the parlor of the Ducharme estate, waiting for the fireplace panel to open.

They heard a pop, then a board squeak, as Thomas slipped through the opening.

"He's gone up. The pulley isn't here," Thomas whispered. "Rachel, it's time to bring Maria in. Can you find her?"

Rachel tip-toed to the laundry room where Maria was humming a song and folding sheets.

"Maria, come with me. I need you quickly." Rachel took the sheets from Maria's hands and led her by the elbow back to the parlor.

"What's this all about?"

Thomas spoke quietly. "Matthew has escaped from prison. We think he's hiding somewhere in the house." They all watched for her reaction. Her face flushed.

"Listen!" Addie said. She looked up. "Footsteps."

"Jonas, keep the women here," Thomas said. "I'm going after him. We can't live in a house this way." He patted the pistol tucked in the back of his belt. "You should have something to defend yourself."

Jonas retrieved a hammer from the drawer. "Thomas, there's a noise in the back passage."

"He must be heading to the caves."

"Stick to the plan, Jonas. Phone for Cole and Chavez. I'll take Rachel as my backup."

Thomas and Rachel followed with their backs along the wall, down the staircase and into the wine caves. They stopped often to listen.

"He's trying to get through the grate. I see him," Thomas said.

Passing the alcove where Zach's crevice led into the tunnel, Thomas slipped through. Once he was clear, Rachel called out.

"Matthew! What are you doing down here?"

Stunned to hear his name, he turned abruptly.

"So it's one of the women coming to take me on."

"Don't underestimate a black belt!" Her eyes glimmered with excitement. Anticipating the action, adrenaline and strength surged into her body.

"Ha! A little five foot four gal against a snub-nose revolver, I don't think so."

He brandished a gun that she recognized. It had been in Thomas's dresser drawer.

"Do you really think it's loaded?" She enjoyed toying with him.

"Look, kid, all I want is my share of the treasure. I know about the medallions and the Heirloom room. You can't imagine how much time I've spent in that house. You're crazy to think I'd walk away from all that. Yeah, it was me that stole the currency from under your nose.

Rachel allowed him to approach and take a hostage hold on her. "I hate to burst your bubble, Matt, but the currency is worthless, it's all marked for destruction. Didn't you notice the perforations?"

Perfect stance, I can't wait for his next move.

Rachel veins bulged with anticipation.

"You don't outsmart me, Rachel, Zach wouldn't have brought it all the way from Brazil if it was worthless. You're clearly trying to distract me . . . Thomas wouldn't send you on his own; so where is he?" Matthew straightened his neck and called sounding cocky, "Hey, Thomas, I've got your wife."

A voice echoed from the tunnel. "Good, all the better for me. I'm betting on her."

Matthew tossed Rachel to the floor and charged at the grate. Squeezing through a side opening, he searched in the darkness for Thomas.

Thomas was poised like a leopard selecting his prey. Matthew tumbled to the ground, then got up and tried another run at Thomas.

"Hey, buddy, it's not going to go like that. Stand up like a man."

Thomas pulled out his pistol from his leg holster." He could see Rachel creeping up behind Matthew with a metal bar in hand. He knew he wasn't going to shoot. In his mind was the Paris image of Madge creeping up behind Eloise.

A crescendo of sirens gave Matthew a brief motivation to escape. Thrusting himself at Thomas's legs, he bolted into the tunnels.

"Rachel, let him go. The police will track him."

A team of officers stormed into the tunnel with two dogs.

Thomas and Rachel arrived at the kitchen with the news that Matthew was on the loose in the tunnel. "Addie, we have to protect the silver cache," Rachel said. The tunnels are no longer sufficient."

Thomas said, "Addie, we don't have many options. I'm sure you don't want the treasure site disturbed but facing reality, it must be secured. It's time to call Wells Fargo bank security."

Jonas picked up the phone and explained the shipment. "It's urgent. Can they come at three o'clock?" He looked at his watch.

Matthew was confident he had made a clean break. The police dogs would be on his scent through the water, meanwhile he was back into the walls, listening to every word.

"Wells Fargo!" he muttered, then made a phone call to Julia. "Honey, call the number Spider gave you. Set up a con for a Wells Fargo shipment of medallions for 2:30 today. You don't have much time before the real driver gets here."

"You're asking a lot, Matthew, on short notice. I'll see what I can do." Julia was at work when she dug into her pocket for the rolled up scrap, then made the call.

She was nervous but pumped herself into action.

"Spider gave me the number. I need a heist of a silver shipment to New York, it's urgent. Turn up with a dubbed Wells Fargo armored truck at the Ducharme estate at 2:30 this afternoon. No earlier and no later. You don't have a moment to spare."

The negotiations were interrupted as the restaurant manager nudged Julia back to her tables.

After taking orders from two tables, Julia's phone rang again. She excused herself to the restroom and pulled out the scrap.

"Alright two hundred thousand. Do it!"

Julia was edgy and distracted during the next hours, waiting for the brown armored truck to pull into the restaurant parking lot. She stood at the window, knowing that her alibi would be solid.

It was hard to take a deep breath as her nerves had her on tenterhooks. Her focus on was intense, and she accidentally sent a plate crashing to the floor.

The manager yelled out. "Julia, where are you? You're not doing your job. What's up?"

"I need a few minutes off. I'm not well."

She stepped outside and dialed the number once more. The driver reached for his phone and she sighed with relief.

"I'm here!" he said.

"Do it and get out as fast as you can!" As the truck pulled to the road, she locked the washroom door to vomit.

The truck drove into the main driveway at the vineyard. It was stolen three hours earlier from the back of a storage lot. The signs were freshly painted, but no one would be close enough to see it.

Three armed uniformed men got out and went to the back of the truck for bankers bags. Jonas and Addie came from the house to meet them.

"Mrs. Ducharme, I'll need you to sign the manifest when we've finished our count. It will be secured until you give us further delivery instructions."

Addie nodded.

Jonas led the guards into the tunnels with Thomas behind. Every bag had the initials of either Jonas or Thomas along with the guard's signature on a seal.

With the last silver medallion counted and packed into twelve bank bags, the Wells Fargo truck eased out of the parking lot. At the diner, Julia Morse stood outside the door, regrets overwhelming her.

"One hundred years," Addie muttered. "I can't help but feel sentimental, already I regret my decision.

Addie and Jonas lingered in the driveway until the truck became a dot in the distance.

Julia answered her phone and listened. "What's the address in New York?"

She said, "My buyer is in Manhattan. I'll call to make arrangements and let you know."

A few minutes later the phone rang again.

"Ms. Morse?"

"Yes, go ahead."

"The destination for the silver shipment has changed."

Julia stepped outside. "No, I haven't agreed to that," she said.

"Your phone has been hacked. This contract and all the contents of this shipment has been bought out by another organization."

THIRTY-THREE

Thomas and Jonas were far in the field, out of earshot of the house. Addie and Rachel worked in the garden, and the crunch of gravel in the driveway drew Rachel's attention.

"A Wells Fargo vehicle is here. Two uniformed men are on the porch and two more armed officers by the truck. What are they doing back, Addie?"

"Mrs. Ducharme?"

"Yes. What is this all about?"

"We're here for the silver medallions. Are we too early?"

Addie's face was ashen. Rachel called Thomas on his cell. "Get back here, Thomas! I think we've been robbed . . . maybe a fake armored vehicle!"

Addie slumped on the wicker chair on the porch. "Can you wait a moment?"

Thomas and Jonas jumped from the tractor and ran to the house.

Jonas said, "Officers, the shipment was picked up earlier by one of your trucks. It must be a misunderstanding, can you check with your office again?"

Rachel slid into a chair beside Addie.

A radio confirmation came from Wells Fargo in Vallejo. "No, this is the first dispatch to the Ducharme estates. The original order was placed by Addie Ducharme."

"Something is wrong, call the police," Jonas said.

The supervisor radioed back. "They're on the way."

Two sirens screeched into the parking lot within minutes followed by a canine unit.

"Mrs. Ducharme, do you know anyone that might do this?"

"Yes! My nephew, Matthew Ducharme. He's an escaped criminal. Your team was here yesterday looking for him."

The officer nodded, and radioed in before proceeding.

"An APB had already been issued for Matthew. Every police unit has a description and his mug shot. Now, start at the moment the duplicate truck arrived."

Thomas handed the officer a small device. "Officer, my trade is as a detective in France, and I methodically placed a GPS tracking device in the last bag. This might help."

One officer activated it, as Jonas led the others and two sniffing beagles into the cave tunnels.

"This is where the Wells Fargo people took an accounting while packing them into burlap bank bags. We were offered insurance forms valuing the pick-up at over $3 million in silver."

"Where did these medallions come from?"

"A century ago, they came from France back in 1844. Since then it remained here in the lava tunnels. Earthquakes over the years sealed it off. Matthew found out about it. Yesterday he managed an escape into the tunnels and we haven't seen him since."

"I have news on the truck, thanks to the GPS. Our forensic team is now tracking it. It appears they've headed out of State, and the FBI will take over the pursuit. We don't just want to apprehend it, we want to see where it's going."

Thomas slipped away to make a long distance call to Ely, a small town in New York State.

"Captain Jamieson!"

"Thomas, is that you? Is everything okay?"

"I need your help."

THIRTY-FOUR

Thomas aimed and directed the telescope, following the single light. As it approached the house, he heard the quiet ticking of the motorcycle engine. He raised his night vision binoculars to confirm his hunch.

"Rachel, it is Matthew! He's with Julia Morse. And her sudden appearance here has been odd. She's Rocky's Julia."

"I'll call the police."

"Hold off for a few minutes. The bike stopped behind the tasting room and they're at the side of the house. He might be breaking in again."

"Where are the security guards?"

"From the cigarette butts behind the garage, I suspect they spend a lot of time there."

"Why is he here, Thomas?"

"It's his obsession with the Brazilian cache. He must have come back for it."

Thomas reloaded his gun and placed it in the pistol hostler on his leg.

"Rachel, take your revolver too. Wake Jonas and I'll go ahead up the right side into the garret."

Thomas exited through the closet door into the passageways.

Stepping slowly, Rachel reached Jonas's door.

Thomas could hear the pulley coming up from the main floor. Pressing himself between columns of two by fours, he held his breath.

Matthew whispered to Julia. "They will be sleeping in the money room." She held his arm for support.

He asked, "You know how to use the chloroform, right?"

"Not a problem." Her heart pounded.

Julia doused a cheesecloth with liquid from a bottle in her jacket. Keeping her hand with the cloth behind her, she tip-toed slowly. Matthew went on ahead to scout the route.

Neither of them had noticed Thomas in the darkness. When Julia passed, Thomas covered her mouth to prevent a noise, then placed the cloth over her mouth. When she was subdued, he lowered her limp body to the floor. Seconds later, Matthew turned and called for her. There was no answer, and he didn't wait.

Thomas listened for breathing and presumed Matthew had moved on, abandoning Julia. He heard the creak of the access panel and the clang of the pulley.

I've got to get downstairs.

Thomas ran through to the landing and tore down the front staircase, stopping when he saw the kitchen light.

"Oh Thomas . . ." Matthew sang in a taunting voice. "Come in, I have something of yours."

Rachel was sitting at the table with Matthew behind her, holding a knife to her throat.

"I'm alright, Thomas."

Thomas rounded the corner and stood in the kitchen doorway. He raised his hands and dropped his revolver to the floor.

"Don't hurt her!"

Matthew's lip curled and snarled as he laughed. "If you follow me, I'll be back one night and slit her throat."

He backed away with his knife pointing toward Thomas. As he neared the door, Jonas was ready and slammed him belly first onto the veranda.

"No, Jonas, he has a knife!" Rachel yelled.

Matthew slashed it wildly through the air for drama and bolted to the door. In an instant, he was on the Harley.

"I'll call the police," Jonas said. "They'll trap him."

The bike roared out and turned toward Charron.

"Julia must still be in the attic," Thomas said. "She was ready to use chloroform on me, but it backfired."

He ran to the stairs, and in minutes was back without Julia. "She made it out on her own."

Jonas said, "She might lead us to Matthew."

"There was a movie about sleeping with the enemy, with the ominous presence of the intruder always in the shadows." Rachel recalled. "Matthew has that presence here in the house. We have to make sure he never returns."

Thomas said. "Jonas! Let's seal the access points. The pulley can be disconnected, the root cellar barred, and the inside panels nailed in place."

A ponytail straggled from under Matt's smoky helmet. He felt new power of being invincible. His black leather jacket was cut off at the shoulder sporting a new tattoo 'To the Death' on his muscles.

He skidded to a stop at the workers' cabin, and Julia slipped her long legs over the back of the cycle. She clasped her arms around him.

"Matthew, this wasn't supposed to happen. I was lucky to find my way out on my own. Why didn't you come back for me?"

Without a word to Julia, Matthew spewed gravel across the parking lot. He turned onto the main highway, in the direction of Vallejo with Julia hanging on tightly.

A mile down the road, he looked back to speak. "I agree with my Boy Scout motto, to be prepared. We're picking up some explosives, a switchblade, hemp rope, butane lighter, and canisters of gasoline. The Ducharmes won't know what hit them when the old house blows."

"How are we going to carry all that stuff?"

"Don't worry your pretty little head. I've found for a place to stash it. I'm too sly and dangerous for Thomas; I'll show him!"

Matthew stopped at Ace Hardware on Lincoln Avenue and loaded up with supplies. He then asked the clerk to see the Swiss Army knives.

Moving a tray of lottery tickets, the man presented a shelf lined with blades and hunting knives. The Victorinox Soldier's Swiss knife was what Matthew wanted. He put it in its leather case and into his jacket. Flicking the box to the side, he paid by cash.

At the bike, he moaned to Julia. "I need a revolver and we need to go to Vallejo, either Metco Defense or Dingo Guns. You choose, Julia."

"Matt, I don't like guns."

"Remember how Rocky died?" he said. "I heard it was a gunshot to the back of the head. He was assassinated, then buried in a forgotten place under a pile of rocks. Not even with a cross to mark the sight. We're definitely in need of a gun."

The Metco store was empty when they arrived. Julie saw it as an overstocked man cave, reeking of heavy canvas and gun cleaning fluid.

As they stalked the gun and revolver cases, a squeamish feeling was building inside her.

Matthew called her over. "Here's a small lady-like pistol for you, Julia."

He pointed to a short barreled pistol behind the glass. It was pink with a marble handle and she was surprised but attracted to it. The 32 Magnum Derringer had the ability to only fire two shots without reloading, but she didn't intend to fire it.

Julia waved for the salesman to open the case. Caressing the pistol in her right hand, she felt the smooth grooves on the handle and raised it to eye level.

"This is the one for me, and the smallest box of ammo. My friend is looking for something heavier." She looked toward Matthew at another case.

The salesman placed them out for Matthew to hold, one at a time and on a velvet tray. A high speed, double barrel 45 Wesson made the cut. He added a calf holster and a black Derringer to match Julia's.

They stopped at an Exxon and he filled the gasoline containers that were strapped in a collapsible wire basked behind Julia's seat. The gas sloshed in the containers as the bike rolled out to the road.

"Matt, this is dangerous. Is the locker far?"

"I'll drive safely. I won't take chances with my angel sitting behind me." He turned to look at her face and the bike wobbled on the shoulder.

The three mile ride was an eternity as the Harley was jolted over ruts and construction bumps.

Julia gasped as a childhood recollection flashed before her. She was five years old living in the mountain range of New

Mexico. Standing with her father as their family home burned to the ground, with her mother inside. In later years, she came across a newspaper clipping suggesting murder and arson.

Tears streamed down her cheeks.

Why didn't Papa try to get Mother out? Is my father the arsonist? This is too much to comprehend right now.

THIRTY-FIVE

Morning dew was on the grass as Addie and Rachel walked to the vegetable garden. Addie wore a floral polka-dot lilac dress and a white crocheted sweater. Rachel had her favorite khaki Capri pants and a beige long-sleeve shirt. Her loose hair was pulled behind her ears with combs.

"When you were a little girl on vacation; you were always the first one to volunteer in the garden." Addie chuckled. "Amy preferred the hammock and riding the tractor."

"Everyone should garden and get their hands dirty. I remember the sweet peas, on the veranda with a big wooden bowl. I'm sure we ate more than we saved. This is wonderful, Aunt Addie, spending time with you."

"Here, put this apron on. It has deep pockets for see' pea shells." Addie pulled a worn apron from her basket.

"What's on the vegetable menu today?"

"All the colors. Carrots, green onions, beefsteak tomatoes, potatoes, parsnips and yellow beans. And sweet peas for snacking, if any are left."

"Food is so much better here."

Thomas hopped off the tractor at the charred service hut. In the distance he watched Rachel. He stopped to admire her physique on the veranda, then jogged to the house.

"Hey, Babe! I've missed you this morning. I spend more time with Jonas than with my own wife."

She put down the bowls and bounded to her feet.

"You're still my knight in shining armor, but I admit I'm feeling a bit homesick." She looked into his brown eyes.

"Once Matthew is securely behind bars, we'll make plans," he promised. She leaned against him.

Thomas said, "I phoned Bert Jamieson about the Wells Fargo shipment. He has access to an intelligence network. They are searching for escaped prisoners with an MO for this kind of thing. There's some black market bidding going on over a silver shipment. Could be ours."

"Did they find the GPS bag?"

"The signal disappeared in Nevada. I've been trying to call Daniel, but I still don't get any answer. My guess is that the shipment was seized in Las Vegas or it's heading to New York. The FBI is tight-lipped about what they know."

Rachel said, "The heist must have been planned by Matthew, but he'd need help outside of California. The Wells Fargo office says a woman made suspect inquiries earlier that morning. That would be Julia, I'm sure."

"We took a lot for granted about her. Considering her father came from the same prison as Dexter Kincaid, she could have criminal connections," Thomas said. "I'll pass that to Jamieson."

THIRTY-SIX

Island off the coast of Normandy, France

Ten steps from the wall to the window gave Daniel his needed exercise. He paced it over and over, stopping each time to look out to the ocean. Captivity had weakened his spirit, and he thought an escape seemed hopeless.

Why did I have Thomas York's passport? There must have been a plan. I remember a pretty girl with auburn hair and blue eyes.

And where am I? There's mainland in the distance; the lights of a town, at night. If I could make it to the beach.

He stayed at the window to look at the shimmering waves. A motorboat approached.

Can't be far from land. There must be a causeway nearby but I'm too weak to swim.

Daniel stepped outside his chambers with a cane and watched the boat come ashore.

Yannick disembarked, and Sister Katrina met him at the dock. Daniel turned his head to pick up what he could.

"Ransom . . . New York . . . Sanderson!"

Sanderson!

His memory flashed back.

What has he got to do with anything here? If he thinks I'm Thomas York, he will kill me. On the other hand, if he thinks I am Daniel Boisvert, he will kill me. I do have memories after all.

When the shock of the words subsided, he focused on Yannick and Sister Katrina again.

"We will need to drug him for the flight," she said. "We'll take him to the mainland on Tuesday and meet with Sanderson's private plane. Nothing bigger than a chopper can land here. I'll accompany him as his nurse."

Napa Valley, California

As a goodwill gesture one year when the crop drought hit, Jacob had given Thorold Delacroix $50,000 to help the farm meet its mortgage payment. The firm condition of no repayment was difficult for Gregoire's family to swallow. On that day, their pride was taken from them and the resentment festered.

When Thorold passed away two years ago, an enormous void was left for Gregoire. Their evening chats had been his inspiration, with daily discussions on how he could build a better vineyard and a better life for Lane and Seebe. He remembered Thorold's advice, 'you need to rely on your right hand man'.

Who's my right hand man? My only son is in a prison for the rest of his life. I've had thieves and murders in my bunkhouse without knowing.

I knew things were taking place, but looked the other way. Easier at the time, but not so easy now. If I were religious like my father, I would be down on my knees.

From his kitchen window, Gregoire saw Ducharme men walking up his sidewalk, Jonas and the houseguest. Jonas had a contraption in his hand. He got to the door before they knocked.

"Well, well, Jonas. I haven't seen you in a snake's age. What brings you to my door?"

Thomas intervened and tipped his hat. "We haven't met directly before, Mr. Delacroix, but I believe we both know each other in passing."

"Do you want a coffee, Jonas and . . . Thomas? I haven't had one since early this morning."

"That's kind. Both black please."

Jonas had been dispatched at Addie's request. The boxes of paper that Thomas and Rachel examined brought up new queries about the property line between the two vineyards.

Jonas laid the analyzer on the table and picked up the coffee. "Mr. Delacroix, I come as a neighbor representing the Ducharmes."

"I'm not sure what you mean, Jonas. But, yes we can have a friendly conversation."

"This morning, we had a surveyor mark out our true property lines. This came about when the old deeds were discovered in the attic. The survey report provided to Zachary Ducharme when he succeeded his father as owner, does not compare accurately with today's survey."

"Are you accusing me of something?"

"No, Sir. My suggestion is that over the years with fence repairs and overgrowth, the Ducharmes have encroached on your property."

Gregoire stood stone faced, eying Jonas as if he were being set up.

Jonas continued. "It represents twenty feet between our west field and your east field. The old wagon is pretty much the marker. We are agreeable to build a new fence to agree with the survey. That includes the area where the French Bordeaux vines were originally planted."

Gregoire's face lightened with pleasure and he challenged Jonas.

"Assuming that is true, the Ducharmes have been harvesting my prize grapes over the years, contributing to the award winning wines." Greed flashed in his eyes for a second, then he backed off.

"No, Mr. Delacroix, let me finish."

Gregoire's tone changed. "Get on with it!"

"Many years ago, Zachary secretly moved the Bordeaux stocks to another location. The vines in that twenty foot area, are weak Beaujolais plants that will come full term in about two years."

Jonas hesitated but avoided mentioning Lane's tampering. "They took a blight about two years ago and had to be replaced."

"Crotchety old Zach, trust him to double-cross me. If that's all you have to say, you can leave now, Jonas."

Jonas wasn't deterred. "We understand the volcanic lava is on your property as well as ours. We have been testing our roots this morning with a soil analyzer to give us an idea of the level of fertility and nitrogen feeding the roots."

"Is that what you fellas carried in here?"

"While we have it on rent, we could test your soil near the Ducharme fence line. A property survey isn't enough, you need a geological survey of what's below the surface."

Gregoire softened, wanting to accept the offer.

"Will this cost me money?"

"No, it's a neighborly duty."

"There's no harm in you showing me what these things do. I'll agree to come with you for testing."

Passing the corn fields in Gregoire's pickup, the scarecrows were flat on the ground and the stubble of crow dining evident. Jonas observed it, but bit his tongue, withholding advice or sympathy.

"Here we are. This will do, Gregoire."

"Do you have any farm tools in the back?" Jonas asked. He climbed on the tailgate to see.

"Only if you count my shotgun. I carry it wherever I go on this farm. And a trowel under the burlap."

Jonas lowered to his knees and dug at the surface to loosen the soil. "Along the fence here, the soil is softer from use and muddier. This should be a good spot to check."

"Mr. Delacroix, what kind of crops do you have in this area?" Thomas asked.

"These are Chardonnay." Removing his cap, he scratched a balding head. "Can't get good help now, the men are probably over at that dang blasted Rusty Nail."

Jonas stood back up with a smile on his face. He lifted the analyzer so they could all hear it ticking.

"Yep, Gregoire, you've got rich lava ash in your soil too. Since we have moved on to your land back here, it's only right that you allow us to make repairs and reinforce your vines and posts. They can't be ignored."

"If this is out of pity, you can keep yours."

"No pity for you, Gregoire, just your Chardonnay grapes. There's an old saying that 'you reap what you sow'. You know what that means, don't you?"

Gregoire sensed he was the target of insult but held his anger. "Can you give me overnight to mull that over?"

Jonas said, "Let me know before breakfast is finished and we have a deal. If you don't come and give me your answer, you're on your own."

"Deal. Thanks for the soil testing."

Jonas stretched his hand forward reciting from Robert Frost. "Good fences build good neighbors".

THIRTY-SEVEN

Jacques Simpson's office, New York

He slammed his phone to the desk and bellowed from his office, "Get me on a flight to Las Vegas! Right away!"

His assistant left his office and was back in minutes. "Mr. Simpson, Sir, the earliest flight is United Airlines at 1:15 PM. Will that be alright?"

"Yes, book it, and put me at the Mandalay Bay."

Simpson had a manicured mustache and thick dark hair worn behind his ears. He dressed impeccably in a navy silk suit and crisp hand-made white shirt. His collar was open, and his hand went to the silver medallion. He caressed the raised letter 'C'.

In his phone, Jacques retrieved the last incoming number, and scratched it on his business card. He opened the wall safe behind the ancient portrait painting of Francois Delevere Courchelles.

"Sorry about this, Great Grandad. I have to rescue your treasure and save a good man. The life of my friend, Daniel Boisvert is hanging in the balance."

Jacques placed six tied bundles of one hundred dollar bills in his business case. He took a long inspection of the Courchelles portrait, and locked his door."

The criminal influence of David Sanderson hadn't waned during the last four years. Instead, he had elevated himself to kingpin at the New York state prison. No one dared to cross him, and favors for him were abundant at the snap of his fingers.

The buzz of his network intercepted transmissions about a silver shipment in Las Vegas, and he made a call from the prison to orchestrate a heist. His sister-in-law was there to visit him in an hour, and he gave her a number to call, the same contact that Julia had been given by Spider.

She dialed from the parking lot and the call was forwarded to the lead man, from the fake armored robbery. The vehicle had been long abandoned and the shipment transferred, but the GPS remained intact.

"I've been asked to give you a message. We understand that you're about to make a sale of your silver shipment to a New York fella. Sanderson says to proceed but dupe the other buyer and put him out of commission."

"Do you mean Sanderson 'the lawyer'?"

"Yes."

"Then what?"

Napa Valley

Lunch was informal on the veranda at the main house, a table of sandwiches, potato chips and lemonade.

"How do I get rid of those Brazilian notes?" Addie asked.

"You can burn the lot," Thomas said. "Last night, through the telescope, I saw a motorcycle in the village lane. The only vehicles that should be back there are the work trucks and tractors."

He looked up to see Coles walking briskly toward the house.

Jonas called out. "Cole, join us for sandwiches!"

"Was it definitely Julia on the motorcycle?" Thomas asked.

Cole took a paper plate loaded with a pastrami and rye, fruit and cheese. He nodded. "A woman at the village saw Julia getting on the bike."

Thomas said, "Either Julia co-operates in trapping Matthew, or she goes to jail. She's smart enough to figure that out."

Rachel said, "Then I suspect she was in on the silver shipment heist."

Addie gasped but didn't say anything.

In a darkened corner at the Rusty Nail, Matt and Julia planned the sabotage of the Ducharme vineyards.

"The medallions are in Vegas, so that's where we'll head right after the barbeque." Matthew laughed at his choice of words. "There will be a crowd, making it easy to be unnoticed when you sneak into the house, Julia. Take the silver and anything else you like from that antique china cabinet. Keep your pistol loaded and ready at all times, and don't be afraid to use it."

"Uh huh." Julia buried her face into her hands. "I don't want the money, Matt. I'm here to avenge Rocky's murder."

Shocked, he looked at her, watching tears trickle down her cheeks.

"We'll get even!"

"Matt, have you ever intentionally lit a fire?" Her question needled into his secrets.

He didn't answer for a moment, then looked at her eyes. "There's nothing like the feeling of watching your own work burn, with fiery orange flames and burst of back flash." His voice shook. "People screaming! Yes, I saw that once—it was truly a thrill." He turned away and mumbled, "Charles and Evelyn."

Pulling back to reality, he deterred Julia's questioning.

"The widow must have family jewels too. In those days, grand parties, receiving lines and fanfare were the style." He laughed again. "We go to the pub, now."

"I get it. I'll look for a jewel chest and the dining room silver. Do you have another sack like your prison pals used for the medallions?"

"I left the Brazilian cache of bank notes secure in the garret where the Ducharmes will never find it. They are bluffing when they say it isn't worth much. Dexter wouldn't have come all this way after forty years for nothing."

"Are we really avenging Rocky's death, or are you obsessed with greed?"

"Both, my dear, both."

My poor Rocky didn't deserve to die here, but I don't believe in 'an eye for an eye'. From the look on Matt's face when he described a house burning, I dread to make the comparison to my own mother.

It's been hard to bear. Witnesses saw my mother at an upstairs window calling for help. Did my father leave her there intentionally? No, I don't want to be like him!

Matthew interrupted her thoughts. "I'll drop you back at the vineyards. Are you still undercover there? I'm going to the storage locker to pick up the gasoline."

"I'll stick close to the estate, but out of sight. I was fired. How are you for money?"

"Gimme what you got right now, and I'll be set for the day."

Julia had hoped he would be a standup guy and refuse. She dug into her zippered pocket and handed him a handful of her tips.

Standing by the side of the road leading to the vineyards, she watched the motorcycle fade into the distance.

The Ducharme contingent gathered in the kitchen to discuss the lava caves and the future of the silver medallions.

Thomas gave them the latest. "The FBI stumbled upon another operative who learned of the silver and is attempting to intercept it, as well. We'll find out soon enough if Julia was involved in the first caper."

"Rachel, does anything else from the attic papers shed light on the treasure?"

"I have an update. The date on the scroll in the trunk was 1844, then it appears the rights to the plundered silver transferred to Francois Delavere Courchelles in 1880. Francois and his wife Genevieve had a large family, mostly girls. As a dowry for his eldest daughter, Anne, he offered the trunk to Jefferson Ducharme.

"In 1920, Anne & Jefferson divided the silver equally among their four sons, with a smaller gift to his five daughters. That explains why the trunk isn't full. There are three sons of Jefferson Ducharme elsewhere in the United States that have established themselves well.

"The neighboring land, which is now the Delacroix farm, was taken over by one of Jefferson's sons, Adam. It stayed in the hands of Adam Ducharme, until his descendants sold the land to Gregoire Delacroix in 2000. Gregoire married Martine who had an aunt that adopted a young girl, Caliste. She came from an orphanage and was nameless.

"Martine passed away leaving her grieving husband bitter. He envied the Ducharme estate as a happy family with flourishing crops, things he never had."

Jonas spoke up. "Today, we made our peace offering to Gregoire to help him get the twenty foot overrun in good shape. He was amenable and had new hope for crop improvements by the lava rich soil."

"Yes, Addie," Thomas said. "It was an olive branch well received.

Jonas glanced at Addie and continued.

"Gregoire's back quarter was in total decay. The man needs to get his pride and inspiration back. We'll send him a few men to help, and our security patrol will watch for poachers and those mangy coyotes."

Thomas said, "The soil analysis reading was excellent; it is fertile and rich with lava ash. There's no reason he can't have a bumper crop and fine wines. Zach could have taught him a thing or two if they had worked on it."

"What about the feast this Saturday night?" Rachel asked. "Should we invite Gregoire?"

"Excellent idea, Rachel." Addie wasn't absolutely convinced and quietly breathed deeply, settling her hands into her apron.

THIRTY-EIGHT

Melissa drove from San Francisco for the weekend, with the three kids singing most of the way.

Their golden retriever, Rooster, was in the back; his real name, Brewster, was difficult when the children were young, so the new name stuck. Rooster was first out of the vehicle when they pulled up, bounding in search of the German shepherds, Barnabus and Samson.

After the Grandma hugs, the kids ran to Jonas, then found Thomas and Rachel inside.

The youngest asked, "Do you live here now, Rach?"

Rachel burst in laughter at the innocence. "You know, Marcy, this is a wonderful place to live, but I have a home far away that I need to go back to soon."

"There's lots of room here, if you want to stay."

When Melissa went to the rooms, Addie nudged Jonas's elbow. "Can I have a word with you?"

"Sure, let's go outside."

"Jonas, you promised to take me on chores around the vineyard." Her hands rested on her hips, and he saw Addie's mischief as she spoke. "Are the Harleys ready to go?"

"Yes, they both run, but Matthew absconded with one."

Addie released her apron and leaned to lace up her work boots. Her wicker hat was already on the table and she tied the string around her chin.

"Time for a test run."

He took her left hand and led her to the bike. "We can circle around starting on the east side. I'd like to check out the workers village and have a chat with Mrs. Wilkes."

"Lead the way, Jonas."

The engine rumbled as Addie settled on the back. With a wobble at first, they weaved across the parking lot and puttered down the east lane.

Mrs. Wilkes was napping in her rocking chair at the first cottage on the left. The sputtering of the engine startled her, thinking it was Matthew returning again.

"Oh, it's you. Jonas."

"Sorry if we alarmed you."

She stepped off the porch. "I sleep with one eye open watching for the escaped prisoner."

"We have a few questions about your tenant, Julia Morse."

"Well, I do too! She doesn't fit in back here. Always eavesdropping and popping into personal conversations."

"It will only be one or two more nights. We'd like to get some information from her before we scare her off."

"Right you are. She's obsessed to find out details. When the weekend comes, she'll be there. That criminal Matthew skulks around here at night but I keep my distance. I'm too old to meddle."

"Thanks, Mrs. Wilkes. Don't mention we were here."

Thomas was concerned about Mrs. Wilkes' safety knowing that Julia had been prepared to use chloroform in the attic.

"Too late about that, here she is coming down the lane."

Julia was approaching on foot, her hair in a tight blonde bob.

Jonas turned to greet her, determined to get her away from the village before the biker returned. "Julia, I'm Jonas Barstow. Would you mind coming to the house for a short chat?"

She hesitated to weigh her options, but nodded hoping to buy some goodwill with her charm.

Julia hopped on the back of the Harley and they puttered uphill to the main house. Addie took the tractor from the cornfield.

"Can I wash up before our little meet and greet?"

"Of course. Take the hall on the other side of the kitchen, the first door before the laundry room."

Julia found her way comfortably, but came back more sullen. She sat with her hands clasped in her lap, and Jonas watched with suspicion as she grasped a tissue.

"I understand you have questions for me," she said. "But first would you be patient enough to listen to my story? I know I'm in some hot water."

Maria brought mugs and two plates of warm, oozing peach cobbler, fresh from the oven.

"My mother used to make this," she said. Tears welled up in her eyes.

Thomas arrived in the kitchen and assessed the silence. He looked around hoping to see Rachel, thinking that these situations require a woman's touch.

"I'm Thomas York," he said. "My wife, Rachel, is Addie's niece. We're staying on the estate."

Julie's emotions switched. "This is delicious," she oozed. "I've been living on hamburgers and fries for a few weeks. This is such a treat."

She scooped the end of the cobbler onto her fork with her finger, and licked the finger clean.

"First of all, my name is Julia Morse. Rocky Morse was my husband. We weren't all bad. He took good care of me and promised me the world, and I adored him. I'm truly sorry for his part in Mr. Ducharme's passing." Her eyes went to her lap.

"My father used the name Spider, and spent time in prison with the real Dexter Kincaid. He heard the details over and over of the robbery and the bank notes, and recanted it to me on my visits. I met Matthew through Rocky and told him my story, and we've been tight since.

"I'd like to explain my childhood phobia. I was used to hearing my parent argue, mostly about money. One night, the arguing stopped suddenly.

"My father came to my room and picked me up. From the yard, we watched the house burn. My mother crawled to the upper window, banging on the glass!" Julia pulled at her hair, her voice raised. "My mother was yelling for help, but my father didn't flinch; he stood in a trance watching her fade out of sight. After that, I went to live with various relatives, but always got a loving birthday card from my Dad, wherever I was.

"In photo albums of my early years, my mother's picture has been cut out. I tracked Spider down and went to see him, to get some of my old school things. When I left, I accidentally took a box of letters and newspaper clippings. There was one of the night of the fire, calling it arson."

Thomas brought a box of tissues. "I'm sorry about your mother, Julia."

"She can't be brought back."

Julia stood up and paced in the kitchen, deep in thought.

"What else, Julia? What's on your mind to tell us?"

She sat again. "Matthew's intentions have an eerie parallel. Just like he murdered his parents, he's ready to light another fire. Here! On Saturday night when you have a crowd of people.

"I pretended to go along with his plans, but he was so anxious for an inferno, I can't take it. Matthew already has the supplies and charges. On Saturday night, when the yard and kitchen will be full of people, I'm to sneak into the house and take whatever jewels, gold or silver I could find. He'd get into the wine caves by the basement and set some dynamite.

"Charges will also be set around the main house."

"For now, Julia, play along with him. You understand, now you're walking a thin line and must continue to be forthcoming. The alternative is a long time in prison."

THIRTY-NINE

Las Vegas, Nevada

Jacques Simpson arrived in Las Vegas from New York on a commercial flight. He stormed through the terminal to the taxi line. In minutes, he was at the Mandalay Bay hotel.

Tossing his overnight bag on the bed, he drew a business card from his wallet with the handwritten number on the back.

The stupid Julia Morse in Vallejo. What enticed her to get involved with such a treasure, and to cross paths with me?

How did she find the Courchelles silver? I'll make one proposal to those thugs and they had better take it. I need this to save Boisvert.

He walked through the ornate lobby, and hired a cab to the Golden Nugget on Freemont Street. His pouch was strapped securely under his shirt.

Stepping through the front doors under a sky of yellow strings of bulbs implanted in the ceiling, he walked past the dinging of slots and the hum of gamblers. At the door of the lounge he spotted three men wearing matching brown shirts.

Let's make this quick.

The lead thief stood to greet Jacques. "Mr. Black, it's a pleasure to meet you."

Jacques didn't extend his hand. "I have a return flight shortly. Let's get this over with; where is the silver shipment?"

"Hold on, Mr. Black. I've got to see your green first."

"No, I am the buyer! You show me the goods. Is this your first time, fella."

Napa Valley

First thing Friday, Jonas and Thomas hauled the banquet tables and chairs from the shed. They spaced the eight round tables in a circle on the back lawn, with eight chairs each. The center lawn was left open for the festivities, songs and flamenco guitars by minstrels in the compound.

Spanish lanterns, bales of hay, pumpkins and squash, and bushels apples had been gathered during the week.

Days preparing secret recipes kept them all bustling, with oldies on the kitchen radio as pots boiled and cakes baked.

Maria and her sister folded and counted the French linen white tablecloths. They'd been used as far back as Jacob Sr. and Margaret for gatherings at the estate.

Addie and Melissa organized the larder that was bursting at the seams. Women from the compound brought salads, Spanish rice, Andalusian bread and corn pone, made the traditional way. Buckets and bowls were ready to overflow with the peel and eat shrimp and Alaska king crab.

"Jonas, can you get one of the boys to take the truck for the wine and beer? I have a list here." Addie's green eyes glimmered. "It's going to be a wonderful party."

"That it will, my dear. The best we've ever had." He hugged her and looked up to see if they were alone. He kissed her quickly, and checked again.

"Jonas . . . I need you here. You know that. The grandkids are leaving in the morning. Could you teach them to sing 'The Old Grey Mare'? Zach always sang it with Melissa when he took her on his walks."

He winked and skipped to the door.

Julia tied a scarf over her hair and put on one of Addie's coats. She turned the collar up before going outside. It was doubtful that Matthew would see her in the dark, but there was too much at risk to take the chance. She climbed into the back of the car and kept her head down.

Jonas drove, with Thomas beside him. They passed a few cars and one motorcycle on the way to the Charron police department.

Cole and two men were left to guard the village, and the security patrol had been alerted to call the police in the event of a night visitor at the main house. Rachel, Addie, Melissa and the grandchildren were asleep.

Thomas called out, "We'd like to speak with the Sheriff."

They heard a voice at the back, then the Sheriff stood up.

"Hello, my nocturnal friends. What can we do for you? You know that you took me out of a lovely nap." He laughed, and Thomas wasn't sure if he should too.

They went to the Sheriff's desk and he cleared some clutter. Thomas relayed Julia's story and the Sheriff noted some dates and details.

"Mr. York, I'll send a couple of patrol cars to check in with your party on Saturday. Of course, if you have concrete evidence or actually see Matthew Ducharme at the estate, we'll dispatch a unit right away."

Julia's face reddened. "Sheriff, can't you see that I've made a serious commitment here? Exactly what is concrete evidence?" Her lip quivered in anger. "Do you mean that we should bring you a charred brick after the Ducharme house has exploded? Do you want dead bodies before you get up from your desk?"

Jonas took Julia's elbow and whispered in her ear. "Julia, let me handle the Sheriff. There's no need to antagonize him."

The Sheriff stayed in control, but stared her in the eye. "Well, young lady, you talk to me again in that tone and I'll cite you for contempt."

"I'm sorry, Sir. But could you re-open an old arson file where Juliette Morse died? She was my mother. It's a cold case from fifteen years ago, and I know who murdered her? I was an eye witness. Would that get your detectives involved?"

The Sheriff stiffened his back and leaned forward on his desk.

"I see you are a passionate young woman, and that is a good quality. In the morning, I'll call Cold Cases and see what they have. Where can we reach you, Julia?"

She turned to Jonas.

"You can reach her through my number," Jonas said.

Thomas and Jonas rose to leave, but Julia remained seated.

"Sheriff. The missing silver from the Ducharme estate . . . I know what happened to it." Julia shook as she spoke.

Jonas interrupted her. "What! Why didn't you tell us?"

"You're walking a thin line, Julia," Thomas said.

The Sheriff raised his palm. "Ms. Morse, do you realize that anything you say here can be used against you in a court of law."

"Yes, I understand. Matthew asked me to make arrangements through my connections. A criminal community is out there waiting for calls like mine. They arranged the heist."

"Where is it now?" Jonas asked.

"Mr. Barstow, let's let her tell the whole story first."

"The shipment was to go to Las Vegas to an underground buyer. But the cons have conned me and started taking bids on the medallions. I can give you the phone number that I had and a few names, but beyond that I know little. Matthew is a wild man, he coerced me. I'm so sorry . . ." Julia turned to Jonas.

The Sheriff drew out a fresh pad of paper and Julia began writing her confession.

Thomas said, "We need her to continue the ruse with Matthew during our Saturday night barbeque. Your officers should be ready. Julia has offered her full cooperation."

"I'll need to make an arrest first, then I'll get a judge to release her on her own recognizance. Can you put up the minimum bond? It shouldn't take long if you wait."

Jonas nodded.

"There's a late café on Main Street," Thomas said. "We need to perfect our own plan to stop Matthew's treasure hunt."

"Thomas, would a sack of disposed South American bank notes appease him?" Jonas suggested.

"He has the other half hidden in the garret. He won't do anything until he has that out of the house. Julia, when are you supposed to meet up with Matthew?"

She looked at her watch. "In five hours. At four a.m., he's coming to talk to me about the plan. He was getting the gasoline today, and wants to hide it on the property."

"Suggest that he store it in Zach's old broken down Ford. It's outside on the far side of the garage with a tarp over it.

Nobody checks that. Once he leaves we'll go in and defuse the contents.

"Are you with us on this, Julia?"

"Yes. I can't allow him to fulfil his plan, but I also don't want him hurt. Someday, I would like to talk with Mrs. Ducharme and tell her how sorry I am for her loss."

"You'll have time for that later," Jonas said.

"We'll bring in extra security to the main house, and we'll screen the guests. We ask that you trust in us. When Matthew is visually on site at the party, you need to go and greet Melissa. That will be our cue. Understand?" Thomas said.

"Okay, greet Melissa. Sounds like a plan."

"Here's a tracking bug. Place it on the motorcycle."

Julia returned quietly to the worker's compound before midnight. Jonas assigned three men to stand guard in the woods near her cabin. They were not to intercept Matthew unless there was a life threatening incident.

The anticipation yielded to knots in her stomach. She waited by the window, then paced inside the cabin. The plan was for Julia to take a walk with Matthew.

In the quiet of dusk, Matthew appeared in the compound on the bike. Julia took a deep breath and straighten her shoulders. She stepped outside and hugged him.

Her voice was low. "Matt, are we still on schedule for the party—for the blast?"

"Sure are, Julia. The fireworks will be seen all the way to Vallejo."

"Where are you hiding out if I need to find you?"

Matthew stepped back and put his hands on her shoulders searching her eyes for truth or suspicion.

"Why do you need to know that?"

"You're my only light in a storm. I want to know where you are."

"It's a fleabag motel between here and Charron. If I'm in, you'd see the Harley out front." He watched her eyes. "Do you know the layout of the house and the access to the wine caves? You'll need to make sure all those doors are open. Wear some gloves and bring a sack. I don't want anything incriminating to come back to you."

"Sure, Matt."

Julia could hardly bear the deceit she was committing. Deliberately she tripped her ankle in a tractor rut on the lane and yelped, hobbling to the bike. She leaned down and secured the bug under the back seat.

"I've twisted my ankle. Will you help me?" Julia looked up at him with a grimace of pain.

"Sure kid." Julia raised her arm up to his shoulder and limped back to the cabin. The night light had been turned out.

FORTY

By ten o'clock Friday morning, the kitchen activity for the party was in high gear, with pans, bowls, simmer pots, and muffin tins lining the table. The children, Hazel, Isaac and Marcy were folding napkins and counting paper plates.

The glazed hams were baking, and a large turkey from the market was browning in the second oven. Potatoes were ready for potato salad, three dozen hard-boiled eggs in a bowl and a tomato sauce was simmering. Melissa was babysitting the lemon pie meringue.

"Melissa, can you make up a batch of Mexican bean stew. Use the four-quart corn pot. All the ingredients are in the larder."

"Sure, Ma." Melissa wiped her hands on her apron.

"Rachel, we need about twelve fresh tomatoes from the garden chopped into eights?"

Marcy's face brightened to hear that, and Rachel didn't miss the hint.

"Come on, Marcy, let's get tomatoes for Grandma. We won't need a basket; we'll gather them in my apron. Ready?"

Marcy raised her arm and Rachel took her small hand. "Coming.'

It was 90 degrees outside and the fans were going in the kitchen. From an oversized cauldron, the room was filled with the aroma of paella dishes of clams, sausage, mussels, shrimp and chicken. chile rellenos, lamb chops and casseroles were on the other burners, and a lineup of chickens were ready for the BBQ spit.

Thomas and Jonas hadn't told Addie yet about Matthew's impending threat to the party. Everything should continue as planned, and as it approached they'd tell her and ensure her safety.

Whatever was going to happen, the children should be confined away from the house. Rachel had an extra banquet table set on the south edge of the lawn.

"Hey, Hazel, Isaac and Marcy, I need you to help me build a fort."

"Where are we going?" Isaac asked.

"Come me with, I have the perfect spot," Rachel said.

"Can I bring the toad?" The girls shrieked and the toad escaped from Isaac's clasp.

"I'm sorry, dear. But I'll race you all to the fort." They all took off, with Isaac in the lead.

"Here it is," Rachel said. "There's a tarp over the table to keep you sheltered, and I'll bring a mat for the floor to keep the ants out of your beds. But you'll need your sleeping bags and pillows."

Cole inspected the wine caves, boarded up the outside access and activated the motion sensor. He had loaded the dolly with four wine cases, requested by Addie.

There was no sign of Matthew on the property, and Jonas felt safe in switching the gasoline. Zach's old Ford was partially hidden by bushes, and Jonas was discreet as he approached it. He looked toward the road and the field, then opened the door. From Matthew's two cans, Jonas siphoned the gasoline into a galvanized container.

He refilled Matthew's cans with a non-flammable diluted solution, and returned them to Zach's car. The gasoline odor remained strong.

Julia swallowed hard as she tapped at the door. Rachel greeted her and brought her into the kitchen. "Addie and ladies. I'd like to introduce a friend of mine who will be staying over the weekend."

Julia smiled and tried a polite curtsy.

Addie's confusion showed on her face and she looked to Rachel for approval.

"I'm happy to have another pair of hands," Addie said. "Do you mind taking over the potato salad. The celery, onion, eggs, mayo and spices are all set. But you'll need a strong arm for mashing."

At two o'clock, the outside security patrol team arrived, understanding that their contract team would monitor and detect movements around the restaurant and the front lawn.

Jonas met with them at their vehicle.

"Case those two buildings for explosives, and check it again every half hour. We are expecting an arsonist tonight. And discuss anything directly with me as there's no need to alert Mrs. Ducharme."

Jack, the lead man, said, "There are five of us and we are connected by wireless communication."

Jonas agreed. "Okay. Send one to stay at post by the garage and someone in the lilac bushes by the garden. The others can rotate in the yard and watch access points. I'll introduce my own men to you in thirty minutes. One will watch the security monitor, and the others can patrol the party and house. I'll bring you a picture of Matthew."

At precisely 9:00 p.m., Julia was to go into the house without drawing attention. She would remain inside until she heard Matthew's crow call, and then begin her search of the main house.

Looking at his watch, Matthew calculated that he had an hour and a half before show time. He felt for a pouch inside his jacket pocket and was satisfied it was in place.

Riding a rusty bike he'd found in the garage, Matthew crept back into the village. Behind the chicken coop, he was relieved to find a wheelbarrow. He worked quickly in the shadows.

The cabins were emptying out as the party-goers had already started into a few cases of beer, and old Ned Barnes had pulled out his accordion.

Last cabin second row.

There was humming coming out of the shower when Matthew stood at the bathroom door casually leveling a rifle over his knee.

"Get dressed! No noise, or I'll hurt you."

Matthew could see she was about to scream and took out a roll of duct tape to quieten her.

"Turn around." He tied her hands together, then her ankles. Slowly he fastened the pouch from his pocket around her neck.

No one noticed the shadow of the man with the wheelbarrow grappling with the ruts on the edge of the lane. At the garage, he knew every fifteen minutes the guards took a smoke break behind the garage. That would be his only opportunity to conceal the wheelbarrow.

FORTY-ONE

Golden Nugget, Las Vegas

Jacques Simpson accepted the wheeled suitcase and opened it on the floor. The silver shone in the room's bright lights and he closed it. He handed the three cons his case with $500,000 cash and they counted the bundles. Jacques poured four glasses of champagne that he had ordered to the room, that he'd opened before they arrived.

In minutes, two thugs lay prone on the bed and the other on the floor. He hadn't touched his glass, and his gun had been at his fingertips as a backup.

It's my guarantee that I won't be followed or expect any harassment. They'll sleep well until morning.

But the clock is running down for Daniel. Sanderson has ordered a pickup.

Jacques hurried to the lobby and hopped to a cab to the terminal. Angels of Providence chartered a private jet to return to New York. He pulled the suitcase onboard and settled into his seat, watching the lights of the Las Vegas Strip.

As he taxied to the runway, he dialed the island monastery off the coast of Normandy.

"I have the ransom. I want to speak with Daniel Boisvert or Thomas York, whoever you've kidnapped. What's next?"

"It doesn't matter which man you think I have. You bring the other one with you to New York. I'll give you forty-eight hours to make your arrangements."

Jacques hung up and looked up the Ducharme's number in California.

I need to bring Thomas York, to close this deal.

Napa Valley

As the sun dropped from the sky, a fluorescent tangerine and rose sunset spread like fire on the horizon. The fiddles had started up a lively jig, the signal for folks to pour in from the worker's village.

Addie looked into the sky dotted with stars.

Life is wonderful, Zach. I wish you were here.

Melissa was standing behind her. "Mom, this is such a wonderful thing that you've done. I will never forget this night as long as I live. I love this land and all the people that make it so joyous. Thank you for having us for the past three weeks. I'd like to stay forever, but I have another life elsewhere. Maybe we'll come for Christmas."

"My three are out there dancing with children from the village."

"I remember the times in the past when you did that. When the party ended after midnight, Papa carried you on his shoulders up to your room totally exhausted."

Emotions were high. Addie broke into a deep sob.

"I miss him," she whispered.

"Me too, Mom. I know he's here in the heavens watching over us."

Jonas watched as each guest exited the cars and trucks. His eyes followed a lone silhouette of a tall man in a cowboy hat. In the light he realized it was Gregoire Delacroix.

Jonas walked toward Gregoire and they shook hands. "I want some folks to meet you," he said. First was Addie.

"Addie, Gregoire has come for our party. I know you were waiting to speak with him."

"I am indeed."

Gregoire shifted his large frame, expecting the riot act from Addie.

"Thanks for the invitation, Addie."

He stretched his calloused hand hoping she would accept his handshake, as Jonas slipped away.

"Gregoire, it is really good to see you. I am so sorry about Lane. You have been through a lot in recent years. I heard the boys got your east corner back in shape. Jonas is an expert in the vineyards, nary does a blight get past him. I hope you'll find time to spend together. Come back for tea any day. Jonas comes up to the house for tea at 11:00 a.m. sharp."

"Addie . . ." Gregoire looked down at his boots. "About Zach, I can't tell you how badly I feel. The Ducharmes have always been good to us. My boy got mixed up with some bad people. Such a tragedy! I should've been more neighborly and not let my Irish interfere."

"Zach's in Heaven, and someday I will join him. You are forgiven by me, now you need to be forgiven by God."

Addie held his rough hands in hers and stared into his hollow brown eyes. They were overrun with thick brow and tears ran down both their cheeks.

"Yes, Ma'am."

"Go on out to the barbeque and find yourself a beer. I know Melissa will want to see you too."

Gregoire was a beaten man with a hundred weight off his shoulders. He sighed his relief and went in search of Melissa.

Matt stopped the Harley at the road. With binoculars, he scanned the property, stopping to focus on the security patrol.

Turning out the lights, he drove slowly to a row of brush leading to the far side of the garage, he eased the bike into the ditch. The music was loud, drowning out the ticking of his engine.

Matthew crouched in the darkness and crept to the old Ford. The point man on the other side of the garage heard the creak of the car door and radioed Jonas.

The guard dogs, Barnabas and Samson were three hundred yards away, coming fast across the field. Matthew pulled the two gas cans from the car. The security man stepped out and Matthew swung a can at his face knocking him to the ground.

Matthew strapped the cans on the back of the bike and took off across the bumpy terrain, turning onto the road. He had lost the dogs, but needed a new plan to get onto the property.

I have to get to the wheelbarrow.

Jonas emerged from the partiers and took a megaphone from the veranda.

"Hello, folks, my name is Jonas Barstow, and I want to welcome you on behalf of Addie Ducharme."

Matthew was on foot at the road now dragging a burlap sack, and stopped to listen.

"As you know, there have been rampant rumors since the unfortunate death of Zach, that the vineyard or caves housed a treasure," Jonas said.

The crowd hushed "There are two levels of treasure to tell you about."

A brief chant started in the crowd. "Show us the treasure."

"Patience please. The first part was a cache of 80,000 Brazilian cruzeiros. It was currency marked for destruction and is worthless."

The voices had a long collective groan.

"Our house was broken into and half of it was taken by Matthew Ducharme, but we were able to recover that portion."

Matthew was angered and enthralled with the story, but continued on his mission. He stuffed the burlap into the bushes where no one would find it.

With everyone's attention directed to Jonas, he advanced toward the restaurant. The guard there was absorbed in the story and didn't notice Matt laying three charges along the front.

The security monitor picked it up and Cole was there in seconds to disable the charges after Matthew had moved on.

Matthew moved up the west side of the house and laid a charge at the back and two at the side, then poured the gasoline without being noticed. He stood in the darkness mere yards from the veranda where Jonas was mastering his guests. The house security man watched and listened to Jonas.

"Here are the banknotes. All stuffed into this bag. I suggest we take this opportunity with a crowd of witnesses to burn the money."

Matthew heard the words.

That money belongs to me. You can't burn it.

The party noise became loud, with the excitement of the money. Some sat at tables while others stood for a better view. The Sheriff's squad of three cars pulled into the driveway and his officers circled the scene.

Matthew pushed his way through the clamoring. He was dragging the burlap sack.

The crowd became silent as he fired one shot in the air. He waved both pistols above his head.

"The whole thing belongs to me," he screamed.

Jonas walked slowly to the bonfire and dropped a handful of bank notes. They fluttered in the air as the fire spit them back and he threw in the whole bundle.

Matthew fired another warning shot in the air and grabbed Jonas by the shirt.

"Where's Caliste Hanson?" he shouted. "Caliste, are you here? Come and face the son you rejected. Come out and explain that to my face!"

His face shook with anger, and he looked toward voices at a corner table.

"Ah ha, I know where she is!" Matthew pulled the sack to stand upright and untied the opening.

The burlap fell away revealing a disheveled Caliste Hanson with a blindfold and duct tape over her mouth.

Matthew hollered again. "Bring Julia to me, she's in the house!" One gun was on Jonas and the other aimed at Addie.

People looked to the house and waited.

"Julia!" he shouted.

The door opened and Julie came to the edge of the veranda.

"Matt, don't do this," she pleaded. "Put your guns down, please!"

He said to Jonas. "I've waited years to come to this place and take back the treasure. You have a lot of audacity to burn what was mine."

Caliste starting squirming but there wasn't any allowance for loose ropes. She stood with wild eyes and tears streaming down her face.

"Let her go, you don't know what you're doing!" Nathan Hanson yelled.

"Hold on there Nathan. There's been talk that my bank notes are worthless, so if I can't have them, then maybe you'd like to give me a ransom. $80,000 is the number." Matthew's eyes were bloodshot as he seethed.

"Matthew, the money was worthless. The bank notes have been destroyed; the batches are perforated. They weren't U.S. dollars. Go and look at one for yourself. Put your guns down."

"Absolutely not, I'm not going away empty-handed."

He lowered a pistol and pulled a device from his pocket. Gritting his teeth, he ignited the switch.

"I light this switch and your house goes kaboom! And this other switch and my Mother goes kaboom!" Matthew detonated the first button.

The side of the house with the extension buckled from the explosion. Jonas was close to the house and was hit by flying glass and debris, knocking him to the ground.

The restaurant wall went next, with windows shattering, less than Matthew had imagined.

"Do I have any bids for this trashy girl that seduced my father and then left him to face the entire blame?" Matthew started jerking in all directions like a leopard. He turned to Caliste and spat in her face.

As he watched, two security guards rushed him.

On his side on the grass, Matthew fired a pair of shots and downed Jack, the lead security man.

"That wasn't smart, Jack. For that, let this fall on your head." Matthew lit a match, holding it close to the ring of dynamite around his mother's neck.

Thomas took a shot that crippled him and he lost control of Caliste. Nathan ran in to scoop her out of the way but the first fuse had been lit. Trying to put it out with his hands, there was a loud BOOM followed by a resonating thud, and flying debris.

When the smoke cleared both Caliste and Nathan were blood-soaked on the ground with people around screaming.

Matthew crawled closer to the house, with his guns aimed at the crowd. On his feet again, he threw a match at the puddle of gasoline near the house, but the match sizzled and sunk into the fluid. Stunned, he tried to detonate one more charge.

Thomas raised his pistol and fired as Matthew turned to shoot, then fired again. A second shot came from a police officer at the side and Matthew fell to the grass. He didn't move, and the officer took the gun from his hand.

Julia screamed and dropped to her knees sobbing.

Addie ran past Matthew's body. "Jonas! Jonas!" "Where are you hurt?"

The medics turned him over to put on the stretcher. Shards of glass and shrapnel protruded from his back.

FORTY-TWO

At 11:00 a.m. sharp, Gregoire got out of his pickup. He stepped around a building crew who were assembling framing on the lawn. Two other carpenters were on the roof.

Jonas was back from the hospital and sitting at the kitchen table. No one talked about Saturday night since the funerals.

Addie heard the knock at the screen door.

"Gregoire, it's good that you're here. The tea is ready."

He said, "Thanks Addie, but I'm also here to ask if you folks need help rebuilding. I have my tools and I've always had a niche for carpentry."

"We'll take you up on that. We've needed to hire a few guys, but any time you can help, we're happy."

He removed his hat and took a seat. "And Jonas, Can we talk more about the geology of the volcanic lava. Addie, here, sang your praises."

Jonas winked at Addie.

"I'm glad you came." Addie said. "I remember the days when Martine came for tea and we had good times."

Gregoire left feeling more of a man.

Thomas and Rachel dressed up for dinner out with the family, but they came down the stairway with heavy hearts. It was time. They were no longer needed here and were ready to go back to Paris.

"I don't know how to break it to Addie, but I'm sure she knows it's the right time too." Rachel whispered.

Thomas drove the rental car, with Addie, Jonas and Melissa in the back. Addie had called ahead to Brannan's Grill on Lincoln Avenue, and they were glad to see it wasn't busy.

"This is a night of celebration." Addie held her heart.

"We have a bit of news as well," Rachel quipped.

"Jonas, how about a cold sparkling wine?"

The waiter returned with a bucket and removed the cork.

"Aunt Addie, you should go first."

Addie turned to Jonas and blushed.

"I don't know where to start, except that I was blessed to have Zach as my life-mate and now I am blessed to have Jonas. He is a part of me and I can't bear to face the future without this wonderful man."

"What she is trying to say, is that we are going to get married," Jonas piped up.

Addie continued. "I know there hasn't been an appropriate amount of widow time, but we were thinking about November, when the yard is back to normal and the house has been fixed."

"Oh, this is wonderful news." Rachel and Melissa jumped up together to hug Addie, then Jonas. "I'm so happy for both of you," Melissa said.

Thomas said, "She's a great catch, Jonas!"

"You'll come back for the wedding, won't you?"

"We'll work on that." Rachel voice softened. "But it's time for us to go home now. Jonas is taking good care of you. We'll look at travel plans tomorrow."

"I understand, dear. I've enjoyed having both of you for the last three months. I can't expect to keep you forever.

At the house, Rachel stood at the window of the Heirloom bedroom. It felt different now. Lingering at the telescope, she saw the vineyards more clearly than before for its beauty. Her eyes welled.

FORTY-THREE

Jacques Simpson's New York Office

Jacques Simpson was ready to call in a favor from Thomas York, a man he had never met but knew plenty about. He stood in his office at Angels of Providence in New York City, about to make the call.

The organization had detected that Rachel had researched his name and the Simpson connection to the Courchelles and Ducharmes, and at this moment the family relationship could work in his favor.

He was also aware that Thomas would know of him as Daniel Biosvert's boss from the London diamond caper.

He dialed the vineyard and spoke to Melissa.

"Hello, I'd like to speak with Thomas York if he is staying there."

Melissa said, "Yes he is in the yard. Would you like to wait?"

She didn't get his name for Thomas, but he came quickly to the kitchen phone.

"Hello, Thomas. My name is Jacques Simpson. I think we are well familiar with each other?"

Thomas interrupted. "Mr. Simpson, Sir, I'm glad you called. My wife Rachel and I are friends with Daniel Boisvert, and we're unable to reach him. Can you help or do you know where he is?"

"I know a lot about you and Rachel. Daniel has given me the story. But I'm also a distant relative of the Ducharmes."

"Mr. York, there's a reason for my call. We do have an urgent situation that involves Daniel's safety. Are you able to get to New York quickly?"

"For Daniel, anything! My wife will be travelling with me."

"Shall I send our jet for you? It can be in Oakland in about four hours."

"Yes, we'll be there."

Jacques added, "I'm sorry our first meeting will be under these circumstances but the situation is quite dangerous. I'll send you details by email right away that you can read on the flight."

Thomas opened the emails from Jacques Simpson detailing the kidnapping and ransom requests. They huddled together reading in silence.

"David Sanderson is behind it?" Rachel asked.

"Yes. But why would Daniel have my passport? He's trying to protect us again. Sanderson must have found my picture while we were in Paris."

Thomas's heart heaved with anger.

"Are we going to Normandy to pay the ransom, or is Daniel being brought to New York?"

"Sorry, Babe, I don't know anything more at this point. We'll find out from Simpson."

Rachel packed quickly and they made her adieus to Addie, Melissa, Jonas and the children.

In the driveway, she jumped out to hug Addie again.

"I'm so sorry about the circumstances when we came, Aunt Addie, but we had a good time. You won't need to worry about Matthew anymore and your house is safe again. We'll keep in touch with the FBI about the medallions."

The Angels of Providence jet was on the ground in Oakland, and both the pilot and co-pilot descended the drop-down staircase to greet Thomas and Rachel.

The pilot, dressed impeccably in uniform, stepped forward. "Hello, Mr. and Mrs. York, I've been looking forward to meeting you."

The co-pilot's hair was tied with a strip of leather, he wore a medallion under his unbuttoned shirt. He offered drinks on the ground, before joining the pilot in the front. Rachel sunk into the luxurious leather and took a sip.

"Rachel, something is wrong here."

"It's the co-pilot, he's not who he says he is," she said. "Did you see his medallion?"

The co-pilot came back and sat on the seat opposite Thomas.

"I'd like to introduce myself, I am Jacques Simpson. My conversations and movements have been tracked and I wasn't free to tell you the plan without alerting our opponents. We are not going to New York, we're going to a small village on the coast of Normandy. We'll refuel in New York and London."

Rachel was blunt. "Mr. Simpson, I need to know why you are wearing the Courchelles silver medallion."

"Please call me Jacques. Yes, I'm a distant cousin of your Uncle Zachary. My great-great-grandfather was Jefferson

Ducharme. When some medallions had been distributed in the family, I came by mine legitimately. "

But I have some good news. I have secured the Ducharme stolen shipment. It is in a cargo bay at the back of the plane. No need to worry about it, I will return it to Addie when our business is all done."

"Are you for real?" Thomas laughed.

"And Daniel?" Rachel said.

"I have ways to intercept the criminal lanes, that's a major focus for 'The Angels of Providence'.

"David Sanderson is sending a jet to Dieppe to pick up his hostage and return him to New York. I believe that he thinks his captive is actually you, Thomas. Whether it's you or Daniel he gets, the chance of surviving is slim. He needs to save face in the criminal world, and no-one is far from his reach."

Rachel looked out the window, knowing that they were back in danger from Sanderson. She wiped a tear and Thomas put his arm around her.

"It'll be alright, Babe."

"I'm sorry that I alarmed you, Rachel," Jacques said. "But from what I know, your strength and acuteness for detail will help us get through this situation. Their plane is expected on Tuesday morning at ten, so we'll be there at nine. I understand that Daniel will be drugged and accompanied by a nurse. I was thinking you could be a flight attendant."

"Anything to help. I've done that before." She winked at Thomas.

"We'll be in New York in four hours for a quick stop, then eight hours to Normandy. There's food and drinks at the bar, and movies at your seats, and blankets above if you'd like."

Flying over Pennsylvania, Jacques came back to sit with them. He described the details of the plan, that would allow Daniel and the nun to board in France, but once in the air,

Katrina would be arrested. Thomas and Rachel assured him of their comfort with the plan, realizing the danger.

Over Ireland, Jacques woke them with some orange juice and a hot breakfast. They'd arrive at the private airfield in Normandy in ninety minutes, and had immigration cards to complete.

Rachel went first to freshen up for her role, returning in an attendant's uniform, with a slim black business jacket and silk scarf.

Daniel was lying on a cot when Yannick and Katrina opened the door to his chambers. Yannick wore an old grey woolen jacket and denim jeans and Katrina wore a blue cotton smock and kerchief. They gave Daniel a fresh shirt for the trip and waited while he washed up.

Katrina led him across the creaky dock to the waiting craft. A surge of pending freedom captured Daniel's soul and imagination momentarily, before his hands and feet were tied to a seat frame.

At the marina, Daniel was led by two men up the ramp to a waiting car. His hopes of escape were gone as he was pushed into the back seat of a rusty 1984 Benz, with a hood over his head.

Twenty minutes later, he heard the drone of a small aircraft, then the hum of another larger plane.

Thomas and Rachel watched from inside the jet as Katrina and Yannick lifted Daniel from the car. His hands and feet were still bound, but Katrina removed the hood.

"His face is gaunt and his body so frail. What have they done to him?" Rachel said.

"He knows the risks of this type of business," Thomas said. "But it's a message to me. This isn't the way I want to live my life, with only a thread between life and death."

Jacques said, "You realize, don't you Thomas, that Daniel's captors thought they had Thomas York. He did this to save you."

Thomas felt like he'd been stabbed in the heart.

"When were you going to tell me that?"

Katrina and Yannick lowered Daniel into a wheelchair. With a syringe from her bag, the disowned nun injected it into his neck, and his world faded away.

The pilot stepped down the staircase to greet Katrina first, and she boarded the jet to make preparations for Daniel.

Rachel welcomed her onboard. She took Katrina's bag and handed her a cup of tea from a tray. Together they went to the seating area set aside for Daniel during the flight.

Twenty feet from the steps, Yannick stopped and pulled out his revolver, suspicious of the early departure time.

"Did Sanderson send you? I'd like to see some proof?"

Jacques was on the steps and joined the pilot on the ground, out of view of Katrina and the plane's windows.

"Yes of course. I have our paperwork here," he said.

With his gun pointed, Yannick walked slowly to Jacques. As they opened the file, Jacques levied a hit to Yannick's head, and squeezed his neck artery until he collapsed. The pilot raised Yannick onto a baggage cart and pushed it away from the runway.

Jacques came back into the cabin to check on the situation and saw Katrina slumped on a leather chair. Rachel gave a thumbs up to Jacques. "She drank up my potion," she said. "Two ground sleeping tablets, two milligrams of clonazepam, with Green Tea and a honey stick. Enough for a full night's sleep. If she didn't drink it, I might have had to use my tiny revolver."

"Daniel was right. You're a smart lady."

Jacques and the pilot lifted Daniel up the stairs and onto the reclining bed. "He should sleep soundly for a while," Jacques said.

Rachel's eyes went to Daniel constantly in the first hour, waiting for him to stir. She was relieved when he shifted and motioned to Thomas.

She placed a cool cloth on his forehead, but his eyes didn't open.

"Daniel. Daniel. It's Rachel. You're going to be alright."

Thomas adjusted Daniel's seat to be partially upright.

"Hey, pal, time for some black coffee."

Daniel mumbled and opened his eyes. The circles under his eyes were dark, and his pupils dilated.

"David Sanderson is going to kill us. You've risked your life to save me and I'm indebted. Sanderson thinks I am Thomas York, but I never give up a comrade."

Jacques was listening and came closer.

"Daniel, you're safe now," he said. "Sanderson will be angry but he won't kill you. When it's done, you can lay charges of kidnapping, confinement, battery and uttering threats to his current forty year sentence. But I expect he'll deny his involvement."

At 7:15 p.m. local time, they touched down at the FBO jet center at La Guardia, four miles from New York City.

Jacques had arranged for a private helicopter ambulance to whisk Daniel to an unknown destination. As he was strapped to a stretcher, he looked to Thomas and Rachel.

"Acknowledge your time on this earth, and remember to leave a footprint." Daniel's eyes projected new energy and his words burrowed into their souls. "Goodbye my friends. We have unfinished business."

Jacques followed the stretcher and leaned over Daniel. "We'll be speaking very soon, but now I have to take care of some business in Vallejo."

Rachel clung to Thomas as the stretcher disappeared.

"It's time to put this behind us, Rachel. But we're back in New York! Let's get an airport hotel, then a quick trip tomorrow to Ely. Paris can wait a couple days."

"I knew that was next. And yes, we think the same."

In the morning they had breakfast with Thomas's father then took the ten o'clock flight. A limo met them at the Somerset airport for the trip across the countryside, back to the little town of Ely.

At 12:15 p.m. they pulled up to the local police station. From the counter, Thomas called to the back, "Is Captain Bert Jamieson here?

Bert looked up. "You're late!" Thomas and Rachel burst into laughter.

"It's so good to be here; let us buy you lunch. I know a good place not far from here," Thomas suggested.

The outer door of the eatery still squeaked and Thomas felt at home pulling on it. The threshold was neatly swept and he couldn't resist a big smile.

"George! Where have you been?" Thomas teased.

"Looks like you've come full circle, buddy."

He greeted Thomas and Rachel with his hug, and Thomas reintroduced Bert.

Bert laughed. "Remember when you sent me here? I have lunch with George every day."

"Bert, I've always been curious about the kid in the train wreck. Did you ever find out who he was?"

"The boy remains unclaimed. Odd how a person spends his lifetime in this world, yet he can disappear and nobody looks for him."

A limo waited at the entrance. "This is our ride," Thomas said. "We're heading back to Paris tomorrow, but tonight we'll surprise Rachel's sister and mother in Albany. In the morning, I'll see my dad."

With a wave to his Ely friends from the open window, he muttered silently.

"I won't be back here!"

He pulled Rachel close and kissed her cheek.

EPILOGUE

In November, Thomas and Rachel took a jaunt back to California for the festivities. Zach's cousin Jacques Simpson brought a big suitcase, tied with a huge white bow.

Addie was startled at his appearance and generosity, and insisted at once that they share in the medallions. But learning about the Simpson project at Angels of Providence, Addie took out keepsake medallions for the family, and donated the silver to the foundation.

The wedding was glamorous, with a garden arch intertwined with roses.

It was not like the Saturday night barbeques, but was for family only and intimate.

Melissa was her bridesmaid and Marcy and Hazel served as flower girls. Each made their own bouquets from the gardens.

Jonas and Addie glowed in their vows.

The sign on the road was 'Barstow & Ducharme'.

Six months later, Melissa returned to the main house for summer vacation. Addie and Jonas were on a cruise and Cole was the main foreman. All the way in the car the kids laughed and giggled while they sang.

"For I am a Pirate King!
And it is, it is a glorious thing
To be a Pirate King!
For I *am* a Pirate King."

It was a tune that Melissa couldn't get out of her thoughts and she caught herself joining in.

Melissa put the three kids in the usual suite, and moved into the panorama room, now bedecked with lace curtains and painted a beautiful maize. Memories flashed to the days when she was small and sat with Zach in a rocker by the same window.

She thought of Jonas, always such a sport taking the kids into the fields with Addie. They were so delighted after playing pirate, with kerchiefs knotted around their heads and homemade patches over their eyes. Such a comical group of vagabonds.

Pirate! I'm such an idiot. The truth is in that annoying little ditty.

"I am the Pirate King indeed." She jumped out of bed and went to the kids' room. "Hazel and Isaac, I need you to tell me the truth. The truth about your Pirate days."

Isaac looked with fear. "Mommy, you're not asking us to break a promise, are you?"

"What Promise?"

"The promise we made with Grandma." Isaac was solemn. "We even spit on it and that means forever."

"Alright, back to bed. We'll talk about it in the morning."

The tune faintly reverberated from little voices across the hall, and stayed in Melissa's subconscious through the night.

When the children finally appeared for breakfast, Melissa was ready to resolve the conundrum.

"Sit at the table and listen to me for a few minutes. Maria will bring you your breakfast when I am finished."

The kids fidgeted in their seats.

"Mom, I know what you are going to ask us. It's about the pirate thing, isn't it?" Hazel took over the questioning. "Let's have our breakfast; then we'll take you for a walk that will answer your questions. We really were pirates last summer."

Melissa was touched by the maturity of her daughter. In no time, the children were ready to go.

"Alright, Mom, come on, and if you want to be part of the group, you need to sing with us," Isaac said.

The four of them set off singing, stopping at the first service hut. Isaac raised his hand to come to a halt.

"This way!" He made pronounced steps toward the back corner of the service hut, then got down on his knees.

"Argh, be cool, so the bad pirates don't come." They all laughed.

Tugging at a loose cement block, he scraped away the soil and dug his hand in deeply. Then a smile burst on his face.

"See, here, Mom, this is Pirate Gran's treasure." He unwrapped a soiled piece of burlap and exposed a beautiful emerald gemstone necklace.

"Mine was rubies, but I don't remember exactly where I planted it. There were lots of days, when we went pirating planting with Grandma."

"You know, Mom, now you have to spit on the promise too. You can't tell anyone, not even Grandma."

Melissa spit on her hand and offered it to the middle of the ring.

Trust in the innocence of a child.

The Paris Network

BOOK FIVE OF THE THOMAS YORK SERIES

In a stark contrast from their idyllic lives on the cobblestone streets of Montmartre, Rachel and Thomas become drawn into a web of a terror plot designed to destroy the core of central Paris.

Instantly, they alert Interpol of the extent of their discovery of planned drone attacks over the city, combined with a network of underground bombs that would collapse the main historical sections of Paris, with the horror of thousands of lives lost.

The protagonists' lives are jeopardized as they conceal a vital item that was recovered from a terrorist drone, and they reach out to their old friend and nemesis from former times, Daniel Boisvert.

As the trio of Thomas, Rachel and Daniel take steps to thwart the attacks, the terrorists step up the stakes with a daring plan to kidnap Rachel for a ransom.

In a modern world of upheaval and terror threats, the unfolding drama reminds us of words of Napoleon, that victory comes to the most preserving, with freedom, equality and fraternity.

The Paris Network – a fast pace, tension and suspense with our characters back in Paris.

ABOUT THE AUTHOR

Born in Barrie, Ontario, Shirley Burton has traveled to research locations of the towns and cities of all her books, walking the neighborhoods and streets of the characters.

Research took her to parts of France and Quebec for her 600-page historical fiction, Homage: Chronicles of a Habitant, portraying ten generations that migrated from France to the New World. For locations for novels, she has researched in Istanbul, Paris, Rome, Greece, London, Amsterdam, Brazil, California, New York, and parts of Canada and the USA.

"There comes a time in life when it is time to take the leap into writing. It's that time for me."

Shirley Burton

shirleyburtonbooks.com

CPSIA information can be obtained
at www.ICGtesting.com
Printed in the USA
BVHW041452051122
650905BV00001B/33